"I don't think we should
see so much of each other."

Roxie's face was a frozen mask, her voice just as
cold when she spoke. "Life is just one big happy
water slide for you. The worst that can happen to
you is that you may get a little wet. And, what's
more, your family owns the slide."

Jake banged a fist on the counter. "You're mad
because my family has money. Is that it?"

Roxie's eyes darkened. "I didn't grow up in a
mansion—I had to work like a dog from grade
school through college. And I resent having to
prove myself against someone who really
doesn't give a damn about the job. Why don't
you just say you're not in the running for the
promotion and leave the field to those of us who
need it."

ABOUT THE AUTHOR

Molly Rice began writing when she was eight. For her seventeenth birthday, she received a typewriter and immediately developed writer's block. She did not write officially again for thirty years. *Where the River Runs*, her first Superromance novel, was written after she had worked at a sternwheeler excursion company. "Nothing," says Rice, who lives in St. Paul, Minnesota, with her husband, "is more romantic than a river, and no setting more conducive to romance than a riverboat."

Where the River Runs

MOLLY RICE

Harlequin Books

TORONTO • NEW YORK • LONDON
AMSTERDAM • PARIS • SYDNEY • HAMBURG
STOCKHOLM • ATHENS • TOKYO • MILAN

In memory of my father, Eugene Victor Stein,
and my sister-in-law Beatrice Schuck Bailey.
To Carol and John Perkins, who were always there.
And last, but not least,
to my husband Eugene Schuck
for his endless love and support.

Published February 1991

ISBN 0-373-70440-2

WHERE THE RIVER RUNS

CHAPTER ONE

JOE HARLEY STOPPED to straighten the sign. It swung from a bracket beside the door: Harley Marine, Inc. Excursion & Charter Boats.

Satisfied, he unlocked the door and went inside.

He hung his coat and hat on a clothes tree near the door and went back to the storeroom to put on a pot of coffee. He checked the thermostat; no sense wasting money on fuel when the office was only going to be used for a brief meeting today. His hand wavered over the control and his throat filled as he recalled how Martha used to fuss when he tried to shave a degree or two off the thermostat to save money. Martha hated frugality at the expense of creature comfort. Now Martha was gone, dead, leaving him alone in the world. He lowered the heat.

Joe returned to the large front office and glanced at the clock over the door. *They should be here soon.*

He went to the windows that faced north. From there he could survey his little water-bound empire below. In the distance, across the Mississippi River, he could see the cityscape of downtown St. Paul.

The frame structure that housed the offices was built on pillars and rose above the docks where the excursion boats were moored. Even after all these years, his chest filled with pride as he gazed down on his two boats, both authentic stern-wheelers.

The *Celebration* had been their first purchase, the start of Harley Marine, Inc. They'd run it for six years and then purchased the *River Princess*, a smaller, sleeker craft. Like assessing the affection one felt for two children, Joe could never decide which of the two paddleboats he loved most.

The *Celeb*, as the very first crew had nicknamed the *Celebration,* could carry four hundred passengers and lumbered through the water like a great rhino. By comparison, the *Princess* appeared to skim the water, like a duck. It was the *Princess* they used when they ran longer charters, going as far south as Winona and, a few times, north to where the Mississippi joined the St. Croix.

Joe's eyes filled, as memories of his late wife flooded his mind. *You always had good instincts, my girl, about business as well as people.*

The door opened behind him. He took out a handkerchief, wiped his eyes, blew his nose and turned.

Roxie Hilton came over and hugged him. Her touch was soothing as she led him to the extra desk on the other side of the door.

"It's all right, Joe," she said, her voice cracking with her own pain. "Let it out." She rubbed his back when he sat down. "We all loved Martha, we're all going to miss her. I especially... I..."

Joe wiped his eyes and smiled weakly at Roxie. "Yes, you were her right hand; she said you'd got to the place where she only had to think she needed something and you were right there to take care of it."

He patted her hand, feeling the inadequacy of words. "I made coffee," he offered.

She shook her head. "Do you want me to get you a cup?"

"Not yet—thanks." He fumbled in his pockets. "I'll have a pipe first." He looked out the door and saw only Roxie's car. "I thought you and Jake had gone to the church together."

"We did, but he wanted to talk to Bill about something so he's riding over here with him." Roxie seemed uneasy, as if she was uncomfortable about what to do or where to sit.

He gestured toward her desk across the room—the desk that had for so many years been Martha's. "Go ahead and sit down, the others should be here—"

His prediction was interrupted by footsteps thumping up the wooden outside staircase. The men were coming up from the riverside.

Jake Gilbert and Bill Tabor came stomping into the front office but instantly softened their steps when they saw Joe already there.

"Captain," Jake said. He moved to Joe, put his hand on the older man's shoulder and squeezed with gentle affection. "How're you doing, Cap?"

Joe gave Jake a smile of assurance and nodded. "Fine, son, fine."

Jake went over to hug Roxie. "You okay, kid?" Roxie nodded and smiled at him weakly. Jake patted her on the back then sat near the window overlooking the river.

Bill Tabor waved at Joe from the seat he'd taken beside Roxie's desk. He'd spent some time with Joe earlier, before the funeral. "Joe, hang in there."

"I'm hanging, Tabe, I'm hanging." Joe sighed deeply and added, "I made coffee."

The two men groaned in unison. Jake held his hand to his throat. "Couldn't you just put pink slips in our pay envelopes like other employers?'' he asked, pretending to choke.

Joe laughed with the others. The laughter felt rusty in his throat but it was a relief after all the grieving he'd done in the past weeks and especially today, at the funeral, and it eased the tension in the room. ''It's the last chance you'll get to drink a real, manly brew,'' he said, trying to prolong the teasing mood.

They all leaned forward, instantly alert to the meaning behind his words. ''What are you talking about?'' Jake demanded. ''You make that stuff every day and then try to trap some poor, unsuspecting slob into drinking it with you.''

Joe shook his head. ''Not after today.'' The others all began to talk at once, bombarding him with questions. He held up his hand for silence. Their voices faltered and stilled.

''I can't stay here without Martha. I knew this while she was dying, but I couldn't leave her long enough to get you together to tell you.'' He wiped his eyes unashamedly and pushed on. ''And because we built Harley Marine together, she and I, I can't bear to sell out and see it go to strangers, maybe even fall apart.''

He looked at Roxie as he held a match to the bowl of his pipe and sucked fire into the tobacco, recalling what Martha used to say about her. *Just pretty enough to make a man's head turn when she passes, but not so pretty she doesn't think she needs manners.* Like most of Martha's characterizations, that one was apt.

Roxie had blond hair that fell in a straight sweep down her back, reminding him of Alice in Wonderland. It made her look much younger than her twenty-seven years. Her most arresting feature was her eyes; almost as dark as chocolate, they made an exotic com-

bination with the fair hair. But she was too skinny.
Even in the baggy corduroy pants and oversize sweat-
shirts she usually wore.

Martha had planned to fatten the girl up.

He squinted behind a curl of smoke. Even Martha's
chicken and dumplings and her homemade doughnuts, thick with powdered sugar, hadn't made a difference. The girl was still skinny.

As if she could read his thoughts and was also remembering how Martha used to fuss over her, Roxie let
the tears slide down her face.

He turned away from the sight and heaved a long,
trembling sigh. Martha's death, just three days ago,
had left him feeling old, tired—too tired to go on living, it seemed at times. And maybe nothing to go on
living for.

As if she were in the room with him, he heard Martha's voice. *Self-pity diminishes a man, Joe, keeps him
from counting his blessings.*

Well, he'd counted his, all right. But somehow
nothing felt good without Martha there to share it.

"I've been thinking about how to do this, how to
keep the business without actually staying here to run
it. I decided one of you should take over as general
manager—sort of oversee the whole operation, have
complete control of the works."

"Where will you go?" Roxie asked. She reached for
the box of tissues on her desk, withdrew one and blot-
ted her eyes.

"I thought I might like to do some traveling for a
change," Joe said, "like Martha and me used to talk
about." His pipe had gone out and he went through the
process of relighting it.

He could see he had their undivided attention. It was a true measure of their worth that not one of them made a move to interrupt him with the questions they must surely have. "Good listeners are good learners," had always been his motto, and those were the kind of people he hired. Working on the river was risky business and every man—to the youngest deckhand—had to be sharp and aware and ever conscious of the rules.

"It will fall to one of you—no doubt about that. But I thought the fair thing would be to have a kind of round-table discussion and each of you tell me if you want the job and why you think you should get it."

His idea was greeted by silence. He could see he'd taken them completely by surprise.

"Ladies first. Roxanne, tell me why you think you'd qualify."

Roxie glanced at Jake. Jake's chin was on his chest, his eyes downcast, his shoulders slumped. She knew what he was feeling; it was a double loss to have Joe leave right after they'd lost Martha.

"Oh, Joe, it's going to be awful here without you," Roxie murmured.

"Different, not awful," Joe said.

"You really want to go?"

"Yes. So if you want to be considered for the promotion, you'd best speak up now."

He knew she wanted it. She had never tried to disguise her ambition—wasn't the type to hide her light under a bushel.

"Well, I've been here five years—not as long as the others..." She took a moment to glance at the two men. "But Martha really took me under her wing, and every time she saw I'd mastered something, she immediately began teaching me something new. I can honestly say there isn't an aspect of this business I haven't been taught."

She hesitated, looking for the right words. "And of course, I've been solely in charge of the office and the charter business since Martha . . . took sick."

"Exactly so," Joe said, struggling to keep his tone even. "And you're doing a great job."

He addressed the men. "In case you didn't know it, Roxie's taken in a quarter of a million dollars in deposits for reservations so far, and it's only April. By the time the season opens next month, she'll probably have us booked solid."

"Not quite," Roxie said, blushing. "There are always people who won't make a decision to charter until practically the last minute."

"Close enough, Roxie, close enough," Joe said. "Did you want to add anything?" He hadn't reckoned on what an effort it would be to show enthusiasm. All he seemed able to feel was sorrow. Clearly he needed to get away.

Roxie glanced at Tabor. "Of course, there's the fact that this office keeps the marina's books, so I'm pretty familiar with that arm of the business, too."

"Yes, that's something to keep in mind. Thank you, Roxie." He turned to the older of the two men. "Now. I guess that brings us to you, Tabe," Joe said. "Want to give us your credentials?"

Bill Tabor was a craggy-faced man in his late forties. He reminded Joe of Robert Mitchum. The horn-rimmed glasses made him look like a big, tough accountant.

Bill lived in a trailer on the other side of the marina. Joe knew firsthand he was a very good chef and that he loved to cook almost as much as he loved the boat business. Martha had said more than once that it was Bill's ability to take care of his own needs that had kept him from doing the kind of serious dating that might have led him to marriage.

Bill cleared his throat and looked out the window for a moment before speaking. Joe knew he was collecting his thoughts, deciding how to word them.

"Um...let's see. Well, I've been with you for ten years, Joe—since you took on the marina. But I've been your neighbor for twenty years and I guess I know as much about the whole business as any of you. I'm the oldest." He grinned at Roxie and then at Jake. Only Roxie returned his smile, weakly. He shrugged and went on. "Not that that cuts any ice—if it did, you'd just be handing me the job right up front. But when you bought the Kenners out after old Hank Kenner died, I'd been his assistant for ten years, and you made me manager and pretty much left everything to do with the marina in my hands. I think I've done all right."

Joe nodded, but didn't say anything.

Bill continued. "In these ten years, we've increased the slips by fifty percent because of the new business I brought in, and I could expand again and sell another hundred over the next couple of years. We're turning people away as it is. I never thought about you leaving the business, Joe, but I can see why you'd want to get away now. Anyway, as for whether or not I qualify for the promotion, I'll let my track record speak for itself."

"Good. Thanks, Tabe."

Everyone turned toward Jake, who had moved his chair so he had a wall at his back.

Jake was a leaner, a sprawler. He liked to tilt a chair on its back legs and let it lean against a wall. He always looked comfortable. A person who didn't know him would not know he could be as fast as a snake, and that behind that air of indolence, he was alert and aware. Jake's boyish looks had a lot to do with the way people always underestimated him. His dark blond hair was sun-streaked from Jake being outdoors so much. His gray eyes Martha used to say reminded her of the color of the river in spring. Women could be fanciful about such things.

Joe remembered when Jake had first come over to the island to beg for a job. That must have been about fifteen years ago, right after they'd acquired the second boat. Jake had to be about thirty years old now. Tall and muscular, he had grown to be a fine man, one any father would be proud of. *I may not have been his father, but I taught him every single thing he ever learned about his craft,* Joe thought, allowing himself a moment of pride at the realization.

Joe nodded toward his young protégé, who had been a surrogate son to him and Martha. "Well, Jake, that leaves you. I know you aren't particularly interested in being king of the mountain, but I think you owe the company your best efforts."

The front legs of Jake's chair hit the floor with a thud. He got up and moved to a window where he could look out over the river as he spoke.

He had his back to Joe. "I don't see why you have to go away. You're young yet, it's not as if you're sick or senile or anything." Joe could hear him plainly and he didn't have to see the younger man's face to know the pain that was written there. It was clear in Jake's voice.

"This isn't about me, Jake," Joe reminded him. "I'm going because I want to. It's about who is going to replace me. That's the only fact we're dealing with here today."

He could not let Jake, or the others, see how moved he was by Jake's emotion. This was a business meeting, and he wasn't going to let it turn into another wake.

He rubbed his forehead, stood up and demanded, "What's your decision, boy? Are you in the running?"

Jake turned. With the weak April sunlight at his back, he looked young and vulnerable—much the way he'd looked as a kid. Joe felt a surge of panic; he would miss this young man almost as much as he missed Martha.

"What do I need the headache for, Captain? I love my job just the way it is. What do I want with purchase orders and invoices and bank meetings..." He waved at the papers on Roxie's desk. "I'm a river man, not a paper man."

"No one's saying you have to give up piloting, Jake. As a matter of fact, with me gone, you'll be senior officer."

The two men stared at each other, almost defiantly.

Jake took a step forward, closer to Joe. Joe could see the unshed tears in Jake's eyes.

Jake's mouth straightened into a grim, bitter line. "Why don't you leave it between Roxie and Tabe? They deserve it. Hell, Roxie wants it so bad you can smell it." He looked challengingly at the girl.

Roxie's cheeks reddened but she stared him down, her chin thrust out with pride.

"You're damn right I want it, Gilbert, old buddy—what the hell use is someone in a job if they don't have any ambition?" She glared back at him.

"Are you saying I'm no good at my job?" Jake's voice rose in anger.

Joe saw it was time to intervene. It was not the first time the difference in their temperaments threatened what was usually a pretty sound working relationship, almost a friendship.

"Break it up, you two," he said softly but firmly, "and let's get on with this without declaring war."

He addressed himself to Jake. "Everything you ever wanted you got from this company, Jake. Maybe what I'm asking now is that you give some of it back. If it turns out you are the best man for the job, don't you think this outfit deserves the best?"

Bill Tabor nodded, understanding Joe's philosophy. Roxie looked at Jake, bewildered, obviously wondering how anyone could think of refusing the opportunity.

"When are you thinking of leaving?" Jake asked, his voice still edged with anger.

Joe's voice softened. "I'm all packed, Jake. I'm leaving today, and I want your answer before I go."

Jake grabbed a handful of tissues from the box on Roxie's desk, turned his back to the others and blew his nose noisily.

When he faced Joe again, his eyes were red-rimmed and his mouth was drawn in a tight line. He looked straight at Joe. "Aye, aye, Captain, whatever you say."

THE LOOK ON JAKE'S FACE stayed with Joe Harley long after the meeting broke up, long after they had all said goodbye to their boss and gone their separate ways.

He recalled the look as he loaded the last of his gear into his van and went back to make sure he'd locked up the house properly. He did a mental check. Everything covered? Yes.

Tabe had agreed to visit the house periodically. Joe had given Martha's plants to their neighbor, and he'd arranged for his mail to go to the office. He planned to keep in touch with Roxie so she could forward anything important. Roxie had check-signing privileges so she would be able to transfer funds to cover the marina account, when it ran low.

So, there's nothing left here for me to do.

Night was falling, the streetlights had just come on, and the moon was rising above the skyline of the city when Joe joined the line of traffic heading west on I-94. He was about to become a tourist, the worst kind of landlubber, but it was the only way he knew to shake the anguish of losing Martha. In fact, it had been her suggestion.

He knew Jake was missing Martha, too, and would probably feel doubly deserted with Joe gone. But Jake was a grown man, with a real family of his own, and plenty of friends, not to mention his lady, Taffy Ellers. Jake would get over his grief and get his act together in time. Joe could only hope that would include Jake's making an honest effort to compete with Tabe and Roxie for the job of general manager.

The way Joe had left it was that each of them would handle his or her own job as if he, Joe, didn't exist, and he would judge who most deserved the promotion at the end of the season, when he returned for a brief visit. "I'll base my decision on which of you best integrates your job with the others," he had told them. A high-sounding statement. Meaningless. He would judge them by some instinct in himself; the same instinct that had made him choose Martha for a bride, and the St. Paul riverfront for their business site. The instinct that had never failed him.

"Strap yourself in, Martha, old girl, we're on our way." Joe patted the vacant seat beside him and signaled his entry to the fast lane.

CHAPTER TWO

A FEW WEEKS LATER Jake stood in the doorway of the cabin, watching Taffy throw clothes into a suitcase. He kept his mouth shut as she ranted and raved about his character deficiencies.

"You're an unambitious, spineless, overage hippie, and as far as I'm concerned, we're finished!"

What could he say? She was right. He had opted for a career as a paddleboat pilot rather than joining his father and brothers in the family business, where he would, by now, have been a vice president. He preferred living aboard his boat, the *Tinker Toy*, though his parents had made it abundantly clear that their twenty-room mansion in Crocus Hill would always be home for any of their children who wanted to live there. That, more than anything, stuck in Taffy Ellers's craw; she'd have given her soul to the devil to live at such a prestigious address.

"Look at you," the petite blonde snapped, glaring across the cabin at him. "You're not even man enough to try to stop me."

"I don't want you to leave, Taffy, you know that," he said. His eyes didn't waver as they met hers. They'd lived together almost a year; he was going to miss her. They'd had good fun and good sex. It was a solid friendship, he'd always believed, neither one making demands the other couldn't meet. At least it had started out that way.

It would take many long, sleepless nights to work out what had gone wrong and how much he was to blame.

Taffy stared at him, her lips tightly pursed in the angry pout that had become almost a permanent feature of her face over the past few months. "You know what you have to do if you want me to stay. All you have to do is grow up and take your rightful place in your family's business."

He didn't lose his temper. It wasn't worth it. Besides, they'd talked this subject to death. He was weary of it. "You mean grow up and live the life you want, don't you, Taffy?"

She banged the lid of the suitcase down, punched the locks on either side, plumped down on the bunk and stared at him. "If you ever do grow up, Jake, you're going to make some woman a hell of a partner."

He felt relief creep into his face. "Does that mean you're going to overlook my inadequacies and stay?" Frustration edged his voice; he wasn't sure he wanted her to stay. Leaving had been her idea but it hadn't really come as a surprise.

Taffy burst into tears. Without hesitation Jake went to her, taking her into his arms. Her head fell against his chest. "I...I don't want to l-leave you, Jake. I...I love you," she stammered through her sobs. "But I want...I want b-babies."

Babies. There was a new subject. And how would he feel about having a child with Taffy? Maybe if he'd had time to consider the possibility. But there wasn't going to be time if she left him. "You love me and you want babies but you're leaving me?"

"I can't raise a family on a houseboat," she cried, nearly screeching. Her sobs increased.

He murmured soothing sounds and stroked her hair but he knew he was making no difference. He could tell from the tension in her body that when the tears stopped she'd get up and leave, regardless of what they said to one another in this moment of emotional upheaval. He wished with all his heart that it didn't have to be this way, but he'd known for a long time that she was as uncomfortable in the relationship as he.

It made him realize that all this talk of love and babies and where they lived was a smokescreen to cover the real truth. Despite the time they'd lived together, they had never really become a couple. Some instincts in Taffy were right on—she was leaving before the relationship deteriorated into absolute ugliness or before they became addicted to all the wrong things in each other. Or before, God forbid, a baby became a reality, even an accidental one.

He realized that one day he would have had to ask her to leave. He was grateful to her for sparing him that task.

He carried her suitcase for her and put it in the trunk of her aging BMW and stood watching, hands in his back pockets, as she slid under the wheel.

"You're going to miss me, Jake." She turned the key in the ignition then pumped the gas pedal when the engine didn't catch the first time.

"I told you not to do that, Taff," he warned, leaning forward to place his hands on the ledge of the lowered window.

Too late he realized that this was no time to be criticizing her driving. Taffy glared at him, burst into tears and turned the key again. The engine sprang to life, and Jake narrowly missed falling on his face as she drove across the marina lot, gravel spinning beneath the car's wheels.

He regained his balance and stood up, sighing in frustration. The worst thing was the ambivalence that struck when these things ended, a part of him wanting things to go on and another part relieved that the affair was over. He knew this ambivalence was what had sparked that last bit of crustiness in Taffy. It wasn't easy to end a year-long relationship, to say goodbye to someone you'd gone to sleep with every night and awakened beside every morning.

He shook his head in exasperation and headed for his own car, a newer model Volkswagen. When it had come to buying cars, Taffy had preferred the BMW even though it meant settling for a used model, while Jake, ever pragmatic about things mechanical, elected to spend his money on a no-frills investment that came with a warranty.

He started the engine, glanced at his watch and made a U-turn out of the lot. He was scheduled to take a short cruise this afternoon and he didn't know yet who was on his crew roster. He pulled onto the highway.

It was a lucky break he'd been scheduled for today; once he was at the helm, in the pilothouse three stories above the river, he'd have the privacy and quiet he needed to get in touch with his real feelings about this new loss.

One thing he was sure of, he wasn't a man meant to live his life alone. He had seen in his own parents and in Joe and Martha Harley that marriage could be wonderful for both a man and a woman—if they were the right man and woman. He knew he wanted that for himself. But he needed to find a woman with whom he could share everything.

It occurred to him then that he could have persuaded Taffy to stay if he'd really wanted her to; all he'd have had to do was tell her about Joe's offer and that he was in the running for the promotion. But Joe had been gone a few weeks and Jake had not even hinted at it to Taffy.

ROXIE SLAMMED the bottom drawer of the metal file cabinet. It sprang open and this time she stood up and kicked it. "You'd better stay shut," she threatened, "I've got plenty more kick where that came from."

"Expecting a plea for mercy?" Jake Gilbert came through the door laughing.

Roxie leveled a look of scorn at him. "And as for *you*—hasn't anyone told you having a phone aboard your boat doesn't do any good if you don't have it plugged in? How the hell am I supposed to get hold of you when I need you?"

Jake smiled and sat down behind the extra desk across the room. He folded his hands behind his head and let the swivel chair tilt back until it touched the wall. "Having a good day, Hilton?"

Roxie bit back a four-letter retort and forced herself to return to her desk in a dignified manner. He seemed to be enjoying her frustration even without any knowledge of its source. Well, that was no surprise; everyone knew Jake Gilbert just played at life. *Just like her father.* She brushed the errant thought away. Why should she compare Jake to Pop? She and Jake were just friends. His lack of ambition certainly didn't affect her life in any way.

She made herself sound calm, authoritative. "Have you bothered to inform yourself of this week's schedule, Captain Gilbert?"

"Yep. It's why I'm here." He peered over at Roxie. "So, where's my crew roster?"

"Need I remind you, Jake," Roxie said, clenching her teeth, "that we can't run a cruise operation on a last-minute basis? What if some of your crew hadn't shown up? Would you have time now, with the cruise scheduled to start in—" she glanced at the clock over the door "—just over an hour, to line up replacements? What if the linens or concessions are short? You didn't show up yesterday at all . . . What if the oil company hadn't delivered oil, or what if Mark had taken ill?"

His chair rocked forward and the front casters hit the floor with an angry thwack.

Roxie jumped despite herself.

"Okay, Hilton. Enough! Something's eating you. Some of it can be laid at my feet, I suppose, but don't try to dump it all on me. I wouldn't be late if I didn't have a good reason and yesterday—you'd know, if you'd look at that schedule you're so steamed up about—was my day off. If you can't run this end of the operation without panic over every problem, maybe you're not right for the job. And remember, you're not my boss yet."

Roxie felt embarrassment heat her face. She had come down pretty hard on him, considering they were, at least for the moment, colleagues.

Furthermore, they were competing for the same job. Maybe it would be more politic to tread lightly with him.

Jake leaned forward, peering through the doorway of the other office. "Where's Mary? Isn't she supposed to help you? You look pretty frazzled to me—like maybe you can't handle the heat."

Roxie took a deep breath, held it, counted to six and let it out slowly. Better. He'd come in at just the wrong moment and instantly become a victim of her frustration.

She stood up and lifted the crew roster and time sheets from the wire basket on her desk. "I'm sorry, Jake. This has been a hell of a day so far, and I guess I'm making it worse all by myself."

He was instantly forgiving as he took the papers she carried over to him. She felt even guiltier when his face creased into his usual grin and he said, "Hey, don't let it get you down, Rox, it's just a job."

She laughed in spite of her irritation. "That's you, Jake. If you were in show business your theme song would be, 'What the Hell, It's Just a Job.' So—" she leaned over the desk to pinch his cheek "—let's pretend you give a damn, and go over the details of today's cruise."

She returned to her desk. She felt better already and realized it was because Jake was obviously not working very hard for the promotion. That would narrow the odds for her nicely. Bill Tabor really didn't know as much about the general business as she did.

Roxie glanced at Jake as she picked up her copy of the cruise agenda and was surprised to see a hurt look on his face.

"What's the matter?" Now where had her vicious tongue led her? Hadn't she made an adequate apology for snapping at him?

Jake was staring at her. "I should be asking you that. Obviously something's got you going but I'm damned if I know what it is, or why you're taking it out on me. When did I ever give the impression I don't give a damn about my job? Piloting the boats on the river is all I ever wanted to do since I signed on for after-school duty, as a gopher, when I was fourteen years old." He came around the desk and sat on its front edge, keeping his gaze locked on Roxie.

"Every inch of those vessels is important to me and every person who rides aboard them, passenger or crew, is important to me."

Roxie stared at Jake. She'd never seen this side of him. Never seen such passion in him though it was true she'd always known he loved his job. Maybe it was too soon to discount him as competition, after all.

On the other hand, he'd made no mention of the rest of the business, just how much he loved piloting.

She saw that his intensity bordered on anger. It did wonderful things to his looks, which were already pretty special. His gray eyes darkened to the color of the Mississippi when storm clouds hovered overhead, and his tanned cheeks flushed to burnt sienna. Even his sun-streaked hair seemed to shimmer gold in the light that filtered through the windows facing the river.

Roxie slumped back and sighed. "God. I'm really sorry, Jake. Clay and I broke up today and I guess I've been taking it out—"

"You and Mr. Wonderful broke up? Today?" Jake interrupted her apology.

"Yes. Over a luncheon at which I had given myself every reason to believe he was going to propose marriage."

Now why in the world did I admit that—and to Jake of all people.

She overlooked his referral to Clay as "Mr. Wonderful," a bit of sarcasm she'd normally chafe at. Her throat seemed to fill up suddenly and she found it hard to swallow. *I'm not going to start crying now, after a solid hour of dry-eyed anger. Not in front of Jake Gilbert. All I need is to break down—and on the job, yet!* She snatched the mug off her desk and gulped the cold coffee. She was choking that down when she noticed Jake was laughing. At her? That would be the last straw for today.

"What's so funny, Gilbert?" she demanded, wiping coffee off her mouth with the back of her hand.

"Not an hour ago Taffy walked out on me. Gone for good. Decided she wants somebody with more swank."

"She said that?" Why was she so surprised? Everyone knew Taffy was a social climber, and Jake the most laid-back of river rafters.

"Not in those words, but yes, that's what it boils down to."

They stared at one another, Jake with the remnants of laughter lighting his eyes and quirking his lips.

"Life's a bitch . . . and then you die," Roxie said, finally.

Silence stretched between them till Jake asked, "So, are you really miserable or just angry?"

She had to think about that, surprised she didn't have a ready answer. "I don't know. Both. Angry." They stared at one another. "What about you?" she asked. "Are you upset?"

Jake shrugged. "I should have been prepared for it, but I confess, it caught me off guard. I guess it's going to take some getting used to—not having Taffy around all the time, I mean."

Roxie turned away, looked out the window. The flags on the pilothouse of the *Celebration*, which was moored at the landing below the office building, were flapping wildly. "Windy today. You're going to have trouble pushing upstream on the way back."

He followed her gaze and nodded. "So don't panic if we're fifteen or twenty minutes late getting back." He brought his gaze back to her. "Montgomery always was, in my estimation, a real jerk. Now he's proved me right."

Gratitude melted the chunk of ice in Roxie's chest. Jake Gilbert was really a nice guy, the kind of person who would know how to stop a little girl's tears and who helped old ladies cross the street.

His remark about Clay reminded her that the two men had gone to school together, though Clay had attended St. Paul's on a scholarship. It was a sore point with Clay, one he brought up repeatedly as he railed against life's many injustices. Not the least of which was the fact that Jake's good family connections were wasted on Jake and would, in fact, have served Clay far better. For a long time Roxie had been inclined to agree with Clay about that. Certainly Jake never showed much interest in the world beyond the river.

"He told me he needed to back off from our relationship. He said his career has reached a place where it's going to demand all his attention and energy. He said he's going to make a name for himself in this state and any relationship would either get in the way or suffer because of it."

Jake's voice became a low-pitched growl. "He's already got the name he most deserves, as far as I'm concerned."

She giggled. She couldn't help it. Jake and Clay had always skirted one another, when they met, like two territorial male dogs. That they disliked one another had always been obvious, but today Jake sounded as if he was really disgusted with Clay for the way he had treated Roxie. That made his dislike of Clay seem more personal, made her feel she had a champion in her corner.

Later, when she was alone again, she'd have to think about what had kept her with Clay in the first place. Why she hadn't seen that their relationship was going nowhere. She'd probably even feel some remorse over the times she'd agreed with Clay that Jake Gilbert's family deserved better than to have a son who was such a maverick. After all, despite their current rivalry and their past differences, Roxie and Jake were friends.

"That's better," Jake said, referring to her titter of laughter. "You don't sound so miserable."

She sobered. "The thing I don't understand is why he needs to be away from me to improve the status of his career. After all, I'm going after an upgrade myself, and that never got in the way of seeing him."

"Come on, Hilton, you know you're one of those people who can do three jobs at once and still keep your eye on a prospect. There's no way you'd let anything get in your way if you were going after something you really wanted."

Lord, was that a compliment or an insult? Maybe she shouldn't have made mention of the promotion they were competing for.

She lowered her face so he wouldn't see the blush she could feel starting, and noticed the schedule she was holding.

"Let's get back to work," she said, clearing her throat and picking up a pen. "It's a public cruise so you only have a crew of three besides Terry, who's copiloting." She made a notation on the margin of her schedule to bring Terry Johnson's hours up to date. He'd need an accurate count when he was ready to apply to the Coast Guard for his pilot's license.

"Floyd's on bar today. Good," Jake commented as he studied his own schedule. "I always feel better when I know he's below."

Floyd Dubrov was head bartender for the operation and in that position was senior officer under the pilots. What Jake appreciated about Floyd was his experience as bouncer at a local club. Floyd was a short, bull-like man. Part Cherokee, he wore his black hair in a ponytail tied back with a leather thong, and a handlebar mustache that gave him an old-fashioned look. He was capable of lifting his own weight and had once put two troublemakers off the boat, before the cruise began, without anyone knowing there'd been a threat.

"Yeah, he's a good man," Roxie agreed.

Jake shifted his hip on the desk edge and frowned at the schedule he was holding. "You've got Donny working again? He must have more hours for this pay period than you do. That's an awful lot of overtime to pay out."

Roxie shook her head. "Can't help it. I needed two on, beside Floyd and Terry, so you'd have a runner to check the engines and someone to keep the bar supplied. Donny is the only nonstudent." She pointed to the wall calendar. "Most of the kids have finals this week, and I couldn't spare Mary."

Jake looked around. "Speaking of whom—I asked before, where is your charming and able assistant?"

"Picking up stuff at the printer's and doing some shopping for the office. She should be back soo—oh, there she is now."

Mary Sanger came through the door carrying two brown paper bags and panting. "Those steps are going to be the death of me," she gasped.

"You don't need to park down there when you've stuff to unload," Jake scolded, relieving her of the groceries. "The parking lot up here isn't going to fill with customers in the few minutes it takes to get stuff out of your car." He was just about to turn away when he gave her a thoughtful look. "Are you putting on a little weight?"

"Yeah." Mary tugged at the waistband of her skirt. "And I can't figure it out. But," she added, "it wasn't very gallant of you to notice."

"Sorry," Jake said, his grin belying his words. He carried the bags to the storeroom calling over his shoulder, "Anything else in the car?"

"Yeah, the printing. A big box of it, as a matter of fact."

Mary leaned through the door of her office and swung her purse onto her desk, then she collapsed onto the chair alongside Roxie's desk. "You wouldn't believe the traffic out there today."

"Yes, I would. I just got back from lunch a little while ago."

"Did you check the answering machine when you got back?" The fatigue in Mary's face lifted slightly to allow eagerness to peek through.

"Yes. Your messages—including one from your mystery man—are on your desk." Mary leaped up, refreshed, and rushed into the other office. "Oh, Lord. Why didn't you say something sooner?" she called from the small inner room.

"Gee, Mare, you've been back a total of two and a half minutes. I'm sorry I didn't tell you sooner. Perhaps you'd have liked me to bring the message down to the lower lot and be waiting there for your return?"

Mary didn't respond. Roxie could hear her dialing.

She was worried about Mary, who was both her friend and her assistant. Mary had started working for the company four years ago, during the summer break from her job as a teacher's aide in one of the St. Paul public schools. At first she'd just helped out with the bookkeeping in the office part-time and hostessed on the boats part-time.

This year, with Martha sick, she'd agreed to come aboard permanently as bookkeeper. She'd asked to keep hostessing nights on the boats until she could save enough money for a badly needed new car. Now Roxie wondered if the double shifts weren't playing havoc with Mary's health. The other thing was, why all the mystery about the new boyfriend? All Mary would admit was that she had one.

"I'm going down to get the printing for Mary," Jake said, coming out of the back room. "I put the supplies away and the milk is in the fridge."

"Thanks, Jake," Roxie said softly. She held her head tilted toward Mary's office, making no secret of the fact she was trying to eavesdrop on Mary's call.

Jake grinned and shook his finger at Roxie. "Shame on you, Hilton." But she noticed he whispered his admonition, and she grinned at him.

"I just want to know who the guy is," she said, "and one of these times Mary is going to slip and refer to him by name."

The door to Mary's office closed with a resounding thwack just as Mary was heard to say, "Hello. May I please speak to Mr—"

Roxie knew that Mary could stick out her leg and kick the door shut; she'd done it often enough herself when that cubbyhole had been her office. If it hadn't been for the window behind the desk, a person could suffocate from claustrophobia in that room. When Mary didn't need the quiet and seclusion necessary to concentrate on the bookkeeping, she used the other desk in the anteroom that was Roxie's office.

Jake laughed out loud and opened the door to the outside. "Foiled again, eh, Hilton?"

She pretended to pout but couldn't hold back a smile. Jake had a way of teasing that always made her feel like laughing. When she was in the mood, anyway. It dawned on her then that her mood had changed since Jake had entered the office.

A nice guy, she thought for the second time. And for the umpteenth time she wondered what he'd had in common with Taffy Ellers. It should have been the other way around; Jake should have been the one to dump Taffy. Which brought her mind full circle.

"I should have seen Clay and I couldn't make it a long time ago," she muttered. She pulled the liquor inventory sheets out of the wire basket on the corner of her desk and began to add up figures on her ten-key machine, posting the totals to a master sheet that would eventually summarize their liquor business for the year.

Journey with Harlequin into the past and discover stories of cowboys and captains, pirates and princes in the romantic tradition of Harlequin.

The door to Mary's office opened and Mary stuck her head out, an impish grin lighting her heart-shaped, freckled face. "I need a favor."

"Sure. All you have to do is make a trade."

"Come on, Rox, that's blackmail. You wouldn't do that to a friend, would you?" She sidled into the front office, the single braid of her dark red hair swinging around to cross her shoulder.

"Wouldn't I?" Roxie held her pen across her upper lip, mustache fashion, and leered at Mary. "We have ways of making you talk."

Jake came back as the two women were laughing and handed Mary her keys. "You left these in the trunk lock. Are you trying to lose your car?"

"She's got a lot on her mind," Roxie teased. "She's in love."

"Nothing wrong with that, is there?" Mary asked, snatching the keys Jake dangled before her. The pink flush in her cheeks accentuated the defensive tone in her voice.

Roxie responded without thinking. "Only if you're looking for plenty of heartache down the road."

And Jake said, "I'd rather be cuddled by a boa constrictor."

They stared at each other across the room.

Jake buttoned his jacket. *She's really been hurt. Too bad. She didn't deserve to get mixed up with a bastard like Montgomery.*

Roxie tamped the pages of inventory together to align them and fit them into a file folder in her lower right-hand desk drawer. *How come it's always the nice guys who get hurt and the jerks get off scot-free,* she wondered.

"The favor is," Mary said, ignorant of the undercurrents that flowed between the other two, "that I need you to take that TexCo cruise for me Saturday night. I have a date."

"You said you didn't want me to hire another hostess when Carleen left the job. I thought I didn't have to go out on any more cruises," Roxie reminded her assistant. She had to turn her back to the two of them in order to replace the master sheet in the journal binder on the file cabinet behind her desk.

"Just this once?" Mary pleaded. "It's a special occasion."

Jake winked at Mary and made a circle with his forefinger and thumb. "Hey, Hilton," he said softly, "it's been a long time since you made a run with us. I...we... The crew has missed you." He looked almost embarrassed as he admitted, "I miss having you bring coffee up to the pilothouse and help me navigate home. Remember how we used to counsel one another on our love lives?"

Roxie turned around, facing Jake. "We didn't give each other very good advice, apparently." She hadn't meant to let the bitterness creep through.

"It felt good at the time," Jake said softly.

"I guess there was a moment or two worth remembering," Roxie was forced to agree. She sat down and sighed. "Remember how we used to razz Martha when she came along on a cruise and couldn't climb up to the pilothouse without someone pushing her up the ladder?"

They laughed at the memory and then fell silent as they thought of the recent death of Martha Harley. She'd lost that plumpness that they'd teased her about as her illness progressed. It had affected them all. And now, of course, they missed her terribly. She had been a loving, maternal friend to all at Harley Marine, Inc.

"Then you'll do it for me, Rox?" Mary asked, breaking the respectful, thoughtful silence.

"Okay. But listen, Mary, if you want to give it up, just let me know and we'll hire a full-time hostess. I'll do it this time. God knows I've nothing better to do."

"Gee, your enthusiasm is so flattering," Jake said. "Funny how you seem to have blocked the good times out of your memory."

Roxie looked pointedly at the clock. "You start loading in thirty minutes, Jake. Don't you think you ought to get going?"

CHAPTER THREE

QUIET REIGNED in Roxie's office after Jake Gilbert left. Mary was holed up in her office doing bookkeeping chores. Roxie was trying to concentrate on her work.

But thoughts of Clay Montgomery kept plaguing her, making her wonder how she could have deluded herself into believing he'd been in love with her.

And what about you, were you in love?

There was the question that made her most uncomfortable. The one that begged the deepest truth—had she loved Clay or only *wanted* to love him? Would she even be able to recognize love—real love—when it happened? She thought about the examples she'd had in her life and winced with pain as her parents came to mind.

Her father, drunk. Falling down, dropping food and drink down his chest, railing noisily at the world for not making life easier for him. And finally, in his frustration, lashing out at his wife because she was there and because he was too cowardly to take his anger to its source.

And Ma, downtrodden. Accepting every lost job, every spent paycheck, every slap and abusive word as if it were all her due. And then going to the local tavern with Pop, proudly holding his arm, as though they were on their way to the Waldorf Astoria, both forgetting they had a daughter to feed or look after.

Starting at an early age, Roxie had done what she could to make a home for her delinquent parents, pretending that she believed what they had was love and that she was helping create the atmosphere of a home for it. It was she who prepared Pop's favorite meals and set them before him, Ma going along with the pretense and taking the credit. On Ma's thirtieth birthday, twelve-year-old Roxie had stolen a bracelet and ring from Woolworth's, wrapped them in old Christmas wrapping and made Pop give them to Ma and say they were from him. It was Roxie who woke them on Sunday mornings, with Alka-Seltzer and coffee to soothe their hangovers, and Roxie who called her father's job—when he had one—to make excuses for his absence or tardiness. Ma's excuse for staying with him? *Why, Roxie, he's my man. I love him.*

"Love!" Did the word mean the same thing when her mother said it? Was it love that was destructive and hurting, or merely the lovers themselves?

At five to three the *Celebration*'s whistle distracted her, and she went to the window to watch the boat readying for departure.

She could see it was nearly full; there were at least three hundred and fifty people aboard. Not bad for the first official week of the season. It didn't hurt, either, that it was unseasonably warm for early May.

Thinking of that, she raised the window slightly, and let in some of the mild fresh air. The sounds of the river wafted up from below, starkly clear on the warm, soft breeze. A screeching gull flew by so close she could hear the vibrations of its wings in the wind. She followed its swoop down to the water where it skimmed the surface, looking for food. A deep breath assured her that the river had not yet acquired the fetid odors that would come later in the long, hot summer.

She looked at the *Celebration* and saw Terry take the stairs to the second deck, two at a time, then scramble up the ladder fastened to the bulkhead of the pilothouse. Because the boat was anchored alongside the dock, facing downstream, the helm was on the river side of the pilothouse and she couldn't see Jake. When the whistle blew again, she closed the window and returned to her desk.

JAKE CLIMBED THE LADDER with the ease born of years of practice and vaulted over the top rung into the pilothouse, Terry Johnson only a sneaker length behind him.

"Come on, Jake," Terry was pleading for the third time in three minutes. "Why can't I take her out by myself? You said the other day that I was ready to solo."

"Not when I've got a full load mostly of little kids and senior citizens and it's windy as hell today." He'd been surprised to see the public cruise almost filled up when he came aboard. Usually things like high winds scared people off, though the *Celebration* was as solid and sturdy a vessel as had ever run on the Mississippi.

"Roxie outdid herself," he said, almost to himself, as he checked dials on the instrument panel and Terry checked in with the Coast Guard by radio.

Terry returned the mike to its holder and looked at Jake, who had just started up the engine that caused the paddle wheel to turn. "What about Roxie?"

"I was just saying, her idea for early spring publics was a good one. She must have bombarded the media with advertising to get such a good turnout."

"Matter of fact, she told me she called a bunch of nursing homes and day-care centers and offered 'em a discount." Terry looked disgusted. "Looks like it worked all right. No one between the ages of five and eighty down there."

Jake laughed and logged in the time. "So we'll have at least one run where you stay in the pilothouse for the whole trip, rather than running up and down the bulkheads checking out the action."

"Yeah. I guess I may as well get us a thermos of coffee. You want something from the concession stand while I'm down there?"

Jake rubbed his stomach, trying to recall what he'd eaten that day. "Tell Floyd to make me one of his special subs, in case I get hungry later," he said. "And try to get back here before we take off."

He pulled the cord to blow the whistle, announcing that the *Celebration* was about to get underway. A shiver ran across his scalp and down his spine, as it always did when he heard the whistle, whether it came from his boat or someone else's.

He still had five minutes before departure. Time enough for any last-minute passengers to come aboard below. He pushed his billed officer's cap to the back of his head and slouched in the swivel captain's chair, feasting his eyes on the hustle and bustle of the daytime river activity below him.

Three tugs at various distances from one another chugged upstream, pushing freight barges ahead of them; a lone boater sped downstream, waving at Jake as he passed; across the river the traffic on Warner

Road repeated itself over and over as if underlining the importance of the city's daily routine. In the distance he could see the coppery green dome of the state capitol building not far from the dome of the cathedral.

The view of the government complex made him think of Clayton Montgomery and then, naturally, of Roxie Hilton. What the hell could the guy be thinking of? The man who had Roxanne Hilton in his corner had a woman with that rare combination of beauty, talent, intelligence and class. Oh, sure, he teased her a lot, and she was a little too ambitious for his taste, but she was one of the few women a man could call a friend. And she was far too good for any man who'd cast her aside for the sake of his career. About the time Montgomery got ready to settle down and realized what a catch Roxie was, maybe it'd be too late and she would have found someone worthy of her.

Thinking about Roxie reminded him of what it had been like when she used to hostess aboard the boat. There'd been a time or two, when she'd been up here in the pilothouse with him, he'd felt like asking her out. But either she was seeing Montgomery or he himself was involved with someone, so it had never seemed appropriate. He'd always thought, though, that despite their constant bickering, they had a lot in common, that they'd have fun together.

A picture of Roxie arose in his mind, obscuring the panoramic view before him. She was one of those blondes that made everyone turn and take a second look because her eyes were the most unexpected chocolate brown. And her hair was that wonderful, natural ash blond, from her scalp to the blunt cut ends that hung down her back almost to her waist.

Today she'd had it up in a kind of bun at the back. He liked that, too. It made her look elegant, showed off her nice bone structure. *Come to think of it,* Jake thought wiggling in his seat, trying to stay relaxed, *come to think of it, if Roxie would dress up more, she'd be as classy looking a woman as I've ever seen.*

He heard footsteps on the second deck staircase below. Terry coming back. He pushed his hat over his eyes, giving himself one last minute of visualizing Roxie Hilton as she'd looked half an hour earlier. She'd been wearing a tan skirt and a cotton blouse of a soft brown color that was perfect for her, emphasizing her blond hair and the color of her eyes.

Come to think of it, he could hardly remember a time he'd seen her really dressed up at work before. She must have worn the skirt and blouse for her unfortunate lunch date with Montgomery. It hadn't registered at the time, but when she'd crossed the office to hand him those papers, he'd got a good look at her legs below the fashionably short hem of her skirt. She had long, well-shaped legs that made a man's mind wander into dangerous territory. Funny he'd never noticed before what great legs she had. Maybe because she usually wore jeans or slacks.

"Clay Montgomery must have bean sprouts for brains."

"What's that about rain?" Terry asked, climbing into the cabin. "Sure, it's windy out there but there isn't a cloud in the sky."

Jake came out from under his cap, pretending to frown. "Sure took you long enough, kid. I've been waiting for you to get up here so we can take her out."

ROXIE WAS LOOKING at last year's calendar book, comparing the bookings with this year's, when Mary came out of her office.

"Are you mad at Jake about something?" Mary asked. She leaned against the door frame.

The question surprised Roxie and it took her a moment to focus on it.

"Don't be silly. Why would I be mad at Jake?"

"I've been thinking about before, when he was up here. You just sort of brushed him off at the end. I got the feeling you didn't like his personal comment."

"I don't like the idea of the crew thinking of me as a fellow playmate now that I'm cruise manager. It's not good for working relations, makes them think they don't have to take orders from me."

"Well, Jake doesn't."

"No, but if the guys see me being too casual with Jake, they'll think it's all right for them to take liberties. That's one of the problems of being a woman among so many men on a job. And especially being a woman in authority."

Roxie cringed inwardly. Had that sounded a little priggish? "You know, with this promotion thing hanging over our heads, it seems more important for the guys to remember I'm one of the bosses."

"Yeah, I know what you mean. I danced with Donny the other night during the NSP cruise and then when I told him to go around and empty the ashtrays on the tables, he got kind of huffy."

"But, Mary, you always seem to have fun on those charters."

"Yeah, it's like going to a party every night." Mary came and sat on the chair beside Roxie's desk. "Roxie, do you mind my asking you something?" She barely waited for Roxie's nod. "The guys in the crew said you never did any socializing during a cruise. Is that true?"

Roxie shrugged, unable to think of a way to express her reluctance to participate in the party when she worked a cruise. That was one of the reasons she used to spend so much time in the pilothouse, once she'd seen to it that the charter group was getting everything they'd ordered and the party was well underway.

"For me, the best part was just being on the river and sitting up in the pilothouse talking to Jake when things were rolling along on their own down below. But of course, that was the shortest part of the cruise. Most of the time you're on the lower decks, running yourself ragged." Her voice softened as she mused, "But in the pilothouse—in the dark—Jake and I could talk on and on about anything and everything."

Mary stared at Roxie, hardly believing what she thought she saw in Roxie's face, heard in her voice.

"You know how, when you're in the pilothouse . . . three stories above the river . . . it's like floating on a cloud and looking down on the most beautiful part of the world passing below you?"

She seemed to be talking more to herself than to Mary. "You feel like, in the whole world, there are just the two of you up there. It's so quiet and special."

Mary shook her head. "I've never been up there, Rox. I've asked to go up, to see what it's like, but Jake always gets a funny look on his face and says, 'Maybe some other time.' And I haven't felt at ease about asking the other pilots."

She leaned forward, her curiosity winning over caution. "Rox, have you ever gone out with Jake Gilbert?"

"What?" Roxie pulled her thoughts away from the days when she'd gone out on so many of the *Celebration*'s cruises. "Jake? Gone out with Jake?" Her voice went up an octave. "Don't be silly. Jake and I...we're friends. I can't even imagine going out with Jake Gilbert. It would be like...like dating—" She stood up suddenly and picked up her coffee cup. "Of course I haven't dated Jake. That would have been the farthest thing from either of our minds, even if we hadn't both been involved with someone else."

But as she went to the storeroom where the coffee maker was set up on the counter, she couldn't help but visualize how lovely it would be to ride upstream at the top of the boat again, alone with Jake in the night, only the stars and lights along the river to pierce the darkness, their voices hushed in the small glass-enclosed space as they shared their innermost, intimate feelings.

As she poured, she pondered the irony that allowed two people to choose their friends so wisely and their lovers so foolishly and she couldn't help but wonder why the intimacy of those moments in the tiny cabin above the night-blackened river had never carried over to the light of day.

For some reason, she felt better about the breakup with Clay as she carried her full cup to her desk.

"All this talk about Jake and the cruises—I forgot to tell you about my lunch with Clay today."

She told her friend about Clay's betrayal and discovered, with surprised relief, that there wasn't an ounce of self-pity in her voice or in her feelings. More than anything, what she felt was anger. At herself, mostly. How could she have been so blind to Clay's true character? Even if he was absolutely one of the most handsome men around, as well as educated and witty. She'd sure allowed herself to become bowled over by externals.

Bill Tabor and Mark Carter, one of the pilots, entered the office just as Mary was voicing her opinion of Clay Montgomery.

"Sorry to interrupt such a ladylike character assassination, Mary," Bill said, laughing. "Hope it isn't one of us you're describing so vividly." Everyone laughed at Mary's blush and the defiant tilt of her little pointed chin. "If it were," she said, directing her remark to Bill with flashing eyes, "you'd know it."

"Is this a social call?" Roxie asked when the others had quieted. She really didn't want them to know it was her ex-boyfriend under discussion. A person had to have some privacy, even in this business.

Despite the initial jocularity, their reason for being there turned out to be serious. They explained their mission as soon as they were seated.

"Have you noticed a boat on the river called the *Shurk*?" It was Mark who asked.

"No." She looked at Mary, who concurred, then asked, "A stern-wheeler?"

"Yes. Used to be the *Pelican* out of Red Wing."

"No. Never heard of either one. Why? What's the problem?" Roxie turned to Bill.

"Well, scuttlebutt says it's not licensed to carry passengers or to run a charter business. But we've seen it loaded with passengers. So we asked around. Seems its new owner is a thug named Harry Minto, who has as much business running a charter operation as I have skydiving from a helicopter."

"So what does the Coast Guard say about it?" She didn't know why they were so worried. Obviously the law would take care of the *Shark*.

"They said they can't do anything unless someone can prove that Minto is actually running an illicit charter business. Minto says he's just taking out parties of friends, that no money is changing hands."

"Must be a real popular guy with so many friends," Bill said with undisguised sarcasm.

"How would you go about proving it?" Mary asked.

"Well, for sure the customers won't admit it if they're getting a better deal from Minto than we, or the other charter companies, can give them," Mark commented.

Roxie pulled the calendar book forward. During the winter months she spent most of each business day selling charters to their regular customers and soliciting new customers. By the first of April almost half the season had been booked for both boats. Over the past week, however, she'd had three cancellations for the *Princess* and one for the *Celebration*.

"I have had a few cancellations," she admitted, looking at the others. "That in itself is unusual, though it doesn't really prove anything about this Minto person."

"Can we afford that?" Bill asked. "Have you got any parties on standby to fill in those dates? How much revenue loss are we talking?"

"Hold it, Bill," Roxie said, hoping she sounded in control. "One thing at a time. First of all, it's too early in the season to say anything is lost. We sometimes get orders for charters just days before a charter group wants to actually go out. What's it called? Spontaneous purchasing? You know how it works. Someone

hears our commercial on the radio and starts thinking, 'Gee, it would be fun to have our office party on
a boat instead of at a restaurant the way we've done it
year after boring year.' "

"So they call us, and they've got maybe three days
to get something set up. Anyway, often we have had to
turn that kind of business away because we're usually
booked solid. So now, instead of sending them to one
of the other companies, we may be able to accommodate them."

She frowned as she looked at the calendar. "As long
as it stops here, I think we'll survive it."

"And if it doesn't?" Mark's voice was quiet, even,
but everyone in the room knew the company could be
facing a real dilemma.

Roxie turned the pages of the book. This had been
sprung on her too abruptly for her to be able to take it
seriously. Still, for the first time since Joe left a month
ago, she needed his advice. If this affected the company's revenue, wouldn't it lower Joe's estimation of
her capabilities?

Tabor craned his head, trying to see the pages. "Are
you booked solid now?"

Roxie felt defensive; was this Bill's way of saying she
wasn't on top of her job? "Of course not. It's only
May. Many customers don't have a firm date in mind
during the winter months. They wait until the season
opens to decide the best date for their parties. And
private parties are more inclined to be chartered on
whim than long in advance of the event.

"The Cavanaughs, for instance." She looked at
Mark. "They've been chartering the *Princess* for their
anniversary party for the past six or seven years—since
before I came to work here—and they never call to

make arrangements until about three weeks before the date. They figure their guests know to keep that date open for their celebration every year, whether it's going to be on the boat or somewhere else."

Bill almost scoffed. "How many of our passengers are like the Cavanaughs?"

Mary piped up, "Don't jump on Roxie, Bill. If this guy is pirating business away from us, it isn't Roxie's fault."

Bill stared at Mary and then turned to Roxie, his expression contrite. "Sorry, Roxanne. I guess I do get a little antsy about the business." He scratched his jaw and looked pensive. "Maybe I've been a part of this company too long—Lord knows this isn't the most secure business, even at the best of times."

"Does Jake know about this?" Roxie asked, surprised he hadn't mentioned it when he was in earlier.

"Not that I know of," Mark said. "Bill and I just discovered it ourselves a couple of days ago."

"Let's table this discussion until all of us can sit down together, then," Roxie decided, closing the calendar book and rising. "Maybe we can brainstorm some ideas. We can probably get together as early as Monday."

"Meanwhile, I'll keep my eyes and ears open over the weekend," Bill said, patting Mark on the back. "And you'll be out on the *Princess*, Mark. You can keep a watch out for the *Shark*."

They were on the way out when Tabor turned to Mary, a big grin creasing his homely face. "And you, little lady, whoever you were talking about when we came in, try to have a little charity in your heart. All that venom might give you freckles."

They could still hear his laughter, harmonizing with Mark's hearty chuckle, after the door had closed and Roxie, turning to look at Mary, was amazed to see the girl staring starry-eyed at the door, her freckles standing out starkly against the flush in her cheeks.

"What are you thinking about, Mare?" she asked, dumbfounded.

"Huh? Oh. Nothing. No one." Mary sounded dazed. She put her hands to her face as if to cool her cheeks and laughed shakily. "I must be coming down with something. Guess I'll go take an aspirin." She hurried into her office before Roxie could say another word.

Roxie looked at the door through which the two men had departed. *Mark Carter? Is Mark the guy Mary's seeing?* But no, that wasn't possible even though Mark was cute as could be with his dark curly hair and that beard that was meant to make him look older but didn't. If anything, the beard accentuated his round, sparkling blue eyes and the rosiness that seemed to permanently stain his cheeks. If he were older, fatter and white-haired, he'd be the perfect Santa Claus, Roxie had always thought. But what did Mary think of him? Roxie couldn't recall ever hearing Mary talk about Mark in a personal way. And why would Mary and Mark have to sneak around? She shook her head. If Mary wanted to keep her love life a secret, that was her right. More or less.

Roxie went to the picture window on the other side of the room and peered out at the ribbon of river moving southward. In the distance she thought she could see the *Celebration*. If she leaned right up against the glass and looked down, she could see the red paddle wheel of the smaller *River Princess* docked below.

Downriver, the bleat of a tug's whistle sounded like music and, as if in accompaniment, a gull flapped down and screeched its shrill notes of avian joy.

She rested her forehead against the glass and closed her eyes. This job was like a wonderful love affair. Sure, it had moments of stress, problems that sometimes seemed insurmountable. There were even times when she thought she'd had enough of her fellow workers. But she knew she'd be devastated to lose this job, to leave this river, to be away from these people permanently.

And what brought all this to mind? She opened her eyes and moved to her desk. All this talk about a pirate boat stealing their business.

CHAPTER FOUR

THREE MEN IN BUSINESS SUITS sat around a table, hunched over a map, in the back room of the Crystal Bar and Grill.

Ernest Givers shook his head and slapped Don Yong on the back as he looked up from the paper. "I gotta hand it to ya, Don, this was one great idea of yours. Now that the narcs are keeping the airports, depots and highways under surveillance, using the river was the only way to go. Only who'd have thought of it but you?"

The third man, Sammy Stone, looked up and nodded. "Yeah, and doing it in stages—from Mexico through the gulf, transferring the stuff in New Orleans and again in Dubuque and then up to St. Paul—was smart, too. Who'd even think of checking out cruise boats?"

Don Yong frowned at his fellow investors. "Don't kid yourselves, we're only one step ahead of the government on this. They've got agents planted on every street corner of the Twin Cities right now. If we get away with it this time, we're going to have lay low for a while, or look for a new route."

Givers felt in his pockets for a cigar. "What about Minto? You're sure he can handle this? I don't like some of the rumors I've been hearing about him."

"That's why he's the man for us. First of all, he's made himself just visible enough so the narcs'll never think he's working drugs, and second, he's slimy enough to do anything he's told as long as there's a buck in it for him." Yong took the cigar Givers offered and bit off the end. He chuckled as he spat out the nub. "Harry Minto likes to think of himself as working with the mob. We let him think that—it keeps him honest."

"As honest as a punk like that can be," Givers reminded.

Yong's eyes grew steely. "He knows what'll happen to him if anything goes wrong. He'll be the first one to get it."

The three men shook hands as they left for their respective businesses, confident that the exchange to be made that evening would go as planned.

HARRY MINTO kicked the pail that stood in his way as he paced the deck of the *Shark*. "Somebody get this damned mess cleaned up—now—or you're all dead meat!"

A freckled, wide-eyed, red-haired boy came scurrying up behind Minto, snatched the pail and hightailed it below deck.

Minto clamped his teeth more tightly around his cigar and grinned. "That's more like it," he muttered. He turned in to the main deck cabin and frowned at the sight of Caryl Martin seated at the bar this early in the day, a glass of Scotch in her hand.

"You're supposed to be cleaning up this garbage heap, not playing host to this lush," he snarled at the young man who stood behind the bar.

"I was cleaning up back here, Harry," George Mayer said.

"I asked him to pour me a little something, since he was back there," the thin blond woman whined.

"Get out." Minto gestured at George with his cigar.

"Harry, please, don't blame George, he was just doing what—"

"Shut up. I told you I wasn't going to have you hanging around here drunk," he said, his voice and expression suddenly calm and cold as ice.

Caryl began to cry. She tried to swallow the great gulping sobs as she got off the stool.

Minto grabbed her arm. "You want something to cry about?"

She shook her head and stammered, "N-no, Harry. I'm s-sorry."

He shoved her away. She fell to the floor, got quickly to her feet and ran out of the cabin.

"Ugly bitch! I'm going to dump her overboard one of these days. All of 'em. All the bitches who get in my way."

He went behind the bar, poured himself two fingers of rum and shouted for Mayer to get back in there and clean up the bar.

George Mayer was below deck, gently rubbing Caryl's back and holding her in his arms. "I'm going to kill that bastard one of these days," he growled. Her hair felt sticky against his chin as she shook her head without lifting her face from his chest.

"No, George, don't ever talk like that. He'll kill you for real if he ever suspects you're trying to help me get away from him."

"You aren't going to have to take this much longer. I promise. I'm going to get you out of here, Caryl."

"I don't understand, George. Why can't we go now? Is it the money? I don't care about that anymore, I just want to be somewhere safe."

"We have to wait till we know it's safe, otherwise he'll find out what we're planning and our chances will be less than nothing." He pushed her away gently. "Go in and clean up. I'd better get back upstairs before he comes looking for me."

She looked so pathetic, creeping into Minto's cabin. For the moment George didn't know how he could protect her or get her away from Minto.

Minto bellowed for George.

"Comin', Harry," George yelled, taking the stairs two at a time.

Minto was on the phone when George entered the main cabin.

"Yeah, we can handle that," he said, shifting his cigar to the other side of his mouth. "It'll cost you five hundred dollars for the three hours." He chuckled at something his caller said, and George guessed the party was expressing surprise at the low charter rate. Minto gestured for George to take the phone.

"I'll let you talk to my charter manager, George Mayer, now. He'll take your order and give you instructions for where to board."

George took the phone and began the ritual he'd learned by heart. "You understand, first of all," he said, turning his back on Minto, "that you'll have to pay in cash; we don't have any credit system."

Minto left the cabin with a jaunty step and threw his cigar butt overboard as he moved toward the pilot-house, whistling under his breath.

Money was pouring in hand over fist, and this was just a front for the real thing, the thing that would bring in even bigger money. Don Yong may not have realized it, but he had given Harry a nice, juicy sideline when he'd set him up on the *Shark*. And now Harry could call the shots. Without the *Shark*, and Harry's part in the deal, the stuff would never make it to the streets. Not that he intended to double-cross Yong and the mob, but the knowledge that he could made him feel ten feet tall.

Knowing he was taking business away from the legitimate companies on the river made the prize all the sweeter. Especially Harley Marine. He had never forgiven that bastard Joe Harley for firing him when he was a kid, just on the verge of getting his pilot's license. He was only sorry he couldn't let Harley know that it was him, Harry Minto, alias Harold Martin, putting the screws to Harley's business.

"OH, IT'S GOOD TO HEAR your voice, Joe, where are you?" Roxie smiled happily and settled comfortably in her seat, prepared for a long telephone visit with her boss.

"Idaho. Beautiful country here—miles and miles of farmland. Thought I'd stop here in Boise, get some rest and make contact with you."

"I'm glad you did. We miss you."

"Sorry to hear that, girl. I was hoping you'd say you were too busy to miss me." Joe laughed.

"Well, yes, we are busy. But there are a million things around here to remind me of you, Joe, so I do miss you. Listen, are you taking good care of yourself—getting good meals on time and plenty of rest?"

"Are you going to go all motherly on me now, Roxie, from long distance?"

Roxie laughed and was glad Joe couldn't see the flush brighten her cheeks. "Sorry, Captain. It's just that I worry about you."

"No need, Roxie, I'm fine." There was a pause while both thought of Joe's reason for being so far from home, in a strange place and all alone. "You know, you sounded just like Martha, fussing over me like that."

Roxie's throat burned and she couldn't think of a response.

She heard him cough softly before he asked, "So, how's everything there? No problems, no emergencies?"

Roxie wondered if the rumors that the *Shark* was a pirate charter boat would constitute a problem. But rumors were all they were. She decided it would be unfair to burden the captain with a worry that might not even bear weight. He had all he could handle right now just working through his grief.

"No problems, no emergencies," she said, making her voice cheerful, "the news here is pretty dull, I'm afraid. Business as usual."

"Jake, Bill, the crew...how's everyone?"

"Just fine. Everyone's in good health—all doing their jobs just as if you were here to keep after us."

"Good. Good. I knew I could count on the three of you, but it's comforting to hear the words, anyway. And Roxie, I don't want you working yourself into exhaustion, you hear?"

"What do you mean? Why would you think—"

"I know how much you want that promotion, girl. But all I expect is that you do your job as well as you have been, and if you come up with some new ideas that promote more revenue, fine. I don't want you working yourself into a frenzy because you'll only make yourself ill."

"Joe. Do you mind if I ask how you will judge us?"

Another of Joe's chuckles preceded his reply. "I guess I'll be judging by the seat of my pants, as we used to say. I'll be back sometime in October—just before the season ends—and I'll know then which of you can best handle the job."

It wasn't much but it gave Roxie heart. She knew she was best qualified, and in her gut she believed Joe would give the job to her for that very reason.

"I'll call again in a couple of weeks, Roxie. I'd like you to have some figures for me then. A projection for the whole of June."

"I'll have it ready for you, Joe. And Joe, at the risk of sounding motherly, take care of yourself, will you?"

They said their goodbyes, and Roxie replaced the receiver and went to the window. The *Celeb* was sitting erectly in her spot beside the levy, her flags flapping in the light breeze. She should have been out on a charter, but last week the chartering party had called to cancel their reservation, giving no reason and showing no regret at the loss of their deposit. Should she have told Joe that? Downriver the *Princess* was moving at a steady pace, doing her daily excursion, carrying a large party of tourists who'd come from Iowa for a long weekend.

She returned to her desk and shook her head. Too early to panic. Cancellations were a part of the business. That they had had more than usual this season didn't really prove anything, and she was sure she could resell the spots they'd lost.

Meanwhile, there was tomorrow, a day off except for hostessing the TexCo party aboard the *Celebration* in the evening. The first Saturday in two years that Clay wouldn't figure into her plans in some way. A free day. A day to do exactly as she pleased.

It was going to be different going aboard the boat this time; she hadn't been aboard since last year, when Martha first took ill. Now it was she, Roxie, who signed the paychecks, she who hired and fired all staff except for the marina. And though the pilots had autonomy aboard the vessels, the crew members would answer to her, as well as to Jake, if their work was unsatisfactory.

She thought about what Mary had said about joining in the fun during a cruise. Not a bad way to begin her new life without Clay—certainly better than sitting home alone on a Saturday night. She visualized herself surrounded by an admiring bevy of Minnesota mining executives.

She grimaced. Some way for an upwardly mobile executive to be thinking. What she should have on her mind were ways to improve her image within the company. Small as it was, it was a well-recognized company that generated a great deal of revenue. At least it always had in the past. She shook her head. "I'm not going to give that pirate boat another thought," she muttered.

Instead she concentrated on the promotion she hoped to get. Almost immediately she imagined herself in a businesslike suit, standing at the head of a conference table, speaking to a room full of male executives. Bank officials or a board of directors. She leaned back in her chair, copying the position Jake had maintained earlier, hands behind her head, and grinned. She didn't own a suit, or for that matter anything much more professional-looking than the skirt and blouse she was wearing.

Mary, leaving for the day, found her that way. "What's happened to put such a smug look on your face, Chief?"

"Just planning my day tomorrow," Roxie said. "I'm going shopping. I think it's time I try on a whole new image. Want to come along?"

"You're going to buy clothes? Real, female-type clothes?" Mary pretended to gasp. "You bet. I wouldn't miss this for the world."

ROXANNE HILTON signed her name with a flourish and stuck the credit card in her wallet.

"You're going to look smashing in those outfits, Rox," Mary said, relieving her friend of one of the silver and burgundy bags. "And I'm glad you decided to buy a few really expensive things rather than a whole slew of junk."

Roxie sighed and mopped her forehead with a tissue. "Whew, I never realized shopping was such hard work. I'm really grateful you were along to advise me, Mary."

"Grateful enough to let me give you some unasked-for advice?" Mary asked, glancing sideways at Roxie.

"Sure. What is it?"

"Let's see if one of the salons in the mall will take you without an appointment and get something done with your hair."

Roxie stopped dead in her tracks, almost causing a collision with a man who was just a few feet behind her. "My hair?" She clutched a handful of it. "You mean cut it?"

Mary took her by the arm and pulled her out of the path of a woman running toward a bus stop. "Don't panic, Roxie, I'm just thinking how unsophisticated your hair will look when you're wearing your new clothes."

"I can always put it up in a twist or a bun."

"Those hairdos are old-fashioned. You've got too much hair, Rox. You need it styled."

The Golden Slipper Salon just happened to have a cancellation. Mr. Henri, who'd been assigned to do Roxie's makeover, cast a dubious glance at her hair, rubbed his hands and forced his lips into a polite smile. "Follow me, please," he commanded.

Roxie gave Mary a last panicked glance and followed the man, feeling as if she were being led to her execution.

"I'll have a manicure while I'm waiting for you," Mary called out cheerfully. *Well, why not,* Roxie grumbled inwardly. Mary wasn't about to take a dose of her own medicine and have that braid cut off.

Henri glanced at Roxie's hands and said, "That's not a bad idea for you, either. I think Miss Jane can find time to do a manicure while I'm shaping your hair."

A cautious truce developed between Roxie and Henri when he told her she had beautiful hair and that he wouldn't dream of cutting it all off.

Placing herself in his hands, while her own rested in bowls of soapy water, Roxie closed her eyes and let her mind wander to the evening ahead.

It would be fun to spend some time with Jake again, up in the pilothouse. He had been right when he said they used to exchange words of advice. She recalled that from the beginning he'd shown a definite coolness when he found out she was dating Clay Montgomery.

All of a sudden she regretted having told Jake about Clay dumping her. Why hadn't she pretended the breakup had been her idea? She never seemed to think of those face-saving lies other people told so glibly. Was that a flaw in her character? Clay would probably say so. His way of getting ahead was different from hers, though no one could say Roxie Hilton wasn't ambitious as hell.

Her thoughts made her shift uncomfortably in her chair.

"We can't have this wriggling around, Miss Hilton, or I won't be responsible for the outcome," Henri snapped.

His warning brought her out of her reverie, and she opened her eyes and almost gasped at the sight of herself in the mirror.

"You've cut off all my hair," she wailed.

"Don't whine," Henri scolded, squeezing the wet hair that hung to her shoulder, "this is still quite long. I'm actually thinking it should be cut to your jaw-line."

"No. Absolutely not," Roxie said, thrusting her chin out. "You may be the expert, but it's still my hair." She winced. "What there is left of it."

When she walked to the reception area, an hour later, she had bangs for the first time in her life. Her hair, cut pageboy-style, just missed her shoulders and swirled around her face every time she moved her head. She had to admit the feeling was sensual though she felt strangely disoriented without the familiar weight down her back.

Roxie walked over to where Mary was sitting and said her name. Mary looked up and blinked. "Yes?"

And then blinked again and jumped to her feet, her mouth agape and eyes wide.

"Roxie?"

"Of course it's me. Come on, I don't look that different."

But Mary disagreed. "My God, you're beautiful," she said, in a hushed tone.

Behind her, Roxie heard Mr. Henri's smug snort of triumph. She hated to admit he'd been right. "Let's go," she told Mary, "I haven't had a thing to eat today and I'm starving."

THAT EVENING, as she stood in front of her mirror assessing her day's accomplishments, she couldn't deny she looked very different than the old Roxie. Her outfit camouflaged her skinniness, the décolleté blouse showing just a hint of cleavage.

As she slipped her arms into the sleeves of a jade bouclé jacket, a shudder of excitement swept over her, making her skin chill. She had never before taken such pains with her appearance, or worn such exquisite clothes. She thought, *This must be how a bride feels,* then blew a raspberry at herself for such a juvenile thought.

"This is strictly business," she said aloud, as she swept up the jade leather clutch and slipped into matching heels, "with maybe a little innocent socializing thrown in to make it interesting."

She couldn't help wondering, on her way to Harley's Landing, how Jake Gilbert would respond to the new Roxie Hilton.

WHEN ROXIE CAME ABOARD the *Celebration*, she was greeted by whistles and applause from those members of the crew who were meeting guests at the gangplank.

The boat's whistle blew, early and unexpectedly, and Roxie looked up to see Jake leaning out of the open pilothouse window staring at her as she looked up. He grinned and saluted her smartly.

She was still smiling when Donny Nader and a strange man approached her. The man was tall and blond with deeply hooded blue eyes that seemed to check her over with a single sweeping gaze. He wore white duck slacks and a navy blazer with graceful ease.

"Ms. Hilton, this is Mr. Danvers," Donny introduced the man. Roxie recognized the name and voice. Danvers had booked the cruise by telephone and discussed details with her.

"Eric, please," he said as they shook hands.

She nodded. "And you know I'm Roxie."

"My imagination didn't begin to do you justice, Roxie, though I guessed from your voice that you were attractive," Eric Danvers said, keeping her hand in his. "I'm delighted that you decided to come aboard. You are joining us for the cruise?"

"Yes. Thank you. My regular hostess needed the night off, so you're stuck with me." She didn't feel able to deal with his compliments. Suddenly she wished she had worn jeans and a sweatshirt. She hadn't even made it past the gangplank yet, and already her smile was beginning to feel strained. She glanced toward the pilothouse, but Jake had pulled his head in and all she could see was his arm moving back and forth as he made adjustments to the helm.

"I'd better check in with Floyd," she murmured, pulling her hand free of Danvers's.

"I'll see more of you later," he said. She wondered if that was meant to be a threat, then wondered why she was having such a cynical reaction to a seemingly nice and certainly attractive man. He stood back to let her continue up the wooden ramp.

"Hey, pretty lady," Floyd Dubrov greeted as she entered the cabin. The bar was to her left and Floyd was behind it, resplendent in the khaki pants and short-sleeved white shirt with navy epaulets at the shoulders that the officers and pilots wore. Sara Winslow, one of the two female bartenders, worked beside him.

"Hi, Floyd, Sara."

"Geez, Roxie, is that really you?"

A spasm of irritation warred with the polite urge to thank Sara for the compliment. "Did I look that bad before?" she asked, softening her remark with laughter.

"There's no comparison," Sara said, unmindful of Roxie's displeasure. "You look like a million bucks."

"I'm not greedy," Floyd said, "I'd have settled for the thousand bucks you looked like before."

Roxie laughed again and went to work.

Some of the charter guests were milling around the bar, waiting for that moment when the gangplank went up and the bar could legally begin serving liquor.

Eric Danvers pushed through the crowd to Roxie's side. "Since this is a private charter, and a free bar, can't you start dispensing drinks now?"

"I'm sorry, Eric, but we only have a federal license, not a state license, so we can't serve liquor while the gangplank touches city property."

Reiterating the rules made Roxie wonder if Minto could be caught violating that law. That would be the easiest way to get him and the *Shark* off the river.

But she had little time to ponder the evils of the pirate boat. The whistle blew again and the cranking of the hoist that lifted the gangplank was heard over the noise of the TexCo revelers.

The MV *Celebration* was a three-story stern-wheeler that, like most of those built today, could be used for parties or excursions.

Because of the number of people in this party, the bars on both decks were in use. Roxie found herself running up and down stairs, lighting the candles on the tables set for dinner, restocking liquor and olives for Andy Carruthers, the bartender working the second-deck bar, and making repeated trips to the ice-making machine on the lower deck.

The caterers had forgotten salt, of all things, and though it was a first, Roxie had to bite back a reprimand as she searched the tiny galley behind the bar for the little cardboard salt shakers they'd purchased the year before when they began the lunch-box cruises.

By the time she'd found a safety pin for a guest who'd broken a bra strap, carried trays of beverages to the members of the band, helped the caterers serve the food and finally helped clear away the remnants of the meal, she was more than ready for a break.

Getting away from Eric Danvers, who'd been dogging her steps all evening, was difficult. In desperation, while dancing with one of Eric's co-workers, she feigned a need to use the ladies' room and fled up the stairway unseen.

In the second-deck galley she snatched a thermos of fresh coffee and slipped out to the deck and around to the starboard side where the ladder hung. There were a few couples out on the deck, braving chilly spring night air. But they were huddled close, as much for warmth as for romance, she guessed, and they didn't pay any attention to her as she made her careful way up the ladder to the pilothouse.

CHAPTER FIVE

JAKE WAS ALONE, as she'd hoped.

His glance covered her from head to foot. "That new hairdo is great. You look gorgeous."

She relaxed as she eased onto the bench and kicked her shoes off. "Hand me a couple of cups." Her hair swung forward as she reached for the mugs. For the first time since coming aboard that night, she had time to enjoy the feeling.

They sipped in companionable silence for a few minutes, the rich aroma of the Columbian brew filling the small cabin. Roxie sighed deeply and slumped back in the corner, lifting her legs and stretching them out along the length of the bench. "Ooh," she said, almost moaning.

"Tired?"

"And sore."

He looked at the shoes she'd discarded. "No wonder. You should have worn sneakers."

"With this outfit?"

"Yeah, I guess you're right. You know—" he pushed his cap back on his head "—I don't think I've ever seen you so dolled up for work."

"I wanted to look good for a change."

His chuckle scoffed at her. "What do you mean, look good for a change? You've been hanging out with that Montgomery jerk so long you've forgotten what you look like."

She hoped he couldn't see her blush in the dim light. "Thanks for the compliment—I think! But do you mind if we don't talk about Clay tonight?"

"Sure, fine with me." He was quiet for a moment then he said, "It's nice having you back. I wondered if you'd get past that mob of oversexed executives and come up here tonight."

"I don't know what you're talking about," she said, looking over the top of her mug, at the night world spread out before them. They were already two thirds of the way back. She could see the lights of the brewery tower in the distance and the lights of the downtown business section just ahead on the right bank.

"Terry said some of those guys were hot on your trail every time he went down there."

She smiled in the dark. "Terry needs to spend more time at the helm and less below, playing espionage agent."

He turned from the wheel and she could just barely make out his features in the semidarkness.

"He said you looked uncomfortable." He nudged one of her shoes with the toe of his sneaker. "Was it because of these?"

"What are we talking about here?" she asked with a short laugh. "My physical discomfort or my mental discomfort?"

"That's what I want to know."

"Why?" She peered through the darkness, trying to gauge his mood.

He took his cap off, threw it on the seat behind him and scratched his head. "I don't know." He sounded exasperated. "I shouldn't have brought it up." He turned to the wheel.

She wondered why they were having so much trouble starting a conversation then realized she didn't really want to talk to him, she just wanted to share the quiet, intimate space with him.

"Jake," she said, her voice reaching softly across the space that distanced them. "I just needed to be with a friend, away from other people."

"Right. You got it." He concentrated on the river in front of him. The lights that guided him through the dark water didn't light the interior of the cabin. He preferred darkness within the cabin most of the time.

Roxie relaxed. Her mind focused on the river as she rested her head against the window and gazed at the wake that ribboned the side of the boat. She deliberately slowed her breathing and began to focus inward.

Was this unusual discomfort with Jake due to the fact that it had been so long since their last time alone together?

Or maybe it was because they were competing for the same prize, the promotion. That is, if Jake really viewed it as a prize. Her honest opinion had been, all along, that he didn't want to compete—that any kind of rivalry was foreign to his nature.

She shook herself and reached deeper within for the black void that would bring peace.

"Damn." Jake's voice penetrated her meditation. "There the bastard is again."

"What?" She leaned forward, trying to see what had upset him.

"That stern-wheeler. I've been seeing it all week." He pointed to his left where Pig's Eye Landing made an island in the river. She could see the lights of a fairly large vessel on the other side.

"Which is it? The *Donnybrook*?" she asked, referring to a mock stern-wheeler owned by a major insurance company president who was a notorious riverboat buff.

"It's a boat called the *Shark*, and I've been asking around and no one seems to know what company owns her or if she's licensed to charter or where she's picking up passengers."

Roxie looked out the window above the bench and saw the other stern-wheeler, boldly lighted and moving at a smart pace through the night. "My gosh! Bill and Mark came into the office yesterday to tell us about it and they seemed pretty concerned, too. Mark said it isn't licensed to carry passengers. They think it's stealing charters from legitimate companies."

He was facing ahead, watching the other boat pass.

"We agreed to get together for a meeting on Monday to see if we couldn't come up with some ideas about what to do about it. Is Monday morning all right for you?"

She heard the rustle of movement as he nodded, better than she could see it, actually. But the river would grow lighter from the reflections of the city lights and the lamps along the embankment, just ahead beyond this next bend, she knew. She remembered how a sort of glow would encompass them here in the cabin, causing Jake's broad jaw to soften, his eyes to change to pewter.

She could barely make out his broad shoulders bent to the helm as he navigated the bend, then suddenly the light came and she could see, after blinking away the night blindness, the true shape of him, the set of his head, the glint in his eyes as he turned to smile at her.

"Practically home," he said. It was what he always used to say to her when they reached this point. She grinned and saluted.

"Aye, aye. Another successful voyage, Captain."

"C'mon up here," he said, holding his arm out.

She padded over in her stockinged feet to join him at the wheel. She'd always loved this part of the trip, viewing the city at night from so high up and right beside Jake at the helm. She could sense the power he felt, could almost feel it herself.

"Look how good the new high bridge looks," he said.

"Where?" She leaned forward.

He put his arm around her shoulders and pulled her closer to his side, his cheek against her hair. "See, over there through those trees? Wait. We're clearing this curve now, you'll see it better in a moment." But he kept her there against him, one hand on the wheel the other on her shoulder.

She breathed in the freshly laundered smell of his shirt and the astringency of his after-shave right there where the skin of his neck began above his collar. A tiny sound in her throat seemed a response both to the fragrance of him and to the pulse that had started thrumming in her neck. She wondered what would happen if she turned her head, buried her face in his neck and opened her mouth to taste that skin.

Oh, cripes, Hilton, are you actually considering nuzzling with the enemy?

"Hey—what's the matter?" Jake's arm seemed frozen in the arc that formed when she broke abruptly out of his embrace and fled to the safety of the bench. She fumbled her feet into her shoes and lowered her eyes.

"Time to get below," she mumbled.

Jake spun around and caught her arms, turning her so she faced him. "I know what you were feeling just then," he said, "I was feeling it, too."

She pulled free, but there was nowhere to go. She was backed up to the bench. She sat on it and shifted. "Don't be silly, Jake," she said, "I wasn't feeling anything." She tried a disdainful laugh. It sounded distorted, as if it had made a wrong turn passing through her vocal cords.

"Roxie, let's not play games with each other, we're too old and we've been friends too long. Something was happening there for a minute. I felt it and I'm pretty sure you did, too." He rubbed her arm gently. "What's to be afraid of, hon? We're not kids."

"No. But we're each just days out of other relationships," she reminded, "and I, personally, wouldn't trust my feelings again this soon . . . if ever."

He looked over his shoulder, checking that they were still on course, made a small adjustment to the wheel and turned to her.

"We already have a relationship, Roxie," he urged, "we've been friends for years. This other thing—" he waved his hand uncertainly "—this is just the flip side of friendship . . . the physical side." A look of surprise widened his eyes. "What if our real feelings have just been simmering below the surface all this time, covered by what we thought we felt for someone else?"

"That's ridiculous, Jake." She began to inch to the end of the bench, toward the doorway. "If that were true, there'd be no such thing as a safe, platonic relationship."

"Are you going to sit there and tell me you really didn't feel anything?"

"No. I'm not going to tell you anything, I'm leaving!" Strange that it should occur to her now, in her anger at Jake, but she suddenly realized what had bothered her about Eric Danvers—he reminded her of Clay.

Under normal circumstances, wearing slacks and sneakers, she could have slid down the ladder, fireman style, as the guys had taught her to do the first time she came aboard, making a quick getaway. But she was wearing a skirt and the dratted heels. She stood in the doorway feeling helpless and foolish.

"I'll lift you down," Jake offered.

"No." She'd made it worse, sounding so frightened. Of his touch? *Jake's?* That seemed as preposterous to her as the thing he'd suggested. She tried to clear the air between them by reminding him of something obvious. "Are you forgetting that you and I are warring for the same job?"

"I think your terminology is a little strong. I can't fathom ever warring with you—you're too small, too lovely. I wouldn't want to be responsible for hurting you."

She laughed harshly. "Don't you think for a minute that I'm too frail—either to beat you at any game or to handle the job."

His grin was downright devilish, showing the even row of gleaming white teeth and an intriguing crease of dimple alongside his mouth. He caught her by the elbows and held her captive, unable to move. "Hey, Rox," he said, almost whispering, "you don't want to challenge me, do you? You might open up the dark side of me—you don't want to see that, do you?"

She shivered. Jake with a dark side. The very idea sent icy tingles over her skin and down her spine. And were they still referring to the race for the promotion? She thought not.

"Let's stop fencing, Jake," she said, "you can certainly understand that I'm feeling a little gun-shy about relationships right now. The prospect of another rejection makes me tremble."

Jake shook his head and frowned. "Rejecting you is the farthest thing from my mind, Roxie." He emphasized his sincerity by caressing her cheek with the back of his hand.

Roxie brushed his hand away and stepped back. "No one means to end a relationship in the beginning, but that certainly seems to be the way they end up. And now, if you don't mind, I really need to get below."

They stared at each other for a moment, Roxie with her mouth set determinedly.

Jake shrugged. "All right. Where were we? Oh, yes. I'll help you down."

He disregarded her refusal and slid down the ladder before she could decide her alternative. He stood below, his arms stretched up to her. "Sit on the floor with your feet hanging down the rungs so I can reach you," he said.

She had no choice. Stocking clad feet would have been just as chancy since she'd get no purchase against the metal with nylon.

He lifted her down and held on when her feet touched the deck. She tried to pretend she didn't feel intimidated by his nearness. But he continued to hold her long after it was necessary. His arms were strong and comforting around her and his chest hard and warm under her cheek.

"Let go of me," she said. She tried not to sound as desperate as she felt.

He let go and she teetered. He put out a hand to steady her. "Do you want to test my conviction?" he asked.

"How?"

His head bent to hers just as she realized he'd probably read her naive question as permission for the kiss that followed.

It was too late to stop him and then, an intake of breath later, she didn't want to.

His mouth was unutterably soft and sweet against hers. Impossible to believe that such a light caress could stir her so deeply. It was as if she could fall right into his gentleness and drown in it.

Awareness first came with the vibration of music and dancing feet below, then the sound of voices raised in merriment and finally the rhythmic splash of the paddle wheel pushing through the water. She drew back, hardly able to focus on where they were.

"I've wanted to do that for years," Jake said, following a long, shaky sigh.

"That doesn't say much for the quality of our friendship," Roxie said. It seemed hard to breathe past the constriction in her chest.

Terry's voice came from right behind her, causing her to jump guiltily. "Who's driving the bus?"

"You," Jake said, his eyes staring into Roxie's.

"Okay." Terry sounded cheerfully calm as he scrabbled up the ladder to take over the helm.

Three things struck Roxie simultaneously. The first was to wonder if Terry had seen them kissing, and the second the realization that this was the first time she'd ever seen Jake make an irresponsible move while piloting the boat. The third was the question of whether Jake was capable of using sex to distract Roxie from competing against him for the job. She didn't know which thought disturbed her the most but she was motivated by all three when she grabbed her jacket from behind the bar and was the first one off the boat when the gangplank went down at Harley's Landing.

ROXIE TOSSED AND TURNED in her bed for an hour. Finally she got up, wrapped herself in a summer robe and went to sit on the balcony.

Jake's kiss had affected her more than she'd admitted to him. And it raised frightening self-doubts. Was she so out of touch with her awareness that she could have thought she wanted to marry one man while harboring sexual feelings for another? The fact that she hadn't recognized this attraction to Jake made her feel uneasy.

She wondered how her friendship with Jake—something she had prized highly for the past five years—would be affected. She couldn't bear the thought of losing a good friend, especially so soon after losing Clay.

She sighed sadly, became aware of the cool air penetrating her robe and returned to her bedroom. Lately it seemed as if life had nothing to offer but losses. First Martha, then Joe, then Clay. She removed her robe and got in bed.

And Jake. If he didn't stop insisting that the chemistry between them couldn't be controlled, wouldn't she lose him, too? At least she'd lose the easy, companionable relationship they'd shared in the past.

Still, her last thought before she fell asleep was a replay of the feeling of Jake's mouth gently searching hers.

BY MONDAY MORNING she was as nervous as a high-school freshman on the first day of school.

Jake was the last to arrive for the meeting and the greeting he called out to her was no different in tone than the one he made to the others. If anything, Roxie thought, his expression was cooler when his eyes met hers. She juggled relief with a surprising sensation of rejection and called the meeting to order.

But conflicting emotions made it difficult for her to concentrate on the task at hand. Looking for honesty within herself, she wondered if she was feeling disappointed that Jake hadn't followed up that kiss with some kind of communication. When he leaned back in his chair, she couldn't help but notice his strong physique and the way his eyes darkened when he was thinking.

Had he really forgotten what had happened between them on Saturday night? As unlikely as that seemed, it was apparent now that he had nothing more on his mind than the business they were discussing.

Yet he'd been so persistent, so obviously interested in her. Then what could have happened to cancel his interest? She wished she didn't care, but the thoughts just wouldn't leave her alone.

He must have realized what foolishness it would be to get involved again only a blink of an eye after breaking up with Taffy. That thought made her realize she ought to feel grateful that he wasn't pursuing her.

She made a conscious effort to keep her thoughts on the meeting as Mary and Mark brought chairs to group around her desk.

Mark began the discussion. "I've had a talk with Harvey Callow over at the Coast Guard, and he says they're aware of Minto's presence on the river but that they need proof in order to curb his activities."

"Proof?" Mary asked. "What kind of proof? Isn't a boatload of passengers proof enough?"

"Not unless someone can prove they are passengers and not just friends. He doesn't do any advertising that describes the *Shark* as a charter boat. What they need is someone to witness money changing hands."

Roxie shook her head. "Doesn't seem too complicated. All we have to do is question people who have booked a cruise with him. We can ask how they got in touch with Minto, what they paid and where they boarded."

For the first time, Jake's eyes met Roxie's, though there was nothing personal or remotely romantic to be found in his level look.

"I don't think it'll be that easy," Jake said. "We can't openly follow his boat and see where they disembark, or stand around questioning his passengers as they come down the plank."

"The thing to do," Bill said, "is think like a prospective customer. How would we find a cheaper way to go, if we were looking for a charter boat? There is a grapevine on the river, we ought to be able to ask around and find out how people are getting in touch with Minto. Or how he's getting in touch with them."

"Callow said to stay away from Minto," Mark reminded, "and personally, I'm not real excited about coming up against him. You, Jake?"

"I don't think the guy's going to do us much harm," Jake said, smiling lazily. "For one thing, the *Shark* isn't as big as the *Celeb*, and for another, guys like Minto usually show up for a season, make their share of mischief and then get into another line."

"We can't afford a whole season of his mischief, as you so casually refer to it," Roxie said, facing Jake head on. "We've already begun showing a loss for June. If I don't make it up, and soon, we'll be losing revenue for July, too."

It took Roxie a few minutes to recover from the jolt of electricity that shot through her as she returned Jake's long, intense stare.

She had to admit, there was something appealing about Jake's lazy self-confidence even when he resorted to sarcasm.

"I didn't realize it was already causing problems," Jake said softly.

"We need a plan, one that lets us check out Minto without his knowledge." Mary's voice cut through the tension.

"Yeah," Mark said, enthusiasm lighting his eyes, "like going undercover the way the cops do."

Jake looked at the two men. "Have you checked to see if any of the other lines know about the *Shark*?"

"No," Bill answered. "But I'll be glad to get in touch with them."

Jake nodded. "If he's operating illegally, he won't have any qualms about which river he runs on. So I'd check the lines on the St. Croix, too."

Roxie was only half listening to the men. Her mind was trying to figure out how a pirate company would solicit business. Since that was a big part of her job, it seemed logical that she would be the one to unscramble that part of the mystery.

She began making notes. Advertising. Radio. Newspaper. Television. Phone soliciting. Letters. Brochures. These were the methods legitimate businesses used. She had taken in a quarter of a million dollars in deposits for the season using them.

She began underlining words, finding she'd underlined the word "newspaper" more than the others, when suddenly the idea popped into her head.

"Wait," she said, almost shouting in excitement. "I think I know a way to pull the plug on Minto without resorting to amateur crime-fighting tactics."

She was gratified to see that she had their total attention. Jake, in particular, seemed to be leaning toward her.

"What if we simply use the newspapers to warn the public? An article about illegal boat chartering will appeal to any of the metropolitan editors. We can choose one, tell our story warning people that such charters are illegal and therefore potentially dangerous, and then send a copy of the story to all the other papers in the towns along the rivers."

Only Mark looked unconvinced. "I've heard this Minto character is a real vicious type—do you think this'd be enough to stop him?"

"If the public doesn't use his services, that in itself pretty much stops him," Roxie pointed out. She waited for further disagreement. When there was none, she said, "Okay. I'll call the city editor at *Dispatch*."

She was already dialing the newspaper when the men filed out of the office, still discussing Minto and his illegal operation.

Roxie admitted that her feelings were hurt when Jake left with the others without saying anything to her. Unhappiness settled over her like a blanket of fog, chilling her thoroughly. This was the very thing she had feared, losing Jake's friendship.

JAKE LEANED OVER THE RAILING to pull the fishing line out from where it had drifted under the boat. He straightened up, reeled in and cast again. The baited hook made a satisfying splash as it landed about fifteen feet from the boat. Jake sat back in the folding lounge chair, propped his feet on the rail and sighed contentedly.

If only life could be this simple all the time. A job he enjoyed and, now and then, a fishing line in the water for recreation.

Behind him, placed on the roof of the cabin, his portable stereo sent out the music of Chopin's "Polonaise." Jake's left hand drummed the bass chords on the arm of the chair as he hummed the melody.

He closed his eyes and let his mind wander.

Above the sound of the music, he could hear the water lapping up against the hull of the boat, one of his favorite sounds in the world. That, together with the metallic clanking of sail hooks against the masts, the ringing of buoy bells, the foghorns on misty nights and the honking of river birds were the chords of the river's symphony.

His thoughts, prompted by the music, turned to his childhood. There had been violin lessons with his brother, Paul, playing piano accompaniment and Beth and Sissy, short for Priscilla, marching around thumping their feet and tooting on make-believe horns.

The image of Beth when she was young reminded him of Roxie. Beth had had long blond hair like Roxie's. But he preferred the way Roxie wore hers. It swirled around her face in a most enticing way. Each time it swirled he caught a whiff of her perfume.

God. She'd smelled so good when he kissed her. He could smell her hair and her cologne and the darker aroma of the coffee they'd shared. He'd held the back of her head with one hand and that wonderful hair had felt like strands of silk caressing his fingers.

No! Mustn't dwell on that.

Jake jumped up, stuck the rod into a holder attached to the rail and went in to get a beer from the small fridge in the galley. He popped the top, took a long draft and returned to the deck.

Uncontrollably, his thoughts returned to Roxie. Right up until the moment he had kissed her, he'd dismissed the chemistry between them as something he could easily handle. And he was sure Taffy's leaving hadn't left any scars. What he hadn't counted on was how deep his feelings for Roxie threatened to be and how suddenly all those feelings were mixed with surprising pain over the breakup with Taffy.

"You're going to have to chill out, take it slow for now," he said aloud. He picked up his rod and returned to his seat. He hadn't liked behaving as if nothing had happened when he saw Roxie this morning. He'd seen the surprise and then the pain in her eyes and he'd felt like a complete jerk.

He'd have liked to go in, sweep her into his arms and give her a resounding kiss on the mouth to show how good it felt to see her again. But something had happened to him on Saturday night, when he'd returned to his boat and stumbled across some of the things Taffy had left behind.

The pain had hit him suddenly, bringing tears to his eyes. He knew he wasn't in love with Taffy—never had been. But he'd lived with her for almost a year and he'd cared for her and grown used to her.

Things hadn't worked out, but it wasn't her fault. Something vital had been missing in their relationship, that special component that made two people a couple.

He knew it existed—he had seen it in his parents' marriage, and in Joe and Martha's. His older brother, Paul, seemed to have it with Cathey, his bride of four years, his sister, Beth, with her fiancé.

The pain he felt was as much for Roxie and Clay as it was for himself and Taffy. Why did some people come together just to hurt one another? He knew suddenly that he never wanted to go carelessly into a relationship again, never wanted to risk hurting a other human being.

It hit him then that he wasn't off to a very good start if he resorted to measures such as those he'd employed at the meeting today. His only excuse was that he'd been under terrific strain to keep his old feelings for Taffy and his new feelings for Roxie apart.

He thought he saw the fishing rod move and jumped up to look over the side. Nothing; the bobber lay on top of the water in the same place.

He went back to his chair and picked up the beer can.

Damn. This had sure been a year for losing people. First Martha, then Joe and now Taffy. Maybe that's why he had felt such a strong, sudden pull toward Roxie. She was someone he'd known a long time, someone with whom he'd shared the incredible loss of the elderly couple who'd been their best friends all these years. And now they were facing personal, romantic failures at the same time, too. No wonder he had been drawn to her.

"And all the more reason to leave her alone," he said, his voice echoing slightly as a maverick breeze caught the vibrations and carried the sound outward. A lone cloud eclipsed the sun's brightness, causing a momentary chill that sent shivers over Jake's bare forearms. He looked at the sky and frowned. He was not a superstitious man—at least no more so than the average river man—but if he didn't know better, he would swear there was an omen in the threatened change of weather.

"Don't be an ass, Gilbert," he muttered, pulling in his line, "this is Minnesota in May, there is no such thing as predictable weather."

Minnesota weather was unreliable and given to change at a moment's notice with no regard for the season. *Sort of,* he thought, *like the heart of a man.*

He grinned at his sappy poetic musings and lifted his radio just as the station began broadcasting the music of Delius, his favorite composer.

CHAPTER SIX

ROXIE TAPPED HER FOOT to the beat of the Charley Daniels band and hummed along as she placed the last of the inventory sheets for April in the folder. The door opened just as she placed the folder in the file drawer.

"Hi, I'm Meg Curley from the *Dispatch*," a small, blond older woman called out above the volume of the radio. She closed the door and strode across the room to Roxie's desk, her hand extended.

Roxie turned off the radio, shook the journalist's hand and gestured toward the side chair. "Care for coffee or a soft drink, Ms. Curley?"

"No, thanks. And make it Meg, will you? I haven't been back in the work force long enough to get used to Ms. Where I come from, 'mizz' was a lazy way of saying 'missus.'"

Roxie laughed, liking the reporter right from the start. "Okay, Meg. I'm Roxie. Roxie Hilton, office manager and cruise coordinator for Harley Marine."

She sat down and nodded as Meg asked for permission to set a miniature tape recorder on the edge of the desk.

"My editor said you have a story that we could use, something about an illicit boat charter operation?" Meg opened the interview.

"Yes." Roxie rubbed her forehead. "I'm not sure how to go about this. We're not even sure the boat in question is running a charter operation. And so we really don't want to name names."

"Okay. Why not tell me what is going on, and together we'll decide how the story should be written. We have to avoid lawsuits, so we're not inclined to point fingers without proof, either."

There was not much to tell, Roxie discovered, as she repeated what they did know. The only facts were that the *Shark* had been seen, frequently, carrying a full load of people up and down this part of the Mississippi, and that the Coast Guard admitted the *Shark* was not licensed to make public excursions or to charter out as a commercial party boat. Beyond that, everything was speculation.

"We've had a few cancellations, which could indicate our customers have found a cheaper way to go," Roxie admitted, "but that in itself isn't proof. None of my cancellations told me they were going with someone else. It may be only coincidence that they've backed out at the same time that this boat shows up in our territory."

"Did the Coast Guard say they'd check it out?"

"I'm not sure. One of our pilots talked to them, specifically to a man named—" she stopped and looked at the notes she had made during Monday's meeting "—yes, here it is. Harvey Callow. Our guy said Callow told him they could do nothing without proof."

Meg leaned toward the tape recorder. "And they didn't say they'd check it out?"

Roxie felt confused suddenly. Were she and the men making a mountain out of a molehill? "I guess not. From what Mark said—Mark's the pilot I mentioned—it sounded like the Coast Guard wasn't awfully concerned. These are federal waters, you know, and a person almost has to be breaking the law on a grand scale for the Coast Guard to step in."

"Like?"

"Well, like using the river to transport stolen goods, or illegal aliens, or dumping toxic waste or—you know, really major things like that."

Meg nodded. "So, is it your opinion that the Coast Guard is going to do nothing about this so-called pirate boat—this illegal operation—because it's not committing a serious crime?"

"Wait a minute!" Roxie rose from her chair in response to the reporter's remarks. "I don't think I said that, Meg. I just tried to tell you the facts as I know them. I have no way of knowing whether the Coast Guard is going to do a real check on Minto and his boat. I don't even know for certain that the *Shark* is selling charters. All we wanted your paper to do was to tell the public to be sure they buy their charters from accredited, licensed companies."

She sat down but stayed at the edge of her seat. "We don't want you to accuse the Coast Guard of negligence. We just thought if you'd print a warning of sorts, the way you've done in the past about people sending for things from companies that operate outside the law or answering ads that promise things they don't deliver...well, something along those lines might keep people from buying charters from Minto, *if* that's what he's doing."

The expression on the reporter's face showed she was less enthusiastic about this approach. Roxie wished one of the men—or even Mary—was there. She did not know enough about the subject to be discussing it without some help. Jake, for instance, would know how to handle this woman. He'd also know more about how the Coast Guard worked than she did. Her heart sank as she realized she might very well be jeopardizing the reputation of the company if Meg Curley slanted the article wrongly or said Harley Marine was falsely accusing Minto.

Besides that, if the paper named names and Minto lived up to his reputation, he might come around seeking revenge.

She shuddered and put a shaky hand to her mouth.

Meg saw she was losing Roxie's trust. Not wanting to alienate a source for a good story possibility, she turned off the recorder and reached over to pat Roxie's hand. "You've got it, kid. This will be merely a warning to the public and maybe a slap on the wrist to this Minto character if he reads the papers."

She stood up, tucked the recorder into her leather bag, withdrew a card from the side pocket and put it in front of Roxie. "My card. If you come up with new information on the guy or decide to go more public with your accusations, give me a call, okay?"

Roxie nodded, relief flooding her body and filling her chest with something resembling liquid bubbles. "My God," she said, nearly gasping, "a person's just a hairbreadth away from slander when they talk to the press."

"Libel. But, yeah, I guess you're right," the older woman said. "But don't worry. We don't practice unethical journalism at the *Dispatch*."

They shook hands again, and parted friends, though with less warmth on Roxie's part than when they first met. But now it was over and Roxie could get back to business. She needed to fill the gaps those cancellations had made in the schedule if she was to win the promotion.

To this end she had sent out letters, complete with self-addressed, stamped envelopes, to excursion and charter boat companies all over the country, asking for copies of their brochures. For a small postage budget, she'd received a bag full of ideas other companies had found profitable, from which she could draw ideas to spark her imagination.

She was soon deeply immersed in studying these brochures, and did not hear the approaching footsteps.

"Planning a trip?" Jake asked.

She was jolted out of her concentration. "Oh! Where did you come from?"

"Up from the sea in a bottle marked Save Me."

Roxie laughed and began shoving brochures into the grocery bag where she kept them. "Why do I get the feeling I'd be better off throwing the bottle back?"

He was plainly curious about the brochures, craning his neck to see what they were as she scooped them off her desk into the bag. "*Are* you going on a trip?"

"*Did* you really come up from the sea in a bottle?"

"Oh, I see. None of my business, right? But if you are, won't it become my business when you're not here to run the office?"

"Uh-huh." She stuffed the bag into an empty file drawer and closed it with a deliberate bang. "And when that time comes, Gilbert, I'll be sure and let you know."

They grinned at each other across the room and couldn't seem to stop. Roxie felt strangely happy, though she knew if anyone came in just then, they'd look foolish as hell. She tried to bring back the bitter feelings she'd had on Monday, when he'd seemed to ignore her, but his presence erased all that.

"So. What do you need to be saved from?"

He sobered only slightly and ran a hand through his hair. "My folks. Seems I forgot all about a date I made with them—reservations made and all that—and now I can't get out of it."

She nodded and pulled the crew's schedule book out of a wire basket. "When do you need off?"

He shook his head. "Uh-uh. It's not that. I'm already scheduled for that night off. The *Princess* isn't running, and Mark's taking the *Celeb* out." He suddenly seemed unable to look at her, gazing first at his feet then out the picture window. "But I...um...well, with Taffy gone..."

It struck her then that he was hemming and hawing because he was trying to ask her out on a date! She stopped smiling and stared at him.

He misread her look. "It's okay—I understand. I really don't need a date...I can go alone...They'll understand and it's really only one ticket to—"

"Don't be silly, Jake. If you were looking for someone to go with you, I'll do it." She couldn't say, "If you were asking me to go as your date." The way she did say it sounded almost grudging, but he was too pleased to notice.

"You will? Great! Great, Roxie, really, I appreciate it."

The trouble was he did not want it to sound like a date. He'd already decided it was too soon for that, and anyway, she hadn't shown much interest despite that moment of sexual awareness aboard the boat the other night. On the other hand he didn't want to attend the dance at the club without a partner. That would raise too many personal questions among his family and their friends.

He was almost at the door when she called out, "Do you want to tell me when it is—the date and time—or should I wait for another bottle to wash up to shore with instructions?"

He felt the grin edge across his features. *Damn!* This was having a powerful affect on his poise. "Friday night," he called, "I'll pick you up at six o'clock."

ROXIE STARED AT JAKE who stood in her doorway, looking as though he had stepped out of the pages of a magazine in a handsome black tuxedo, then looked down at herself, clad in a two-piece cotton print. She groaned, waved her fist in his face and ran, swearing, to her bedroom.

Jake called out, "You sure picked up the vernacular of the river. Hasn't anyone told you swearing isn't ladylike?" Her answer was muffled, coming as it did from a room at the end of a long hallway, but its implication was made clear by the tone of her voice.

Jake laughed and began a leisurely stroll around the spacious, sparsely furnished living room. "Some setup," he yelled, stopping at the long, low counter that separated the living room from the kitchen. On the bar was an aquarium filled with exotic candy bars instead of fish.

He crossed the room to oak-framed sliding glass doors that opened to a small balcony. The view of the river was magnificent.

Jake was about to call out another comment as he moved toward her bookcases when she came into the room. The words died in his throat and he stood still, mouth agape, staring at her.

She had changed to a white, floor-length, brocade satin dress with a mandarin collar that transformed her into someone he'd never seen before. It clung to her body, showing off the long, sleek lines of her figure. She was like a trim, sleek, well-balanced craft.

Roxie did a slow spin, asking, "Is this better?" She held her breath, waiting for his reply.

He didn't answer immediately, then he shook his head. "You're the most gorgeous thing I've ever seen." His voice was hushed with awe, and Roxie knew he really meant it.

She grinned self-consciously and said, "You're pretty gorgeous, yourself, Gilbert." She took his arm and urged him to turn around as she had done. *This is no rented tux,* she thought. It fitted his broad shoulders and his narrow waist and hips perfectly.

They faced each other, grinning again, feeling good about being together.

"I'm grateful now that I let Mary talk me into buying this dress. I honestly didn't believe I'd ever have occasion to wear it."

"I'm grateful to her, too," Jake said, his eyes glowing as they made another survey of her figure, "and that you agreed to come to this thing with me."

Roxie nodded. "I'm really glad you asked." Her grin turned to a soft chuckle. "We're acting like polite strangers."

"I know." He looked sheepish for a moment and then grew serious as he gestured at the room. "We are strangers, in a way. I didn't know you lived here, for instance. Last time I was at your place was the party you gave for Mary's birthday, two years ago, when you lived in that apartment out in Highland Park. It's a lucky thing I remembered hearing that you'd moved and looked up your address. This is a pretty swank place."

"I only moved here this year." Roxie looked around, shrugging her shoulders. "As you can see, I don't have enough furniture to fill it, but the price was so good, I decided to go for it and furnish it gradually."

"Well, at least you have a place to sit down to eat." He pointed to the low stools that ran the length of the bar counter and were bolted to the tiled floor.

"Yes." She hugged herself, rubbing her arms, though she was really quite warm. Jake was having the most incredible effect on her tonight. In his black and white formal attire, his hair shining almost gold under the soft recessed lighting around the walls, he looked wonderful.

"I'm not sure I want to take you out and introduce you to the studs I know looking like this," Jake said, taking her arm. "But the fact is, my parents are meeting us at the club and they won't like being kept waiting."

"The club?" She looked up at him, startled. She had assumed they were going to an elite restaurant. And he had mentioned tickets. She had thought that meant the theater, or Orchestra Hall.

"The Minnesota Club," he said, naming one of the most exclusive private clubs in the state.

She drew back and put a hand to her mouth. "Jake, I...I'm not sure..."

"Come on, Roxanne," Jake said, taking her arm again, this time with a firmer grasp, "you're not going to go all snobby on me, are you?"

"Snobby? Just the opposite. I'm not sure I'd fit in at the Minnesota Club."

"And you don't think that's snobby? My parents may have more money than yours but they're real people with real problems and real pleasures. This dinner dance tonight is one of their pleasures, and I don't think you should begrudge them that. Besides—" he almost leered at her gown "—if you don't fit in there, they ought to close the doors."

He moved her toward the small foyer, cutting off any other arguments she might have. And since the club was only a short walk from her apartment, any further doubts were not allowed time to develop.

The senior Gilberts were waiting for Jake and Roxie in the lobby of what used to be a private men's club. They greeted the younger couple warmly, acting as if they'd known Roxie for years, scolded Jake mildly for being late, and led them into the lounge where the rest of their offspring were already milling with the crowd.

Jake's brother and sisters had visited Jake at Harley's Landing, so they knew Roxie, and greeted her as an old friend, which helped her feel at ease.

When Jake got caught up and carried away by some of his old childhood buddies, Roxie was kept too busy to notice. She was enjoying the champagne a waiter brought her and laughing happily at the banter between the Gilbert siblings and their parents.

When dinner was announced, Jake returned to her side to escort her into the main dining room and pressed her arm close to his as he leaned down to whisper, "You're knocking 'em dead, Roxanne."

She tried not to blush, not wanting him to know she was moved by his remark. "Why not," she said airily, "they're just folks, like you and me."

He laughed and led her to a large round table set for twelve. A brass holder topped the centerpiece of flowers and contained a card that read Paul Gilbert, Sr.

Marlene Gilbert, Jake's mother, assigned seats to each of them, thoughtfully making sure Roxie was seated where she would be most comfortable, between Jake and Martin.

Martin had worked one summer as a deckhand for Joe when Roxie first came to the company, and she'd got to know him fairly well.

"How do you like working with your dad?" she asked him as they spooned up the delicate consommé that was offered as a first course.

"I love it," Martin said. He raised his voice. "Of course I don't have the beautiful fringe benefits on my job that Jake does."

Jake placed a proprietary arm across the back of Roxie's chair and leaned forward to speak past Roxie. "It's just as well you don't, kid. You need to keep your mind on the figures in your spec sheets."

Roxie exchanged a conspiratorial smile with Mrs. Gilbert and poked Jake in the ribs with her elbow. "Eat your dinner, Jake."

Later she could only recall that the entire meal had been beautifully prepared and delicious, right down to the apple flambé the waiters had fired up at the end of the meal. The entire Gilbert party were warm, gregarious and entertaining, directing most of her attention to the conversation rather than to the food.

After the delicious dinner they moved upstairs to the ballroom, where a small orchestra played dance music from the forties and fifties.

Roxie began the first dance with Jake but soon his father cut in, saying, "Roxie needs to learn to lindy from an expert."

"Everybody has to be expert at something," Jake said, laughing, as he relinquished her to his father.

It didn't take long for Mr. Gilbert—who insisted she call him Gil, as everyone else did—to put her at her ease and to teach her the dance. After that, the rhythm of the music suggested the moves and she relaxed and enjoyed the dancing.

Every now and then she remembered to look for her escort in the crowd, but Jake always seemed to be dancing with someone and would wave at her cheerfully from across the large dance floor.

And then, around ten-thirty, the orchestra started a medley of romantic show tunes and Roxie found herself in Jake's arms, moving around the floor in a slow, lilting waltz, his hand holding hers against his chest so that she could feel the warmth of his body, the beat of his heart.

"I missed you," he said, sounding surprised.

She realized that he was even more handsome at close range. His complexion was healthy and tanned, a result of all the time spent outdoors. Up close the curve of his mouth was even more sensual, more compellingly attractive. Her senses came alive as she recalled that mouth pressed to hers in a searching kiss.

She tilted her head back. Brown eyes met gray. "You didn't show it," she said. "You looked like you were perfectly happy where you were."

"There's happy and there's happy," he said, tightening his arm around her waist and drawing her a fraction closer. "I personally don't enjoy dancing just for the sake of exercise. I see it as either a social amenity or—" he bent his head and breathed deeply at the skin of her neck "—or an opportunity to make love to a beautiful woman."

Roxie drew back, moving her body away from his.

"You're very... very different tonight," she said.

"No I'm not." He grinned and pulled her back.

The warmth of him had begun to feel familiar.

"But I guess I seem different to you because you've never seen me in this setting."

Her body curved into his as he tilted her into another spin. "And you may never see me here again."

She caught her breath and laughed lightly. "Why not? You seem to be having a good time and your family is obviously delighted to have you with them."

They twirled to a stop and the music ended, but Jake kept his hold on her and his face grew somber. "I don't want you to get the wrong idea, Roxie. I'm here tonight because, in a weak moment, I let my mother con me into a commitment. But this isn't my life anymore—or my life-style. That was the mistake Taffy made. As much as I enjoyed tonight, I don't want you to think that I would let myself be lured back to this." He waved his arm to encompass the room, the occasion and the people. He grinned at her.

She thought he was warning her not to expect anything from him and punched him playfully in the shoulder. "No fear from this quarter, pal. I don't have any designs on you or your family's life-style."

He had the good grace to blush. "Did that sound a little—"

"Pompous? Conceited? Arrogant? You bet!"

"Gross misinterpretations, all."

"Gross?"

"Well, slightly exaggerated, anyway. I just meant that I prefer a simple life and I don't want to find myself falling back into this—" he waved again "—sort of accidentally or unconsciously."

"I don't want to argue with you, Jake, you have a right to choose the way you want to live your life." The music started again and they began to dance, almost without thinking. "But I am curious as to why you're so adamant. Can't you enjoy the social benefits of your family name without going into the business?"

His eyes darkened to tarnished pewter and his jaw tightened. "It's not that simple, Roxie. First of all, these people accept me right now because I only show up in their midst about once a year. If I were on the scene regularly, they'd begin to feel obligated to help me improve my station in life. After a while, when I kept refusing, they'd begin to find me an embarrassment."

"Your parents?" She was astounded.

He shrugged. "Maybe. At least they'd begin to find themselves apologizing for me, or defending me. There's no point in putting any of us through that. I'm happy where I am. And by keeping my forays into high society to a minimum, everyone else is happy, too."

She didn't intend to belabor her point. His was well taken and none of her business, really. If she felt any regret for his choice, it was that it seemed such a waste that his social graces weren't used more than once a year. He seemed to fit in here so perfectly and everyone showed such pleasure at his presence. *And God, he looks so absolutely beautiful in a tux.*

Later, when she was dancing with one of his brothers, she spotted Jake across the ballroom and her heart lurched at the sight of the rakish grin he sent her way.

It took all her determination to remind herself, as the party ended and they were bidding people good-night, that this was not a date and that this whole evening was just a once-in-a-lifetime fluke, never to be repeated. And that that was the way she wanted it.

CHAPTER SEVEN

ROXIE GOT UP to adjust the blind on the window to keep the sun off her newspaper. She filled her coffee cup.

A smile tugged at her lips as she recalled last night, her evening with Jake, the dinner dance at the Minnesota Club. Jake had said she was gorgeous and he had reiterated the compliment three or four times during the evening.

Still, she couldn't help but compare herself to some of the other women at the dance and to the type of women Jake dated customarily. Women like Taffy Ellers, for instance. Now *there* was the kind of figure Jake had always seemed to prefer, curvaceous and voluptuous.

She reached for the bread on the counter. It made her hungry just wondering what it would be like to have the kind of figure that turned men's heads. However, experience had taught her that while overeating might make her the envy of her friends, it would never give her those curves she equated with real beauty. She sighed and closed the bread wrapper.

At the back of a dresser drawer, she found the horizontally striped knit shirt she was convinced made her look a little less skinny. She put on a pair of worn jeans that were baggy and shapeless, and added socks, sneakers and a short denim jacket. She looked as round as clothes could make her look, she thought, and was ready to tackle the list of errands she had made for the day.

But first she had to straighten the clutter in her room—evidence of how late she'd returned home and how tired she had been once she'd undressed and creamed off her makeup.

The white gown lay in a crumpled heap near the closet door. She picked it up and held it to her chest. Could she still detect the fragrance of Jake's after-shave clinging to the fabric?

She sat on the edge of her bed, holding the dress, remembering the way the evening had drifted from the noise and excitement of the party down to the quiet, serene, comfortable aftermath of shared coffee and reminiscences in her apartment. At first they'd talked about the party, about his family.

And then Jake had said, "I can't seem to get up and go."

"Too tired to drive across the river?" Roxie asked. She'd got up and was quietly tidying away the coffee things, hoping that the busywork would keep her mind off how handsome he'd looked in his dinner jacket, how much she'd enjoyed his company.

"Too comfortable just being here with you." He proved it by shifting on his stool so that his back leaned against the wall and lifted one leg onto the next stool. "I always forget how good it feels to just sit and talk with you."

He'd pulled his tie out of its bow and opened his collar when they first came into the apartment. A line of golden chest hair peeped over the neck of the T-shirt he wore under the dress shirt. In that slightly disheveled state, he looked rakish and even more sexy. With his leg stretched out in front of him, she could see the bulge of thigh muscle pulling the black pants fabric taut. It had taken incredible will to turn her gaze from that sight and she remembered how dry her mouth and throat had suddenly felt.

She remembered she'd said something inane about how it would be a lot more comfortable for entertaining once she got some real furniture.

He had mistaken that as his cue to leave and she did not try to change his mind. It was late and she looked forward to being alone with her thoughts. She walked him to the door and he hung his arms over her shoulders and pressed his forehead to hers. "You're a good sport, Roxie. Not many women would have come through for me the way you did, on such short notice, and done such a gracious, charming job of it, besides." She felt the quiver start in the pit of her stomach. Was he going to kiss her again? She moved forward a fraction of an inch, almost involuntarily.

"It wasn't a job, Jake," she murmured. "I had a wonderful time."

His arms fell to his sides and he nodded. "Thanks again, Rox." He kissed her then, but it was just a friendly peck on the cheek. "See you on the river."

He'd gone, abruptly, leaving her to wonder if she'd somehow, at the last minute, offended him.

She clutched the dress tighter and fell back on the bed, her face breaking into a huge smile.

Two minutes after she heard the elevator doors close, her phone had rung. It was Jake, calling on the house phone in the lobby. "I meant what I said, Roxie, I don't know when I've enjoyed an evening more, thanks to you."

He hadn't given her a chance to retort but hung up and left her holding the phone with a dazed look on her face, a warm sensation creeping up through her chest.

She sat up with a frown and tossed the gown onto a pile of other clothes waiting to go to the cleaner. What was she thinking of? She got up and began making the bed. She had done a good turn for a friend and that was just how Jake had seen it. She was foolish to read anything more into it.

She thumped the pillow extra hard and threw it at the headboard. When would she ever learn not to read more in a man's empty, politic words than he meant? Hadn't the humiliation from Clay Montgomery taught her anything?

And though they hadn't brought the subject up once the whole evening, there was still the matter of their professional rivalry. The fact was, they'd be lucky to be able to maintain even a platonic friendship once the competition really took off.

JAKE TUCKED THE VIOLIN between his chin and his left shoulder, adjusting it so that the chin rest fit comfortably, and picked up the bow in his right hand. The music on the cassette paused for a brief second, leading into the violin solo, and as the strings resumed the music, Jake began to play. He stopped abruptly, pushed the rewind button on the tape player and put the violin in the cushioned case. He turned a screw set into the end of the bow, pushed the frog back and forth to tighten the hair against the spring of the bow and tightened the screw.

Once again he went through the manipulations of setting the instrument just right against his shoulder. He turned the tape on.

This time he played to the end, pure exaltation softening his features, causing a glazed look to form in his eyes as he became absorbed in the music and in his instrument. His fingers, long and sensitive, moved deftly, knowingly, along the fingerboard, and his right hand drew the bow hair up and down and across the bridge, creating the haunting harmonics of the Paganini composition. He didn't need to read this piece of music, he'd played it over and over from the time he was a teenager. Most of the time he played it with his eyes closed, making it easier to lose himself in the beauty.

As the tape came to an end, when the last note had been wrung from the violin, Jake returned instrument and bow to their compartments in the case, and used the handkerchief with which he'd lined the chin rest to wipe the beading sweat from his face.

"Hard work emulating Zuckerman," he said, and laughed with exhilaration. Some people ran every day, or worked out in a gym. Others meditated to get their endorphins up. Jake played the violin, exerting every ounce of energy—physical, mental, emotional and spiritual—to get the music right, to get the instrument to become a part of himself so that together they sang the music.

He closed the case and placed it carefully at the back of his closet. He admitted to himself that he was a closet musician and always had to laugh inwardly at how accurate that image was. Even his family didn't realize how often he still played, and certainly it wasn't something he wanted bandied about the river where he would be teased unmercifully. Classical violin was not the music of choice of most of the people who hung out along the river.

He was making himself a sandwich and some soup and thinking about Roxie again. He wondered what she would think of his playing the violin. He recalled that he'd just been about to check out her record collection, her taste in music, when she'd come out of her room dressed like an Oriental princess, making him forget everything but how beautiful she was.

She had been a source of pride to him the whole evening. Not once had anyone asked about Taffy and his family had taken to Roxie as if she was one of them.

But her background was very different from his.

He knew she'd been raised on a small, poor Wisconsin farm. A farm her parents had finally just walked away from. The land had lain fallow and barren over the years, and the buildings had decayed. Her father sounded like a weak man—maybe a drunk—and her mother not much better. He had the impression that what little nurturing she got from them, she'd dragged out of them, and that she had fought hard to attain a college education with no help from her parents. It struck him then that the little he knew of her past justified her intense career ambitions and made her seem less of a professional barracuda.

Anyway, last night there had been no sign that Roxie came from a different background or that she felt out of place among his family or their peers. Best of all, she hadn't seemed the least impressed by any of it, either. He didn't like making comparisons but he couldn't avoid recalling that the few times he'd had Taffy around his family, she'd been unable to behave naturally in the presence of anyone she considered a celebrity.

He poured the tomato soup into a foam cup, put the sandwich on a paper tower and carried both on a tray to the deck where he could enjoy the river view as he ate.

"I'm the one who was out of place," he admitted aloud as he chewed and swallowed.

He groaned as his thoughts turned again to Roxanne, and then to his failure with Taffy.

He stood up abruptly. He knew one way to get past all this soul-searching—people.

Other people.

He carried the tray to the kitchen, dumped the food into the garbage can, grabbed his jacket and leaped over the rail on the starboard side of the boat onto the plank leading to land. Maybe he'd get lucky and find they had that new Isaac Stern album at Great American Music, and if not, the ride out to Rosedale was always a good way to clear out the cobwebs. After that, he would head over to Harley's Landing. That ice maker on the *Princess* still needed work and he might as well get at it today, while she was at the dock.

"HEY, CREW, hand me that wrench, will ya?"

Roxie looked down at the long, muscular legs of Jake Gilbert, sprawled on the deck in front of the ice machine. Today they were encased in jeans but she had a vivid picture in her mind of the way he'd looked in his dress clothes last night. She stuck the wrench into his hand and laughed.

"I'm not crew but I'll be glad to help out."

Jake banged his head, swore mildly and slid forward. "Roxie? Sorry, all I could see from under there was sneakers and jeans. I thought you were one of the guys."

She shrugged away his unnecessary apology. "So this is how you spend your time off? Building up your pool of brownie points?"

"Ha!" He wiped his hands on an oily cloth and looked surprised when they didn't come clean. "This is the kind of work I've been doing around here from day one, and making pilot doesn't change that. Everybody pitches in and does what he can aboard a boat. Besides, no use paying good money out for a service guy when I can probably fix it myself for half the cost."

He got to his feet and looked around for a clean rag. Roxie spotted a box of them behind the bar and handed him one.

"So, what are you doing here today? You don't usually go into the office on Saturdays, do you?"

She wasn't ready to tell him about the brochure idea hunt she was on. "I was out doing errands and thought I'd stop here for lunch and then pick up some papers I want to go through tonight."

Saturday night and she was going to stay home and work? Jake noticed the bag she was carrying for the first time. "Lunch?" He gestured with the rag.

"Yes." And then, mostly out of politeness, "Would you care for half a roast beef hoagie?"

He grinned. "Divanni's?"

Her weaknesses were well known around the landing.

"Yeah."

"Where?"

"Rosedale."

"I mean where are you going to eat?"

"Oh." She giggled. "I thought up on the observation deck, where I wouldn't be in anyone's way."

"Sounds good. I'll join you in about five minutes."

Today was an especially good day for Roxie's little boat-deck picnic. The temperature had soared to sixty-two by noon and there was just enough of a breeze to give character to the surface of the water. She sat on the deck leaning against the wall of the cabin and lifted her face to the sun while she waited for Jake.

It was an added bonus that he was here and wanted to join her for lunch. She really hadn't expected to see him. *Why not? This is his territory, after all.*

Okay. Maybe she'd hoped to run into him. So what? They were friends—they'd had fun together last night—and it wouldn't be the first time they'd shared an impromptu sandwich over the years.

"My contribution." Jake surprised her out of her reverie, plunked two cans of beer on the deck and sat beside her, crossing his legs. "Do you need a glass?"

Roxie shook her head, almost unable to speak. He looked even more appealing today with his freshly scrubbed face, strands of his hair wetted in the process, and wearing jeans and a *Celebration* T-shirt. His hair formed a cowlick and she fought the urge to lick her finger and press it down. *The many facets of Jake Gilbert,* she thought. And wondered why, after being merely a close acquaintance, at best a casual friend, for so long, he'd suddenly become so omnipresent in her life.

"My kind of woman," Jake said, taking over the task of unwrapping the huge sandwich. Politely he spread the wrapping, exposing the two halves of the hoagie, and waited for Roxie to take first choice.

She took the slightly smaller one and nibbled delicately.

Jake was less fastidious. He took a large bite, humming a sound of pleasure as he chewed and swallowed. "Perfect," he mumbled before taking another.

Roxie watched his Adam's apple move up and down and the little bone in the side of his jaw rotate, and felt a spear of excitement clutch at her throat and move down to her belly.

Jake gestured with his sandwich. "You're not eating."

She took another small bite and found there was no room in her throat beside the lump. She forced the food down with a swallow of beer and gave up all pretense of eating. Jake finished his half and eyed hers hungrily.

"You're not hungry?" he asked.

"No. Go ahead," she said, offering her uneaten food.

She watched as he placed the corner from which she'd nibbled into his mouth and her stomach lurched again, as if his tongue had touched her own.

"That was wonderful," Jake said a few minutes later, crumpling up the wrapping and putting it in the bag. He swallowed the last of his beer and crumpled the can with the same ease. "I didn't intend to eat your whole lunch," he said, looking only slightly abashed.

"It's okay," Roxie said, "I only thought I was hungry when I was at Divanni's. Maybe it was just a reflex action." Like wanting to use her finger to take that little dab of mayonnaise clinging to his bottom lip and put it in her own mouth. And not because she was hungry for mayonnaise.

"I know what you mean." Jake sat back against the wall and sighed with satisfaction. "Whenever I pass a Pizza Hut I automatically get a craving for pizza."

It was beginning to get too warm. The sun was reflecting off the enameled metal of the bulkhead and the deck. Roxie dabbed at her forehead with her napkin. "Guess it's time to get going," she said, getting to her feet.

Jake stood, bringing the bag with him. "I owe you a meal," he said, smiling at her.

"No, of course you don't," Roxie said, and shoved her hands deep in her pockets so she wouldn't be tempted to wipe his lip.

Their eyes met and held. As if he could see his reflection in her eyes, his tongue snaked out and caught the white speck.

"Well, you're going to be hungry later, and I did eat your lunch, so will you let me take you to dinner?"

"I told you Jake, you don't owe—"

"Right. I know. But the fact is, I'm sort of at loose ends tonight, since tonight's cruise was canceled, and I don't want to eat alone."

So you'd be doing me a big favor, he thought, and jeered at himself for that implication.

"Sure. Okay. I guess that beats sitting home alone and working." *Oh, that sounded gracious as hell, Hilton,* she thought then realized that he hadn't even noticed.

He grinned from ear to ear and said, "Good, I'll pick you up at seven."

She started to nod then shook her head, remembering their most immediate problem. "Jake, doesn't it bother you that I'm doing my damnedest to win that promotion from you and Bill?"

He shrugged and stuck his hands in his pockets. That, and his grin, made him look even more boyish than the cowlick and jeans. "I'm just inviting you to dinner, Hilton. I don't think that implies we're getting too chummy, do you? We can always resume hostile conditions after dessert.''

She had to laugh at his whimsy.

CHAPTER EIGHT

"THIS HAS GOT TO BE the most romantic place in the city," Roxie said, looking around the candlelit room.

"It's the view, mostly, that makes it so romantic," Jake said, drawing Roxie's attention to the wide expanse of glass that afforded them a panoramic view of the city stretch.

"Yes, I could hardly take my eyes off it during dinner."

"I noticed that." He lowered his voice. "I could hardly take my eyes off you."

"You're . . . very kind."

"You're very lovely."

They stared at each other, seeing themselves reflected in one another's eyes in the candlelight. Roxie took a deep, quivering breath and drew her gaze from Jake's reluctantly.

This was getting out of hand. It wasn't just the romantic ambiance of the room, or Jake's preoccupation with her appearance; there were her own feelings to contend with. She was the more realistic of the two, but here she was, blushing at his flattery, gazing into his eyes, fluttering every time he said her name or touched her hand.

She decided it was time to direct the conversation.

She pushed her plate away to make room for her elbows on the table and rested her chin on her palms.

"You know, when you guys took the boat down to winter quarters, I never heard how the trip went."

Jake slouched in his chair and studied her with half-closed eyes. "Is this polite conversation?"

She felt herself blushing. "No. I really want to know about the trip."

"No one's shown you the log or told you anything about the winter season?"

She shook her head sadly. "No. Just when you guys brought the boats back up from St. Louis, Martha died." She could almost talk about it now without choking or resorting to tears. "I kept track of the trip down there via the weather reports from the Coast Guard and the television, but then Martha took that last bad turn, and I was left with most of the work."

The candle sputtered between them, casting shadows across Jake's handsome face as he leaned toward her and lowered his voice sympathetically. "You've really had your hands full since we left for the winter, haven't you?"

She put her hands in her lap and straightened her spine. "I was able to handle it," she said in a cold voice. This reminder of their basic conflict threatened to spoil the evening.

"Hey, don't get so defensive, I wasn't implying you couldn't—just that you've always had Martha to work with in the past and you haven't always had to start the season off with a funeral and a new job."

"What about the trip," she reminded.

"Yeah." He squinted across the candlelight, trying to figure out what had upset her. She could be touchy about certain things, he'd noticed over the years, particularly anything to do with the job. He wondered if that didn't suggest the job wasn't as good for her as she thought it was.

Aloud he said, "Well, we didn't have any terrible storms, fortunately. But we went aground on a sandbar about fifteen knots from where the Mississippi joins the Missouri and had to be towed out and then we had engine trouble and, since Joe wasn't along, we had to find an engineer to do the repairs."

He sipped coffee. She noticed again what beautiful hands he had and forced herself to raise her eyes and concentrate on what he was saying.

"Other than that...oh, yeah, Andy came down sick right after we docked at St. Lou and we had to take him to a hospital emergency room. Turned out to be a virus but they kept him overnight and he wasn't up to snuff for about a week after that so we ran short crew during the first tourist herds."

"I've always envied you the trip down south every winter," she said, sliding a finger up and down her wineglass.

"Even the winter of the big storms when we went aground in New Orleans?"

"Even then."

"Yeah, sure," he scoffed, "you say that now but if you'd been aboard, you'd have been scared out of your mind."

She shook her head. "I don't think so."

She looked up and he could see that her eyes were aglow with excitement.

"I think it would have been gloriously exciting. I would have loved it."

"Maybe you would have." He studied her face thoughtfully and visualized what it would have been like to have her along.

He could imagine her with lightning highlighting her face, gale winds pulling at her clothing and tossing her hair. He sensed the electric charge that would run between them as they worked together to batten down the hatches. For some reason the imagery reminded him of their kiss aboard the *Celebration* that night, his sudden intense need to be close to her, her instantaneous and total response to him.

"Martha always said it wasn't fair that I never got to go down for the winter trip, and that someday she'd see to it I got to go." Her eyes darkened and she looked at her glass then lifted it and swallowed the remains. "I guess I won't ever get to go now."

Jake took the bottle from the ice bucket on the table and filled her glass. "Maybe you will."

She shook her head. "Who'd run the office?"

"Aren't you training Mary to take over?"

Roxie looked confused. "Well, with her doing the bookkeeping and hostessing so many of the cruises, when would she have time to—"

Jake returned the wine bottle to the bucket with a crash that made Roxie wince and look around to see if anyone had noticed. "Are you telling me that if you got sick, there is no one who could take over?"

Roxie swallowed hard and closed her eyes, unwilling to see the righteous anger in Jake's. He'd hit on a problem that she'd been meaning to work on. Of course she was in perfect health so she really didn't need to worry.

"I don't see what you're so upset about, Jake. I'm very healthy and I'm not planning to be away from the office for any reason in the near future."

He leaned across the table, glaring at her. "What about vacation time—when did you last have one—

when did you plan to go on one—who's going to take over for you when you do go?"

She shrugged. "I just figured I wouldn't have one this year. Martha's illness sort of precluded the usual scheduling of things like vacations and I figured I'd have Mary trained by next year."

"Not at this rate!" He sat back, shook his head and looked disgusted.

Despite her feeling of defensiveness, Roxie could not help but appreciate how masculine and compelling his jaw was when it was set in anger.

"Has anyone ever told you you're beautiful when you're mad?" she teased, hoping to lighten the mood, to restore his humor.

"This isn't a joking matter, Roxanne," Jake said. "You want that promotion so badly, and you haven't even learned the first rule of executive command."

Okay, if he was going to insist on keeping up this tirade, she wasn't going to try to carry the evening alone.

She let sarcasm express her displeasure. "No, *Captain Gilbert,* but I'm sure you're going to tell me whether I want to hear it or not. So, what is the first rule of command?"

"Learning to delegate authority. If I didn't learn anything else from my father, I certainly learned that. And isn't that what Joe has done in his absence?"

She didn't like hearing it—and especially not from Jake—but the words rang true and she realized he was right.

"Maybe you know more about running a business than you've let on, Gilbert," she said, softly.

A look of alarm crossed his face. He ran his hand through his hair and shook his head at her. "I'm sorry. I had no business coming down on you like that."

Why was he backing down? Was it her remark about his knowledge of running a business or the fact that he felt he'd been attacking her?

The busboy diverted them by coming to the table to clear their plates, followed by the waiter who recommended strawberries Delmonico for dessert.

They finished their dinner in relative silence, exchanging pleasantries until it was time to leave.

THE NEWSPAPER RAN THE STORY in the Friday morning edition. Roxie opened the paper with trembling hands and read the article. Meg Curley had not only referred to Harley Marine; she had named Roxie as her source, and she didn't pull any punches.

"What we want is to warn the public that to charter unlicensed boats for their cruises is both illegal and dangerous," Hilton, cruise coordinator for Harley Marine, Inc. said.

"Those pirate boats can't get insurance, if they don't have their vessels inspected by the Coast Guard." When this reporter asked if Ms. Hilton was referring to a specific boat that was pirating business away from them, she admitted that she was and that the presence of that boat, another stern-wheeler, on the Mississippi was her reason for granting this interview.

Roxie slumped back in her chair with a moan of disbelief. "What the hell made her go this far?" she demanded of the empty room. The rest of the article, when she was able to finish it, wasn't much better. She reached for the phone automatically, then drew back. Who would she call? Jake?

She had not seen him all week, not since their dinner, which had ended so strangely. If he was avoiding her, she didn't know why and wasn't sure that she'd change things if she could. There was too much chemistry between them and this was no time to start something with him.

Bill Tabor? But wouldn't he love to use this against her to assure his own promotion?

Joe was the logical person to turn to and he wasn't here. That left Mary. What could Mary do? And for damn sure she wasn't going to incite that Meg Curley to any further writing by speaking to her again, even in outrage against the article.

But she didn't feel able to cope with the normal demands of a workday. She dialed Mary's number.

"Turn the phone over to Jeannie at the answering service," she told her assistant, "she knows the drill if anyone calls wanting information about charters."

Mary agreed then asked, "Are you ill?"

"Just slightly. Read the morning paper. I can't talk about it right now."

"Will you be out for the whole day?"

"I don't know. Maybe. I'll be in touch."

Roxie replaced the phone, walked over to the balcony doors, slid one open and stepped into the warm, morning air. The sun was burning its way through a thin cloud cover and promised to shine in full, hot glory when it escaped its shroud. The early morning dew that usually lay like beads of perspiration on the balcony rails had already dried. She touched the seat of a lounge chair and, satisfied that it was dry, sat down. She thrust her feet onto the railing, closed her eyes and forced herself to start her relaxing exercises.

She started with her toes and had worked up to her thigh muscles before her mind began to sort things out.

What was happening in her world all of a sudden? Only a week ago she'd felt on top of it all, so willing and ready and—damn it, yes! able!—to run the whole show. Martha had done it all these years and made it look easy. Indeed, that was why Roxie had been able to learn with such facility. Martha never made a big deal out of anything.

Martha had thirty years of running things under her belt when you came along.

Yeah. That was true.

She sighed and concentrated for a couple of minutes on her breathing.

And what was the very first thing Martha taught you?

Her body tightened slightly and she made herself go limp again.

"To help the customer design his cruise and write up contracts," she whispered.

And then?

Payroll. So no matter what emergency befell Martha, the crew would always get their pay on time.

Does Mary do contracts? Has she ever done payroll? Does anyone but you even have power to sign payroll checks now that Martha and Joe are gone?

Roxie's feet thudded to the balcony floor and her eyes popped open. Jake was right! She'd been foolhardy in her neglect. What if she had had any kind of unexpected illness or accident? Who would pay the crew? There was no way to get in touch with Joe, he was on the road most of the time. Granted, Bill Tabor could—if push came to shove—pay the crew out of the marina checkbook but that was pretty drastic, since even his people depended on her for their paychecks. And come to think of it, Bill did not have the authority to transfer funds from one checking account to another, so he wouldn't always have the balance to cover a complete payroll.

So you've been a fool. So change it. "Yeah," Roxie said aloud, "quit groveling in self-disgust and start acting like a professional."

But she'd start tomorrow. Today, she'd given herself a day off and she might as well make use of it. She'd been planning to landscape the balcony with plants one of these days; why not get started on it today?

Her intercom phone rang, just as she was tamping the soil down around the last planter, and she ran inside to answer it, wondering who'd stop by, unexpectedly, on a work day.

"I CAME TO APOLOGIZE," Jake said, looking boyishly contrite.

Roxie held on to the door jamb and willed her heart rate to return to normal. She breathed deeply and stepped back to let him enter.

"It's taken me a whole week to get up the nerve to apologize."

"How did you know I was here?"

"I went to the office first—Mary said you weren't feeling well, that you were taking a few hours off. I came to see for myself that you were all right. And I wanted to say I know I got a little carried away when I criticized you for the way you do your job. Actually, you do run that office very well and you do a hell of a job finding customers."

She felt her heart swell up with some new, happy emotion—whatever else was happening between them, they were somehow wired to one another in a way that kept sending these wonderful vibrations from one of them to the other, back and forth.

"I was just thinking," she said, as she led the way to the living room, "that you were absolutely right. I have a lot to learn about running a business on my own."

There was that foolish grin again—not just on his face—she could feel it on her own. She wrapped her arms around her waist and hugged herself, holding in the feeling that threatened to explode out of her.

Jake couldn't stop grinning. He couldn't recall ever having these feelings about another person. She had a peculiar effect on his mood and on his imagination. Right now he could imagine replacing her arms with his own and wiping that grin off her face with his mouth, turning her look of happiness to a look of *pleasure*.

He took a step forward and stopped. Maybe he'd be making a mistake. Maybe she wasn't interested in more than friendship. But then why did he feel as if he could hear her voice, inside his head, saying, *Kiss me, Jake. Please, I want you to kiss me.*

Roxie didn't see how she could contain herself much longer. She wanted to throw herself into his arms, to hug and hold him close. She wanted to run her hands through that thick, crisp hair, to feel again the breadth of his chest and shoulders beneath her palms, to press the length of her soft, feminine body up against the hard, masculine length of his.

She took a step forward and stopped. All he'd done was apologize. He hadn't said anything more personal than that she was good at her job. That being the case, why did she seem to hear his heart beating from way over there, and why did his eyes seem to be begging her to let him love her?

"Jake?" It was only a whisper.

"Yes?" He covered the few feet between them in two strides. "Roxie?" His hands cupped her face and slid through her hair to hold her head. He tilted his mouth towards hers.

"Yes, Jake, yes," she breathed and opened her mouth to receive him. As their mouths met, she heard a deep, guttural sound through the roar of her blood pulsing in her ears and even as she was wondering what it came from, her mind was distracted by an onslaught of sensation such as she'd never known before.

He broke off the kiss, panting, and stared into her brown eyes. "Should I stop?" He could hardly form the words.

"No!" She clung to him then let go. "I don't know. I..." A fleeting memory of Clay was just that, gone before she could truly identify it. Her body trembled at Jake's nearness.

His eyes held her gaze and his thumb stroked provocatively at the underside of her chin. "I'll stop, Roxie, any time you say." And even as he said the words, his thumb kept moving; now dipping into the hollow at the base of her throat, now caressing her collarbone, now edging toward the slight curve of her breast.

She stared into his eyes, seeing the rise of his desire, and tried to make her lips form the words that would stop the sensuous stroking. A low moan escaped her lips instead, and she moved closer to him.

His thumb came to the crest of her right breast and hesitated. Roxie felt her body move forward the necessary inch and sighed happily as her breast filled his waiting palm.

Jake thrust his other hand through her hair and drew her forward for another mind-blowing kiss. *Careful,* he warned himself as his hand squeezed her breast. It was small enough to fit his hand perfectly. *A perfect handful.* The touch of her erect nipple against his palm sent waves of electric desire directly from his hand to his groin. He needed something to ease the pain that grew out of his need and he caught her hand and brought it to his throbbing manhood.

They moaned in unison as her hand closed around the denim-covered bulge that expressed the magnitude of his desire. Gently Roxie squeezed, thrilled by the responsive contraction she could feel against her palm. Her body ached. She whimpered and removed her hand so that she could fit her body against his.

Jake slid his hands around and down to her buttocks to hold her against him for a moment longer. The kiss ended as he considered whether to ease her to the floor, right there on the carpet, or lead her down the hall to her bedroom.

Roxie read his indecision and a cool wave of sanity chilled her.

Her mind flashed to a night, just over a year ago, when the company had had their annual end-of-the-season party. She remembered she'd come upon Jake and Taffy, almost hidden beneath the stairs near the ice machine. Jake was sitting on a table with Taffy standing between his legs, her arms wrapped around his neck, and they were staring into one another's eyes, their foreheads touching. They were too preoccupied with one another to see her, and suddenly she'd been gripped by a spasm of jealousy. At the time, she'd convinced herself that it was because Clay was out of town and she had no date for the party.

But now she realized it had been the proprietorial way Jake had held Taffy, a way Clay had never held Roxie. A surge of bitterness welled up in her throat as she thought of the years she'd wasted on Clay. And the image of Jake with another woman, so fresh in her mind, was another dose of cold water. She drew away.

"No, Jake, I can't."

"You can't?" He frowned, desire fogging his mind. "Why not? Are you . . . Have you . . . You're not sick, are you?"

Her chuckle contained a note of residual passion but it helped clear some of the haze. "No. It's not that. It's just that I'm not ready for this with . . . with anyone."

Especially you.

Jake let her go with a puzzled frown on his face. "Was I only imagining that we were feeling the same things?"

"We can't always act on our feelings. Anyway—" she moved away "—mine are all mixed up right now."

That he could understand. "Why don't we go out to lunch? It's almost noon."

Her eyes widened with surprise. Where had the morning gone? And how come he wasn't mad at her for cutting him off right at the crucial moment?

"You want to take me out?"

He ignored her question. "Your eyes are the color of chocolate." His voice was thick with suppressed desire.

Roxie's feelings were just barely contained; any minute she knew she might lose control and throw herself into his arms. The sane part of her mind told her the safest thing to do would be to get him out of the apartment.

"Lunch sounds great," she said, turning away. "I'm starved."

CHAPTER NINE

JAKE DRAPED THE SEAT BELT over his shoulder and locked it in place then checked to make sure Roxie's was secure. "Do you mind if we drop by my parents' house before we go to lunch?"

Roxie looked at him, surprised. "No, of course not."

Roxie watched familiar scenery slide by as they drove along Kellogg Boulevard toward the Crocus Hill area where Jake's parents lived. She glanced at him. The expression on his face was cheerful, and his hands, one resting on the window ledge and the other on the wheel, looked perfectly relaxed. No one would guess that only moments before they'd been locked in a deeply passionate embrace. Was such emotional control typical of all men? Her hands were tightly clasped in her lap to hide their trembling.

Jake shifted gears and the car climbed Ramsey Hill to Summit Avenue.

That control must be what men mean by "cool"— it's part of their macho image.

Jake turned the wheel sharply to the left and drove up a narrow street that curved to the left, forming a kind of alley behind the block of huge mansions. He parked beside a high stone wall. Once out of the car, Jake unlocked a wooden door set into the stone wall.

"Wow," Roxie breathed, when the door opened into the back yard. A huge emerald-green lawn was bordered by flowers. In the very center, a large black marble fish seemed to rise up out of a fountain, spurting water into the air. Near the fountain, steps led to a lovely white gazebo trimmed in black wrought iron.

A deep screened porch ran the entire length of the back of the house. White wicker furniture with plump green, white and peach chintz pillows promised comfortable seating.

Jake led her across the porch and through another screened door into a large kitchen where a small, dark-haired woman leaned over a restaurant-size stove.

"Kelly, may I present Roxanne Hilton," Jake said, properly presenting the young woman to the older. "Roxie, this is our cook, and one of our best friends, Catherine Kelly."

"Miss Kelly," Roxie said, taking the proffered hand.

"Just Kelly," the cook corrected, "and I'm happy to be knowing you." There was only a trace of accent but enough to let it be known that Kelly was from Ireland. That, and the translucent skin, plump red cheeks, black hair and blue eyes that sparkled with humor.

A television set on the third shelf of a bookcase, otherwise filled with cookbooks, was tuned to a popular soap opera.

"Where's Mom?" Jake asked. He went to one of the long, ceramic-tiled counters and lifted the head off a pig-shaped cookie jar. "Mmm—my favorite. Want an oatmeal butterscotch-chip cookie, Rox?" He held the pig's torso toward Roxie.

"Before lunch?" she said.

At the same time Kelly asked, "Have you had lunch yet, mister?"

The two women exchanged a knowing look and laughed in unison.

"Some things never change," Kelly pretended to scold, "and your mother just went to get her glasses, the better to see our show that you know we always watch at noon."

Roxie noticed that one end of a long, butcher-block table was set for two, with a plate of tuna salad and a glass of iced tea at each setting.

Kelly saw her glance. "I've plenty more if the two of you will join us for lunch?" She glared at Jake. "And if you'll promise to keep your mouth shut while our show is on and make none of your sassy remarks about our taste in TV."

"Why, Jake and . . . Roxie, isn't it? What a wonderful surprise!" Marlene Gilbert came in from a door at the other end of the room, polishing a pair of glasses with the edge of her apron.

Marlene caught the expression on Roxie's face and laughed. She curtsied, holding out the edges of the apron. "Mrs. Paul Gilbert, Sr., lunching in her stately home on Summit Avenue."

"You look wonderful to me, Mom," Jake said, pinching her cheek then bending to kiss the same spot.

She pretended to box his ears and said, "You could have warned me you were bringing company."

"Who? Roxie? She's not company, Mom, she's my paramour."

He raised his arms to fend off the slaps of his mother and the cook, laughing and shouting protests at the same time. Roxie just stood there hoping her face hadn't turned beet red, and tried not to laugh at the sight of the two small women trying to punish the large, muscular man.

"Your lady's going to think we're daft," Kelly said, giving Jake a last slap and going to the built-in freezer. "You want iced tea, Roxie, or coffee?"

"Are we staying?" Roxie looked at Jake, suddenly hoping he'd want to stay. The salad looked cool and lovely, and she was enjoying the domestic feel of Jake's ancestral home. On the television set, a character she recognized was scolding a handsome, elderly gentleman.

"Uh-oh! Stanford's going to catch it now," Kelly said. Marlene turned her attention to the set. Kelly gestured behind her, not taking her eyes from the set. "Get two more plates down, Jake."

Jake shrugged and grinned at Roxie before going to a cupboard for the additional china. At the first commercial, Kelly filled glasses with ice, arranged tuna salad on their plates and got a basket of rolls out of a warming drawer in the pantry. By the time the soap opera resumed Jake and Roxie's lunch was ready.

Marlene Gilbert took a moment to apologize. "It's sort of a ritual, do you mind?"

"Not at all," Roxie assured her.

Roxie noticed even Jake was interested in the soap. She was content to look around the wonderful kitchen and take in all the little details that made the room efficient as well as charming.

The room was four times the size of her kitchen and could easily accommodate the Gilbert clan for informal meals. There would be no problem preparing for large dinner parties here. A ceiling fan swished around over their heads, stirring Roxie's hair pleasantly.

There was silence while the show was on; conversation only took place during the commercial breaks.

The meal ended concurrently with the end of the day's episode. Roxie spooned the last of an exquisite mousse into her mouth and sighed with contentment.

"Yum," she said, grinning at Jake as the two older women chattered excitedly about the events on their program.

"Yes, you are," Jake said softly, nudging her knees with his own.

Roxie covered her blush with her napkin over a contrived coughing spasm.

"Wouldn't you like to show Roxie the house?" his mother asked, as she rose from the table and began to gather up the dishes.

Jake led her through a swinging door and then through a butler's pantry, which led into a large, open space that Roxie saw was the front entrance hall. An impressive oak staircase rose from the center of the hall, and a balustrade ran along both sides of the second floor. She suppressed a gasp in a deep, quivering breath as she looked up at the magnificent chandelier that hung from the vaulted ceiling.

Jake laughed. "People always react like that. Gorgeous, isn't it?" He squeezed Roxie's arm and drew her toward a set of golden oak sliding doors. Roxie was still trying to catch her breath when the doors opened onto a living room as big as the lounge at the Minnesota Club.

Floor-to-ceiling windows gave a view of Summit Avenue, and a grand piano seemed to take up hardly any space at all.

There were four seating areas in the room, each a separate space, each beautifully furnished without overpowering the room. Roxie's eyes were drawn first to the massive fireplace, flanked by matching sofas, and then to the huge oil painting above the mantel. It occurred to her that the cost of the ornate, gold-leaf frame would probably furnish her whole apartment.

"The library's through here," Jake said, gesturing toward glass-fronted French doors, but Roxie made no move to follow him.

"What's wrong?" Jake asked, turning back.

"Nothing. Jake, would you mind if we skip the rest of the tour and just go home?" There was no way she could explain, at that moment, how overwhelmed she was by what she'd seen of his family's home.

He was immediately concerned. "You don't feel well? I knew it. It just wasn't like you to take a day off if you—"

"Jake, please!" she interrupted. "I'm not sick, really. I just want to go home."

Jake did his best to hide his disappointment. "Sure, Roxie, whatever you want. Let's just go say goodbye to Mom and Kelly."

The women were on the back porch, knitting and chatting, when the young couple found them.

"Thank you so much for your hospitality, Mrs. Gilbert. And thank you for that delicious lunch, Kelly." Roxie put her hand out to Jake's mother but the woman ignored it and gave her a hug.

"Come and visit again, dear, we loved having you."

Jake kissed his mother's cheek and then her mouth. She put her arms around his neck and held him close for a minute. Roxie saw that her eyes were glistening with unshed tears. "Come home again soon, son, we miss you."

When he bent to kiss Kelly the woman said, "Go on with yourself," but she blushed prettily and clung to him for a moment. "Skin and bones," she muttered, "and probably living on preservatives and poisons."

Jake laughed. "I promise I'll give them up and eat nothing but fast foods from now on."

Jake was still smiling as he and Roxie walked to the car.

"Did you enjoy the visit?" Jake asked, as they drove onto Summit.

"They were very nice," Roxie said evasively.

Jake didn't seem to notice her sudden reticence. He turned to her and smiled broadly. "They liked you, too, as good as ordered me to bring you back."

They were nearing Roxie's apartment.

"We never had a chance to talk at lunch as I'd planned. Do you mind if I come up and visit for a little while?"

She didn't know how to refuse him without appearing rude. "I guess not."

It seemed a lifetime since they'd left the apartment to go to lunch. And now her beloved home somehow seemed tiny and less charming. She went to the counter and straightened the salt and pepper shakers.

Jake shoved his hands in his pockets and watched Roxie. Something had put a burr under her saddle, he realized.

"What's happening, Roxanne?" he asked, seating himself on one of the counter stools. He folded his hands on the Formica countertop, prepared to wait all day if he had to to find out what was bothering her.

"I don't think we should see so much of each other...outside of work."

Jake swiveled on the stool so he could lean back against the wall and propped his hands behind his head. "Why? I thought we were getting along pretty well. Did I miss something here, folks?"

Roxie's face was a frozen mask, her voice just as cold when she spoke. "Life is just one big happy water slide for you, isn't it? The worst that can happen to you is you get a little wet, which is the object of the damned slide in the first place."

"Am I supposed to know what you're talking about?"

She seemed to have had an additional thought. "And what's more, it turns out your family owns the slide."

"You're mad at me because my family has money. Is that it?" He banged a fist on the counter. Were women inconsistent or what? Taffy had been mad because Jake didn't share his family with her. Roxie, it seemed, was mad because he did.

"I'm not mad. I'm just more aware that it would be foolish to get involved, and I don't want us to become involved sexually."

"Yes, you do."

"What?"

"Yes, you do want me to make love to you and that's part of what you're so ticked off about. But okay, have it your way, I'll concede for now that you don't. So. What's my family got to do with it?"

Roxie got a water bottle out of the fridge and reached in a cupboard for a glass. She kept her back to Jake as she poured and drank. When she turned back, her eyes were darkened by hostility. "You don't really want that promotion, do you?"

Jake shrugged and frowned, not sure where this was leading.

"Then why don't you stick to your guns and tell Joe you're not in the running and leave the field to those of us who need it?"

Jake was beginning to get angry. "I'm not sure where you're coming from. What is all that supposed to mean?"

"Some of us didn't have the luxury of choosing a career that's fun—some of us were forced to look for work that paid enough to live on. I didn't grow up in a mansion on Summit Avenue—I had to work like a dog from grade school through college just to get a job that paid enough for *this*." A wave of her hand diminished the rooms she loved. "I resent having to prove myself against someone who really doesn't give a damn about the job."

Jake looked at her from under his furrowed brow. When he responded to her tirade, his voice was calm.

"Roxanne, a few weeks ago you put me on hold because we'd just each broken up with someone else— okay." He held up his hand. "That's fine. I agreed." He nodded.

"Then you put the kibosh on us because we were rivals for the same job. Well, I didn't see what that had to do with our basic friendship. I assumed we'd be friends no matter which of us got the job anyway, but—" again he held up his hand "—I went along with you." He frowned and sat forward. "Honest to God, I really care about you, Roxie, and I need to know where we stand."

She rubbed her throat. It didn't ease the ache. "I don't trust you, Jake. I feel as though we're on different wave lengths, as if I'd be begging for heartache to get involved with you."

He groaned and threw his hands in the air. "I wait for a revelation and you throw another clinker in the works. What is it with you?"

She had no time to answer. He came around the counter in a blur of motion and pulled her into an embrace that locked her against him, knocking the wind from her and making her unable to move. His kiss was a ferocious demand for capitulation, threatening to continue until she suffocated or succumbed; he didn't seem to care which came first.

The white rage in Jake's head cooled and fragmented into tiny explosions of reality. He let her go, and she stumbled and righted herself against the counter.

"I'm not even going to dignify that with an apology," he said, touching his mouth where his own teeth had bit into the lip. "I'll go."

She grabbed his arm as he was about to turn away. "Wait."

"For what?"

Suddenly she was very clear about one thing. She couldn't bear it if he left. She had a feeling he'd give up if she let him go. She ran her hands through her hair.

"I can't get my feelings straight yet, but I know I don't want you out of my life forever."

He looked doubtful. "No more games, Roxie? No more weak excuses that just confuse both of us?"

"I...I'll try. I guess I still have some hang-ups I need to work through. But Jake, don't you think getting involved in a physical relationship will confuse things more?"

Jake's smile was gentle, caressing. "Try to trust me, Roxie. I promise, I have no intention of hurting you—ever."

She couldn't doubt the sincerity in his voice or in his eyes.

She went to him and clasped her hands behind his neck. "I want to," she whispered, and pressed her lips to his.

He sighed against her mouth and let her take the lead, not pressuring her with demands. The kiss was sweet, tentative, tremulous. It made Jake's insides flutter nervously.

Roxie drew back, a cautious smile tilting her lips. "Truce?"

He nodded and cleared his throat. "Would you like to have dinner with me tonight, aboard my boat?"

She hesitated for only a moment before saying, "Yes, I'd like that."

He lifted a strand of her hair and ran it through his fingers; it felt like silk. "Around seven?"

"Fine." She felt her hair snag against Jake's work-roughened palm and she held her breath, wondering if he'd wrap the hair around his hand and pull her to him.

He released her hair and stepped back. "I'd better go. I have to see Mark before he goes out on his run."

God, anything was better than losing her altogether. She was so mixed up, so confused by her feelings and, he guessed, by her past relationships. He probably wasn't much better off. But at least he knew that somewhere down the road, this woman was going to become his permanent and only partner.

"Okay, see you later." She sounded so blasé to her own ears. Good, he wouldn't know how she was trembling inside, wishing all her fears and doubts would disappear and leave her free to throw herself into his arms and beg him to love her all night long. She smiled at him and clung to the edge of the counter.

Jake was at the door, his fingers to his lips in a farewell gesture, when the phone rang.

Roxie laughed, watched the door close behind him and lifted the receiver.

"Hello."

A deep, steel-edged voice knifed across the wires.

"The next time you get your name in the papers it'll be in the obituary column, unless you lay off me and my operation."

The dial tone hummed against her gasp of dismay.

CHAPTER TEN

ROXIE WATCHED JAKE pour wine into glasses at the small table on the deck of the *Tinker Toy*. She twisted her hands in her lap and looked out over the moonlit water. She should tell someone—Jake, probably—about Minto's call. She didn't feel able to keep it to herself.

But she didn't want word of it getting back to Joe. When he'd called yesterday, he had sounded happier, at peace for the first time in a long time. He had told her he was at the Continental Divide and that the feel of the mountains was as healing as anything he'd ever experienced. She'd been cautious about relaying the number of cancellations they'd had for June. It was the first time she'd ever lied to Joe about anything. Well, not lied, exactly, but certainly withheld the truth. She felt confident she could refill the slots before she spoke to him again.

Jake handed her a glass and winked at her. "The river's beautiful at night, isn't it?"

"Yes. Beautiful."

"So, why do I get the idea your thoughts are far away from here?"

She decided to obey her impulse. Jake was the one to tell. She could convince him not to let Joe know about it just yet.

"Jake, that phone call I got as you were leaving—it was Minto. He...he threatened me. I..."

Jake set the wine decanter on the table with an angry thud and stared at her. "Did you call the police?"

"No. I don't think that would be such a good idea."

"Why not?" he demanded.

"I think...I think we'd just better drop it, is all," she said, taking a sip of her wine. "I think he'll leave us alone if we don't make anymore waves."

"He can't be allowed to get away with breaking the law and then threatening you on top of it," Jake snapped.

"Jake, the article has probably already nipped his business in the bud, and he isn't going to bother me if I leave him alone."

"I'm not afraid of him. I'll go after the bastard."

"Without his guessing you were acting on my behalf? Jake, I'd never be able to sleep at night again for worrying about what might happen next, either to you or to me."

Jake felt thoroughly frustrated. He picked up his glass and swallowed the contents. "This really goes against the grain, Roxie," he said, reaching for the decanter.

"The path of least resistance," she said, and when he lifted his questioning gaze to hers, she added, "Sometimes that's the best way to go."

It occurred to him that she might not be referring only to this problem. "I'll go along with you, up to a point," he bargained.

"Yes? And what is that point?" She was relieved that he seemed willing to go along with her.

"I want you to stay here tonight, in case he decides to call back."

"Come on, Jake! Give me a break!"

His grin was crooked. "This isn't a come-on."

"I just don't see what good it will do. He indicated that he wouldn't make a move on me unless I gave another interview."

"Nevertheless, you'll be up all night worrying if you're alone at your place. You'll jump every time the phone rings."

"I won't."

"What makes you so sure?"

"I was thrown by the surprise, the unexpected venom. Now that I've been exposed to his nastiness, I'm sort of armed against it."

He didn't really believe that but he could see that she did. Still, he didn't like the idea of her going back there alone. "I'll sleep out here on deck, on a sleeping bag. I've done it before."

She raised an eyebrow. "You'd really sleep out here?"

"Scout's honor!" He raised two fingers to his brow.

"Were you?"

"A scout? Sure." He sprawled back in his chair and grinned at her. "My mom insisted we try everything for one year. If we didn't like it, then we could quit."

"Everything?"

"Yeah. You know, music lessons, baseball, scouting, dance class, swimming..."

"Dance class?" She almost laughed out loud.

He reddened slightly. "Yeah. What's so funny about that?"

"You mean, like ballroom dancing or ballet?"

"Either." He was feeling defensive now. She didn't have to make such a big deal of it. He and his brothers weren't the only boys who took those classes.

"Either? You mean you could choose which you preferred?"

"Yes."

"And which did you choose?"

He stood up and went to the door to the cabin. "I'll get our dinner. Why don't you light the lantern?"

She couldn't help it. Even before the door closed behind him she was laughing again, picturing the Gilbert men, all very tall and ruggedly masculine, in white tights, *en pointe*. And Jake's refusing to answer her question made it seem all the funnier. Maybe if he hadn't sounded so defensive it wouldn't have amused her so much; after all there were some very attractive men in the ballet world.

Anyway, it had helped ease the stress caused by Minto's threat. Laughter was the best medicine in the world for restoring emotional order.

The candle lantern Jake had asked her to light hung from a hook under the eave of the cabin, over the table he had set on the deck. Straw place mats covered two sides of the table and a third, in the center, held salt and pepper shakers and soy sauce. A glass in the center of the table held chopsticks.

She saw why when he came out carrying a tray with an assortment of open carry-out boxes.

"I remembered that you like Chinese food," he said.

"I'm glad you didn't go to a lot of trouble to prepare dinner," she said, but felt strangely moved that he'd remembered and picked up her favorite cuisine.

It turned out that he'd chosen some very spicy and exotic Szechuan dishes for her, and plain old chicken chow mein for himself.

"What are you laughing about?" he asked, sounding injured.

"You're just so adventurous, Jake," she said.

"I can be, if you just give me a chance," he said with a licentious grin.

"Sure, if your sexual appetite is like your taste in food . . ." She let the words trail off.

"There's no comparison," he said, and was surprised at how foreign his voice sounded. "I like my food domestic and mild, but my women exotic and wild."

Her laugh sounded strained. The moon was climbing rapidly skyward, bathing her in its glow, making the night appear darker in the shadows. Her chopsticks sounded like chattering teeth as she attempted to pick up a piece of shrimp. "I'd never have guessed that about you."

They ate in silence for a few minutes.

Jake spoke at last. "I think we should tell the captain about this, Roxie."

"No!" She almost shouted the word. "All that would do is spoil his trip. And if he decided to come back because of it, what could he do about it?"

"Maybe figure a way to put the kibosh on Minto's operation."

"If there's something that can be done, we could do it ourselves," Roxie pointed out, attempting to sound reasonable.

Jake raised an eyebrow at her. "You're not thinking of doing anything about it yourself, are you?"

She hoped he had accepted her refusal to bring Joe into their confidence. "All I'm going to do is let it drop, Jake." She picked up a pea pod with her sticks. "And spend the night here, where I don't have to think about any of it, anymore."

Jake saw he'd won at least one point. He decided to settle for that, for now, and continued with his meal.

"The moon is so beautiful over the river," Roxie said finally, lifting her gaze to meet his.

"I ordered it just for our dinner."

"Clever. It makes the perfect background for an Oriental meal."

"It's for afterward."

"Afterward?" Her throat seemed to clog up, keeping the word from surfacing in her normal voice.

"Yes. I thought afterward we'd lay a blanket out on the deck and make love." The words sounded teasing but his eyes had darkened to pewter gray as he said them, and he was not smiling.

She cleared her throat and pretended to ignore his remark.

"Can't take a joke?"

"Of course." *Can't let you guess how appealing your idea sounds.*

Moonlight turned her blond hair to silver and smoothed the planes of her face so that she looked like a beautiful marble statue. Her lips glistened and her eyes caught the candlelight and reflected it back to him.

"How's your dinner?"

"Hot," she breathed. She sipped wine but it only seemed to increase the spiciness and she took a bigger swallow.

He watched the way her throat moved when she swallowed. She was wearing a sundress that bared her neck and shoulders. In the moonlight her skin looked like alabaster. He wanted to reach out and touch her.

She glanced at the deck beyond the table. There *is* room there for a blanket, she thought suddenly. The thought made her hands tremble, and she placed her chopsticks across her plate.

"Not hungry again," Jake asked, "or isn't the food good?"

"It's good," she murmured. She picked up her chopsticks, ate a little more and reached for her water glass.

"Well, if you're through, maybe we'd better get on to the next thing on the agenda."

His reflexes weren't quick enough to catch the glass that slipped from her hand.

"You seem a little nervous tonight," Jake said, as he bent to pick up the glass.

"I . . . no, just clumsy. Thank goodness it didn't break."

Jake held it up. "It's not fine crystal. I don't think it would have depreciated the collection if one of the set got broken." He put the glass on the table and ran the back of his hand along her cheek. "You have amazing skin," he said softly, "it feels just as soft and silky as it looks."

"I feel as though I should break into a face soap commercial now," she said, blotting at the wet spots on her dress. Her laugh sounded strained.

He went to his chair. "Would you like more water? Or anything?"

"No. Thanks."

He pushed his plate away to make room for his elbows on the table. He noticed how, when she nodded, her hair seemed to send out crackles of moonlight in every direction. He cleared his throat. "Did I tell you how much I like your new hairdo?"

"No. Yes. I guess." She smiled shyly.

When she smiled he thought he could see that tiny dimple in her right cheek, just there, near her mouth.

"I do. Very much. I loved it before, but now it has a wonderful life of its own. It works with your every movement."

God, he could be so poetic at times. She didn't even know if she liked that, hadn't heard it much from any of the men she'd dated. Clay, for instance, was too pragmatic to stoop to anything as romantic as a poetic turn of phrase.

"I'll tell Henri, he'll love your description of it."

"Henri?" Jake almost bit his tongue. Geez, the way the name bolted from his mouth, he sounded like a jealous lover.

She laughed, that little girlish sound that hovered somewhere between a throaty chuckle and a giggle. "My hairdresser."

Jake's turn to nod. "You thought I was going to suggest going to bed, didn't you?"

The question, coming out of the blue, startled her. If she'd been holding a second glass of water, she'd have dropped that one, too.

"Will you stop that!"

"What?" His smile was gentle.

"Don't sound so innocent, you know what I mean. Stop sneaking up on me with innuendo and off-the-wall remarks."

He lifted his glass to her in a toast. "Nothing off the wall about going to bed—or making love, if you prefer."

"I prefer we change the subject." He could make her feel so . . . so frustrated. *So vulnerable.*

"Okay."

Well, he didn't have to go to the other extreme and sound quite so indifferent. She shivered despite the warmth of the night and the heat from her spicy food.

He stood up. "How about a little music?"

"Sure." She looked at him and her throat tightened at the sight. He was so tall, so fit and strong and lean. She could see his arm muscles flexing as he loaded the dishes and boxes of leftovers onto a tray. He did the domestic task easily. Clearly he was used to taking care of himself.

"Did you all do chores when you were kids?" she asked, curious about his childhood.

"No. We had lots of live-in help when I was young."

He said it so casually, as if everyone had people to wait on them when they were growing up. Still, she winced as a fleeting memory of the run-down shack of her childhood blazoned across her mind.

"How did you become so domestic?" She gestured toward the cabin, the interior of which was as clean as a whistle.

"Captain Joe and Martha taught me that. It's mandatory aboard a boat that everything always be ship-shape—first, because of limited space, second, to maintain sanitary conditions, and third, to avoid accidents."

He took the tray inside and came back carrying a coffee pot and two mugs. At her nod he poured and set a cup down before her. "The other thing is, my folks made it clear when I first went to work at Harley Marine that if I was going to work outside their community, I was going to have to make do just like any other working stiff. It went with the territory." He grinned. "I liked the territory so much, I decided it was worth learning to push a dust rag around and do a few dishes.''

He went over to the portable radio and moved the dial until an instrumental version of ''I'm In The Mood For Love'' filled the air. He offered his hand to Roxie. ''Care to dance, m'dear?''

''There's not much room,'' she said, eyeing the narrow strip of deck dubiously.

He pulled her into his arms. ''Well then, we'll just have to dance very close.''

That ought to have warned her. Instead, she snuggled into his embrace and let the music, the beauty of the night, the romance of the boat and Jake's physical nearness all seduce her into submission. By the time the music ended, her senses were inundated with Jake's clean and masculine fragrance, the solid feel of his body against hers and the sensation of floating in a world occupied only by the two of them.

''Are you ready for dessert?'' he whispered into her ear.

The question, asked in a husky near-whisper, suggested all sorts of things to Roxie, none of them to do with the final course of a meal, and set off alarms in every part of her body.

''I could hardly finish dinner,'' she said, drawing back. She pointed vaguely in the direction of the table without taking her eyes from his face.

He stared at her. *Why don't I just take her in my arms and let nature take its course?*

''What—what are you d-doing?'' *What a silly question. You're about to be kissed, the only question that applies is are you willing to let it—*

She made a sound against his mouth that could have been either a moan or a muffled word. He deepened the kiss. This time he recognized the sound for a moan, and groaned his appreciative response.

Damn they were good together. Each time they came together this way, they were instantly responsive to one another's chemistry.

He could hardly believe that they had known each other for five years and that he'd just, in the past few weeks, begun to notice her. More amazing, it had only taken those few weeks to begin to fall in love with her. And Roxie? How did she feel about him?

He interrupted the kiss, needing to look into her face, to read her emotions. She sighed and the sibilance wafted warmly against his lips.

"Do you want me to stop?" he asked.

"No, oh, no."

He led her inside, past the galley and over to the bunk. He stood beside the bed, and kissed her.

Roxie let her body lean into his, threaded her hands through his thick, luxurious hair and opened her mouth to receive his tongue. So what if they were rivals for the same job? So what if it was too soon after Taffy and what's-his-name? So what if they came from entirely different backgrounds? He was delicious, indescribably delicious and so damned sexy she wanted to crawl all over him and chew him up and swallow him and do everything she'd ever fantasized.

"Yes, do that," she moaned, moving to help him pull the top of her sundress down. His hands were unbelievably gentle.

"How do you do that?" She was almost purring. She didn't want him to stop, *ever*.

"What?" he whispered. He bent to kiss the delicate skin of her neck just below her ear. He'd never known a woman with such lovely, touchable skin. And her fragrance was making him salivate. He wanted to taste her. No, more than that—to gobble her up, to fill his mouth with great gulps of her.

"That," she groaned, "barely touching me and yet—sending—" she swallowed to relieve the dryness in her mouth "—sending such electricity over my body."

Jake looked into her eyes but kept his fingers playing over her taut breasts. If he looked at her breasts now, he'd explode. "Violin."

"You—you play the violin?" She pulled at his shirt, letting him know she wanted his chest bared to her eyes and hands and mouth. He pulled it over his head and drew her into his arms. Their flesh met and vibrated with feeling.

"I love the violin," she said. She thought briefly of Charley Daniels, of how she loved his bluegrass fiddling and then the thought was gone and her mind and senses were filled with only Jake. She caressed his pectoral muscles, ran her fingers around his nipples, tugged gently at the mass of hair that covered his chest.

"Do you?" His voice shook. He wrapped her hair around his hand and caught her lips between his own, sending his tongue to explore the deepest recesses of her mouth.

Their breathing orchestrated their movements as they undressed one another, shutting out all the sounds of the night and the river around them.

They were naked, their bodies melding together as they sank to the bunk. "I'll have to—to play—for you—sometime."

"Yes." He had knelt beside her, laid her on her back, her head hanging over his arm, her hair brushing the mattress, and begun kissing his way down her body. She felt as if she was going to faint with pleasure even as her own need to dominate rose within her. She wanted to ravage him, to be rough where he was gentle, to overpower where he seduced, to thrust where he merely enticed. "Jake. Oh, Jake, I want you so." She pulled him down on top of her.

"I'LL MAKE THE COFFEE," Roxie said, snuggling more deeply against his side.

"No." He shook his head and turned to kiss her. "God, you're even more beautiful now. Lovemaking certainly agrees with you."

She pushed him away and sat up, her hand going automatically to her face, her hair. "I'll bet I look like something the cat dragged in," she said, "and you don't have to flatter me to get out of making the coffee. I said I'll do it." She swung her legs off the bunk and looked at him over her shoulder. "Do you want cream and sugar?"

He caressed the silken length of her bare back. "Uh-huh, I certainly do." His hand snaked around to the front of her, to caress her breasts and belly, then crept lower to emphasize his meaning.

She slapped his hand away. "Oh, you really are outrageous, Jake Gilbert."

He twirled an imaginary mustache. "I certainly hope so."

She got up and fled the small inner cabin. "Is everything you say a double entendre?" she called back.

"Some people smoke after sex," he yelled. From the galley she could detect the note of satisfaction, of happiness in his voice. Well, that was fine. She was feeling pretty happy herself, and she didn't think it was just the residual contentment of good sex, or even the first flush of falling in love.

She put her hand to her mouth to stifle a giggle. "Love?" she whispered, reaching for the coffee canister. *Uh-huh, love.* Well, she knew by now she could trust that inner voice to hit the nail on the head and to speak only the truth.

But could she trust her judgment? She filled the aluminum pot with water at the miniature sink. Could she tell the difference between lust and love, between need and true caring? Was she one of those women who needed to give a name to her emotions in order to justify them? Did she need to justify lovemaking with love? Was there a difference? And if there was, would she recognize it? She put the basket with the coffee onto the stem and slipped the whole thing into the pot. *I can't handle being hurt again.* And somehow, she knew, Jake could end up causing her far more pain than she'd ever experienced before. *And are you such a coward that you'd avoid the relationship to avoid the gamble?* Was she such a coward? She had always thought of herself as rather brave, a person willing to take risks.

Why, look at how she'd handled the threat from that worm, Harry Minto. The mere thought of that ominous, dangerous voice on the phone gave her the shivers.

She was reaching for the matches on the shelf above the stove when an arm caught her around the middle. She screamed and dropped the matches.

"Hey, hey, what's wrong? I was just sneaking up to give you a hug." Jake couldn't believe the intensity of her reaction. She was shaking. He lifted the blanket he'd skirted around his lower torso and wrapped her in it, pulling her, blanket and all, into his arms. "Shh, it's okay," he soothed, "I'm sorry. I shouldn't have surprised you. Shh, it's all right."

It felt so good to be comforting her. He wanted to protect her from all harm for the rest of her life. Sometimes she was like a little girl, reminding him of his sisters when they were little. She brought out the same protective, big-brother urges in him.

He smoothed her hair and kissed her brow. "Better?" The shaking seemed to have eased.

"Yes. Sorry to get carried away like that, I don't know what got into me."

"I think that's another subject," Jake said, grinning at her.

She punched him in the chest. "Enough with the post-sex humor," she said, laughing shakily. But it did help to get her past that moment of shock when the unexpected touch of her lover had made her think that someone had crept aboard the boat to attack her.

She slid her hands around his waist, becoming aware for the first time that he was naked, and let her hands move lower.

Their mouths met, kissed, then clamped together in a tearing surge of passion, and all thoughts of acting the brother to Roxie fled Jake's mind.

CHAPTER ELEVEN

ROXIE WAS LATE getting to work on Monday morning. Too much exercise over the weekend, she thought, smiling happily as she parked her car in front of the office.

She ran into the building, threw her sweater at the clothes tree, tossed her purse on her desk and called out, "Mary, come in here, will you, please?"

Mary came out of her office still wearing the glasses she used for book work, holding her accountant's pencil in her mouth and carrying a stack of ledger sheets.

"Oh...you're really deep in your work," Roxie said, "I'm sorry."

"S'okay." Mary spoke around the pencil. "Whassup?"

"I'm afraid I need your undivided attention. I'm going to teach you my job."

The pencil fell from Mary's open mouth and she bent to pick it up then collapsed on the chair beside Roxie's desk. "Your job? Now? Why?"

"I'm afraid I've been really negligent—if Jake hadn't brought it to my attention—" She rubbed her forehead but the frown remained.

"I don't get it. What's the big deal? Are you planning to be out of the office or something?"

"No. But what if it became necessary?"

Mary looked blank. "Like...like if you became ill?"

"Yes."

"Well, then, I'd—" Her eyes wandered to the metal mesh baskets on Roxie's desk, the ones marked, Contracts pending, Cruise breakdown, Cash bar inventory, Party bar inventory. "I guess I could muddle through." She leaned forward, took a paper from the top basket and scanned it. "This is a contract, right?"

"Yes," Roxie said.

"Okay, well, it looks fairly simple to me—I just sort of fill in the blank spaces with the right info, don't I?"

"Yes, but do you know the right information, or where to look it up?"

Mary scratched her head. "Gee, I've been working here part-time for four years and full-time for three months, you'd think some of it would just have sort of rubbed off on me."

"Probably did—but we need to sit down and pull it all together in an organized way." Roxie was discouraged by the dubious look on Mary's face.

"Don't you want to learn to sell and coordinate the charters? It could mean a juicy promotion for you if I move up. And meanwhile, once you're able to handle my job as well as the bookkeeping, you'll get a nice raise."

Mary began to tap her teeth with her pencil. "I don't know, Roxie, I signed on as a bookkeeper because I have a natural talent for figures and numbers... Do you think this is my cup of tea?"

"I don't know, Mary," Roxie said honestly, fighting a feeling of exasperation. It seemed incredible to her that anyone wouldn't be jumping up and down with excitement at the prospect of learning more, of moving ahead.

"We'll have to give it a try and see how you do and if you like it. If you don't we'll have to hire a third person for the office. And I think we should start right away, so you'd better call around and find us another hostess to work full-time on the *Celeb* on a regular basis—you're going to be too tired at the end of the day to go out on those cruises."

Mary proved to be a good student, and after a couple of days, Roxie tossed her some notes and said, "You write up this contract and follow through on the cruise breakdown."

Mary grinned and took the notes from Roxie. "Sure, Chief, love to."

Roxie studied the younger woman. "You do like this, don't you?"

"Uh-huh. More than I thought I would. It's fun, actually."

"So, does that mean you don't miss hostessing on the boat?"

"It's kind of nice having my nights free." She smiled and said, "My fella appreciates that, too."

"Aha." Roxie hadn't had a chance lately to keep up with Mary's mystery romance. Maybe this was it. "So you get to see more of your boyfriend now."

Mary's freckles stood out even more when she blushed. "He's not my boyfriend, exactly."

"No? What, then?"

"Well, he's my... my... We are seeing each other as—but he isn't... I don't think of him as... as a *boy*friend."

"My goodness, Mary. I've never seen anyone so flustered over a word before." A terrible thought occurred. "Mary, he's not married, is he? Is that the reason for all the mystery?"

"No. Of course not. God, Roxie, you can't think I'd ever fool around with a married man."

"No, I'm sorry, I shouldn't have thought it for a minute. But it's hard to think that there's any other good reason for keeping a romance a secret in this day and age."

Mary headed for her office. "My guy has a good reason and I have to go along with his wishes whether I agree with the need for secrecy or not."

So the secrecy was her friend's idea. Well, that was one more small clue that might lead to the solution. Roxie followed Mary into her office. "Are you free for lunch? Now that you understand this end of the business, I'd like your input on some ideas I've got for expanding."

They called the phone service to take their calls and within minutes they were seated at Boca Chica, juggling oozing, spicy tacos and half a dozen boat company brochures.

"Where did you get these?" Mary asked, wiping sauce from her lips with her napkin.

"I wrote away to various excursion boat companies around the country asking for their mailers."

"Great idea, Rox," Mary enthused, sorting through the brochures. She held one up. "Look at this one. Look at how they've carried the theme into the decor of the main salon."

Roxie held up another. "How about this one— they've lined the outer deck with Japanese lanterns and used a garden-party motif."

"This is really exciting, Rox, I think we should do it. When will we start?"

Roxie wiped her mouth and hands and sat back looking thoughtful. "As soon as I can sell Jake and Floyd on the idea."

Mary looked surprised. "Why do you need their approval? I thought all that sort of thing comes out of our office."

"Yes, normally. Normally, it would be decided in the office with Joe's approval—but now I'm running over into Jake's territory, and Floyd's department would be affected as well." She frowned. "Jake could nix the whole idea."

"Well, he wouldn't though, would he? Why should he?"

Roxie shrugged. "I guess it would depend on how much he wants to keep me from leaping ahead in the race for the promotion, and this just might generate enough extra revenue to do the job. Anyway, we have that staff meeting tomorrow, we can bring the subject up then."

"WEEKLY DINNER PARTIES on the *Princess*?" Jake echoed.

Roxie kept her hands busy, readying brochures for mailing, and avoided Jake's eyes, which would only remind her of their weekend together.

Somehow Saturday had drifted by in a haze of shared domestic chores that more often than not ended in giggles on her part and intense clowning on Jake's, and without discussing it, another overnight stay. By Sunday morning they were both exhausted from two nights with very little sleep. They agreed that Minto would probably not call again, and Roxie went to her apartment. She couldn't remember ever enjoying a weekend more.

"Like a restaurant?" Floyd asked, drawing Roxie's attention. "But we don't even have a regulation galley aboard the *Princess*, at least not one equipped to handle a dinner."

"No, no," Roxie said, "you didn't let me finish." She stole a glance at Jake. When he looked up and their eyes met, his smile was friendly. Only the glint in his eyes told her, he, too, was remembering.

Roxie sighed and tried to concentrate on the subject at hand. "Not like a restaurant. There wouldn't be any cooking aboard. It would all be catered, just like the private parties are now. Only this would be open to the public."

Jake's chair rocked slightly as his foot kicked the front frame of the desk. "What happens if you have the caterer aboard with all that food and the public doesn't turn out."

"It would all be done with advance sales," Roxie said. "I'd advertise it in the paper and on radio and set it up for, say, Tuesday nights, and have a cut-off date. All reservations must be made and paid for by Friday of the previous week, for instance."

"Do you think people would be interested in a dinner cruise on a Tuesday night?" Floyd Dubrov asked.

"Good point, Floyd," Jake said.

"That is a good point," Roxie admitted. "But I'll have to pick a night that is open every week on the *Princess*'s charter schedule. And people do celebrate birthdays and anniversaries and such on week nights. As a matter of fact, our advertising could suggest that people don't have to wait for the weekend to have a romantic evening or to do something exciting and different."

Jake watched Roxie from under his eyelids. God, she was a beautiful woman. She seemed to grow more so as summer went on and her skin took on the golden glow of a suntan. Lately she'd taken to wearing more feminine clothing, skirts and blouses, suits, tailored dresses—very professional but also very enticing. When she uncrossed and recrossed her legs, he had almost fallen off his chair. When she'd put her hands behind her head, causing her breasts to outline themselves against the soft fabric of her blouse, he'd had to sit forward to hide the evidence of the excitement she engendered.

Mary, who had been quiet until then, said, "How about, 'Add another Saturday night to your week'?"

Everybody applauded that idea. "Very nice, Mary." Roxie's excitement was beginning to grow as the others began to show some enthusiasm. Everyone but Jake, that is, she thought. *He looks as if he hates the idea.* She pushed on anyway.

"And I could use our regular mailing list to notify our customers that we are now offering an alternate service to private charter," Roxie added. "For instance, Mr. Miler, from Winters, Inc. He might like to know that a cruise is available for wining and dining out-of-town customers without chartering the whole boat."

She allowed herself to look Jake's way then. His face was closed. She couldn't read his reaction. Maybe this competition was finally beginning to take on some importance to him. But, oh, how she suddenly wished everyone else in the room would disappear so that she could be alone with him.

"So, Jake. You haven't said much, what do you think?"

Jake was sitting forward, his arms on his knees. "I'll have to think about it for awhile," he said, finally. "I admit the idea has merit but it must also have draw-backs—I need time to consider those."

The front door flew open just then and Bill came rushing into their midst.

"We've got a real problem," he said without preamble. He picked up the straight chair beside Rox-ie's desk, turned it and sat with his arms folded across the backrest, his legs straddling it.

"Is this so important it can't wait, Bill?" Roxie asked, frowning. "We're in the middle of a meeting." The men always exaggerated their dilemmas. Roxie had learned to take their crises in stride.

"Beau Henderson was just over at the marina, said they've had four more cancellations for the end of June and three in July."

"Beau Henderson." Roxie frowned. "From Red Wing Marine?"

"You got it," Bill said. He looked at Jake and shook his head. "You were right, Minto's all over both riv-ers. Henderson said Dillers, up on the St. Croix, has filed a complaint with the Coast Guard."

"I hope they have better luck with the Coast Guard than we've had," Floyd said wryly.

"So, Roxie, what's to keep our reservations in-tact?" Bill asked.

Roxie picked up a pencil, leaned back in her chair and began tapping the pencil against her teeth. "We're already feeling the crunch," she admitted. "We've had three more cancellations for this month and another in July. That averages out to about a ten thousand dollar loss, with food and music."

Floyd blew out a gusty sigh. "How does the guy do it?"

He didn't need to clarify that he was referring to Minto.

Roxie felt the frustration swell up in her, and her insides began churning. "Why didn't that article keep people from dealing with him?"

Jake said, "Maybe it did—some. But there are always people who are natural looters who take advantage of this kind of situation."

"Looters? What have they to do with this business?"

It was Floyd who explained. "You know, people who take advantage of blackouts and go in and loot stores—people who normally might not even shoplift."

"Oh, I see. They read there's a boat operating on the river that is pirating legitimate business, and they decide to take advantage and save a little money."

"Yup." Floyd pushed his billed hat back and scratched his head. "So what do we do about it?"

"Get in touch with the Coast Guard again. They certainly can't think all those passengers are Minto's personal friends."

"They're going to want proof," Bill said.

"Well, damn it! Let them get it." Roxie threw the pencil in a fit of pique. "It's their job, isn't it?"

"Whoa," Floyd said, holding his hand up. "Let's not get apoplectic here, Rox, nothing's that serious."

"Oh, no? What about your job, Floyd? There isn't time this year, but next year that river rat Minto could eat up our entire season if he's allowed to get away with it now. And even this year we're already talking a loss of twenty-five thousand dollars in canceled trips, and God knows how many more before the season ends."

"Don't they forfeit their deposits?"

"Yes," Mary contributed, "and that's what's so scary. Minto must be giving them a hell of a deal to make it worthwhile for them to throw away in some cases as much as five hundred dollars."

Floyd scratched his head again and looked pensive. "How can he afford it?"

Roxie drew a blank, then suddenly it came to her in a flash of intuition. "No overhead!"

"What?"

"Well, don't you see? No one knows where he operates out of, and nobody has been able to locate his office. He probably operates out of his pocket."

She scrambled around in her desk. "Yes, here it is." She pulled out a copy of a newspaper clipping. "This came in lieu of brochures I wrote and asked for." She gave the paper to Floyd, who was nearest her chair.

It was an article published in the *Wall Street Journal* about a man who owned a couple of stern-wheelers, had been running them for public charter on the Mississippi in Iowa for twenty-five years, and had never had an office. He paid cash for everything and eliminated the need for a bookkeeper. When the reporter asked where he kept his business records, Captain Jones had pointed to his pocket.

Floyd laughed and passed the clipping to Bill. "He must have a hell of a memory."

"The point is, there are legitimate businesses that don't bog themselves down with a lot of overhead, so maybe this Minto is doing just that, which means he can afford to take on passage for a lot less than we can. He doesn't have to pay rent, taxes, utilities, office staff, printing costs—he just needs a phone and a note-book.''

"Okay. Suppose you're right? We know that a legit-imate outfit, like Captain Jones's, can just hang a sign on the dock and wait for customers to show up. But how does Minto do it? Where does he make contact with customers or they with him? How does he adver-tise?'' Floyd asked.

That was a little tougher. For a few minutes there was silence as they all thought about it.

"Word of mouth,'' she said.

"What? What's that, Roxie?'' Bill asked.

"They're probably using word-of-mouth advertis-ing. Sort of like a river grapevine. Isn't that how street crime is advertised? One person whispering to another that a certain commodity is available at a certain place?'' She grew excited as she warmed to the idea, her belief that she was on the right track increasing. "Yeah. And why not the reverse? Someone puts out the word they're looking for a cheaper way to go, and not fussy about licensing and certification, and Minto gets in touch with them.''

The others were agreeing that Roxie might have hit on something when Jake saw the look on her face and read her mind.

"No way, Roxanne,'' he said, sternly. "You're not getting mixed up with that thug, I forbid it.''

"You what?'' Funny, she'd never noticed that his eyebrow arched arrogantly when he was angry. It was a habit she had herself.

"I'm not kidding, Roxie. You're not to do anything foolish, like trying to contact Minto on your own.'' He was straining toward her, his back to the others. "Roxie, you've already had a threatening phone call from the guy, you sure don't want to come up against him in person. You leave this up to the men.''

Roxie had no intention of having a scene with Jake in front of the others. She wasn't going to take a chance on losing face. Furthermore, she didn't want questions about the phone call from Minto. So, though her mouth was set in a grim line and her eyes flashed fire, her voice was quiet and calm.

''I wouldn't dream of it, Jake. You men can handle this one, and of course, Mary and I will keep our eyes and ears open and let you know if we learn anything you can act on. Right, Mary?''

Mary looked from Roxie to Jake and back to Roxie and then nodded, confused. When she saw Roxie's warning look, Mary shrugged and said, ''Sure, of course. We'll let you guys know if we hear anything.''

''I mean it, Roxie,'' Jake said, as the men rose from their chairs. ''You're not to go near that guy, do you understand me?'' He leaned toward her, one hand splayed on her desk.

Roxie looked down and felt herself grow warm as she recalled the feel of that hand threading through her hair. ''Wouldn't dream of it,'' she said softly, and looked away from the warning in his eyes and the way his hair fell in a soft wave to shadow them.

She was grateful that Bill brought up the subject of the new wharf taxes the city was levying, and the subject of Minto was dropped. The meeting broke up a few minutes later.

''Okay,'' Mary demanded, the minute the door closed on the last of the men, ''give! What are you planning?''

Roxie put a finger over her lips and went to the passageway and listened, making sure that Bill, who'd gone through the back, was out of the building. Con vinced they were alone, she turned to Mary.

"Get me this morning's paper," she said in a low voice.

Mary went into her office and came back with the *Dispatch*. Roxie almost snatched it out of her hands in her excitement, rustled through the last section and folded the pages back when she came to the beginning of the want-ad section. Running her finger down the column, she held her breath and let it out on a shout of triumph as she found what she was looking for.

"Here it is!"

"What? Here what is?" Mary scrambled around the desk to see what Roxie was so excited about.

The ad was minuscule. It read, *Take your party on a river cruise for less,* and gave a phone number.

As Mary read the ad, Roxie dialed the number. "It's a tape," she said, whispering all the same. "It says to leave a name and number at the sound of the tone and the call will be returned as soon as possible. There's no name and nothing about chartering a boat."

Roxie hung up and drummed her fingers on the desk as she tried to think what to do next.

"You aren't thinking of leaving your number, are you?" Mary asked, putting the paper down. "I've heard the guy is a real scum, Roxie. If he gets wind of the fact that you're not on the level..."

She didn't have to finish. The implication was clear.

"No, I guess not." Roxie sighed. "But I sure am tempted. I'd love to be the one to catch him, but I guess that'd be foolhardy." She wrote the number from the ad on a piece of paper and drew a circle around it. "Maybe I'll tell Jake about it and see what he thinks."

"Actually," Mary pointed out, "you don't even know that the number is Minto's or that the ad is about private charters on the *Shark*."

But more than intuition told Roxie she was right. What Mary couldn't know was that she'd recognized Minto's voice on the tape.

CHAPTER TWELVE

MARY SAW that Roxie was preoccupied with Jake, their heads together over the brochures, and she slipped quietly into her office. Just as quietly she picked up the phone and punched in a number.

"Hi," she said to the man who answered, keeping her voice just above a whisper. "I'm just checking about tonight. We're going to do the stuffed chicken breasts, right?"

"Yes," the man said. "How is the new work going today? Are you comfortable with the charters now?"

It was hard holding a normal conversation while trying to keep her voice to a whisper. "I'll tell you all about it at dinner."

"Are you going to pick up the chicken?"

"Yes, I'll get it on my lunch hour."

"You should eat lunch on your lunch hour."

"I've got to keep my weight down somehow." She lowered her voice another half decibel. "Those breakfasts we've been sharing should take care of my nutritional needs for the whole day."

"I offered you the alternative of staying in bed," the man said in a throaty, seductive tone.

Mary put her hand to her mouth to suppress the gasp of excitement his words elicited. As if he knew the effect he had on her, his laugh came through the wire low and smug.

A sound of chairs scraping in the other room caught her attention.

"I've got to go," she whispered, "see you tonight."

She hung up the phone and grabbed her pencil, determined to look innocently busy if Roxie or Jake happened to glance in at her in passing. She knew Roxie was hell-bent on learning the name of her secret lover, but Mary was just as determined to honor his wishes even though she didn't really understand his reasons for wanting to keep their affair a secret.

"I've got to run off some fliers, Mary," Roxie called out. "I'll be in the back."

"Oh, I'll help," Jake said in a suspiciously loud voice, "I've got an hour to kill, anyway."

Mary put her hand over her mouth and giggled. "Who do you think you're kidding," she whispered behind her hand. Talk about secrets; Jake Gilbert and Roxie Hilton had a lot to learn about clandestine behavior if they really meant to keep their feelings hidden from the rest of the world. Especially from Mary, who was one of Roxie's best friends. They were as transparent as glass. The past few weeks, every time they were in the office together, you could cut the sexual tension with a knife. And Jake, the most independent, self-reliant, masculine man in the world, followed Roxie around like a little puppy.

"Like now." She grinned, shook her head and bent to her work. But the vague sounds of movement and talk from the back room distracted her. It didn't sound like the old mimeograph machine was running. Now if they'd already purchased the new photocopier Roxie kept talking about, Mary wouldn't know if it was running or not. But the old mimeo clunked like wheels on a track. Everyone knew when it was running.

No, the sounds she was hearing were most likely the sounds two people made who couldn't keep their hands off one another but couldn't afford the luxury of taking time off from work to be alone.

It made Mary think of her own romance. It hadn't been love at first sight, or popped up unexpectedly. It had sort of grown over time in a quiet, lovely way. Not the wild, insane passion Mary had come to expect after watching too many late night movies on television, but a very sweet, deep, compelling emotion that made her feel like the most protected, most loved woman in the whole world.

As for Jake and Roxie—well, romances were probably as different as the people involved in them, and Jake and Roxie's relationship was more of the storybook kind, though she was sure it was the real thing.

Meanwhile, even as Mary was contemplating Jake and Roxie's relationship, Roxie was wondering about Mary.

"Something's going on with her," Roxie whispered, "and I'm going to find out what—rather who—it is, if it's the last thing I do."

Jake pushed her farther into the storeroom, slipped his hand under her skirt and nuzzled his face into the softness of her neck as his fingers found the smooth flesh between the tops of her stockings and her panties. "Stop worrying about Mary's love life and concentrate on ours, woman."

She moaned softly and collapsed against the hard arousal of his body, fitting herself to him eagerly. "Yes." She whispered the word into his ear then bit the lobe as he moved his fingers under the scant bit of lace that covered her.

Jake kicked the door shut behind him then leaned against it, Roxie in his arms. He was kissing her now, over and over, each kiss lasting longer, probing deeper, arousing both of them to nearly uncontrollable heights as his hand caressed her until she bit his shoulder to stifle her cries of pleasure.

"Let's go to my place," she begged, forgetting in the heat of the moment that Jake had a run in less than an hour. She leaned her sweat-dampened forehead against his shirt. He smelled of fresh air and clean laundry with just a hint of masculine sweat and after-shave mixed in. She breathed deeply and sighed her hunger for him.

"Let's do it here," he almost growled in her ear. They laughed together and drew apart to enjoy the pleasure of looking at one another.

"God, you're beautiful," Jake said, staring at her flushed face. Her eyes had become much darker and glittered with excitement. Damp wisps of hair escaped from the barrettes she wore on either side of her head and framed her face like gold lace.

Roxie lowered her long dark lashes to hide the shyness his flattery evoked and ran her hands up and down and over his shoulders. "You're pretty gorgeous yourself, you know," she whispered, raising her eyes once again to meet his gaze.

"I love you so," he said, his muffled voice sending shivers across her skin.

"I've got to get back out there before Mary comes looking for me," Roxie said regretfully, suddenly aware that the phone was ringing for about the fourth time since they'd retreated to the back room.

He let her go and pulled out a handkerchief to mop his wet face. "When are we going to be together again?"

"I don't know." Belatedly Roxie turned on the mimeograph machine and tucked the tails of her brown and blue plaid shirt into the waistband of her blue denim skirt. "With your charters every night this week..."

"You could come along."

She laughed and shoved him playfully out of her way as she bent to take a stack of paper out of the box under the machine. "Sure, and you could run the boat aground, and two hundred passengers with it."

She reached behind him to open the door, to let some air into the room. He caught her arm and pulled her against him. "It's got to be soon, I'm going nuts wanting you."

She sighed and nodded, feeling her own need make jelly of her knees and send darts of desire to the hidden place between her legs. "I could wait up for you tonight."

He groaned and kissed her, every ounce of his desire present in the kiss, in the hard, aroused length of his body. "It'll be really late—after midnight. You'll be exhausted tomorrow."

She moved away from him to the comparative safety of the grumbling old machine. "I'll be more exhausted if we don't spend some time together again soon."

"You could take a few days off now that Mary knows how to—"

"No!" Her answer was too quick, too abrupt. She tried to calm the surge of defiance caused by his suggestion. She'd been expecting this, that's why she'd been so quick to go on the defensive. "Mary has enough of her own work to do, especially now. I'm not going to dump on her just so we can play around."

"Is that how you see this? Playing around?"

"No, of course not," she snapped. She wiped her brow and hoped he'd blame the flush in her cheeks on the temperature in the room. "I didn't mean that, it's just that I can't see turning over a major operation to a comparative newcomer. Mary only started learning my work a few weeks ago, it's too soon to expect her to carry the ball by herself."

"We're talking a day or two here, Roxanne," Jake said gravely, "not a month or even a week. It's not as if the place will fall apart during that time." His gaze held fast to her face. "You still haven't learned to delegate authority if you can't let people solo when they've learned how."

She knew he was right and yet she couldn't let go, couldn't relinquish her hold on the job. *Maybe you can't admit that you're not indispensable,* her inner voice queried. Roxie jerked away from that thought and frowned at Jake. "I think I'm the best judge of when Mary's ready to be left alone with the work. I have every intention of taking some time off and entrusting her with the office."

"When?"

"Soon." She turned her back on him and began feeding paper into the machine.

The machine was so loud she didn't hear him come up behind her. His hand on her shoulder made her jump. "Don't wait too long," he said, almost shouting to be heard, "I wouldn't want to see you suffer from burnout."

She gave him a dirty look but softened it by reaching up and kissing him briefly on the mouth. "See you tonight?" she mouthed. He nodded and left the room with a backward wave.

MARY DRIED the last of the lovely white bisque bowls they had used and placed it beside the others in the cabinet over the sink. "I don't understand why you're still insisting that we keep our relationship secret. Joe's gone and no one else around here's going to care," she grumbled.

Bill Tabor rinsed the stainless steel sinks with a spray hose and shook his head. "Joe will be back at the end of the season."

"So what?" Mary threw the dish towel at the rod hanging over the counter. It missed and fell. She left it there, ignoring Bill's frown of disapproval. He picked up the towel, shook it and folded it neatly over the rod.

Mary persisted. "You said yourself you're going to tell him then, so what's the difference?"

"I want to tell him in person—and before the others find out. I owe him that."

"Sweety, you make it sound as if we're doing something wrong. Is that how you see us?"

"No. Of course not." He drew her into his arms and buried his face in the softness of her neck.

"Listen, Bill," she said, stroking her fingers over his thick, curly, graying dark hair, "I know lots of couples closer in age who don't have as much in common as we do and who don't get along as well. Why can't you just thank God we found each other and get on with enjoying our life together?"

Because I'm old enough to be your father, he thought. *Because other people will think I'm an old man making a fool of himself over a young girl.*

Aloud he said, "I wish it were as simple as that." He couldn't resist pressing his lips to her sweet mouth that pouted up at him even as his mind filled with all the arguments against their relationship. Her face glowed beneath the dusting of freckles that made her look even younger than her twenty-four years. He felt sure that if they were seen together, people would mistake her for his daughter.

He attempted to take her mind off the subject with a peace offering. "I've got a trifle in the refrigerator. Raspberry."

"Ooh, Bill, how can you be so cruel? Just look at this." Mary pulled her shirt up to show that she'd been unable to close the snap at the waist of her jeans. "You're going to feed me right into blimpsville and then you won't want me anymore."

He scooped her into his arms and kissed her soundly on the mouth. "You're still small enough for me to tuck in my pocket," he teased.

Her arms around his neck, legs dangling over his arms, Mary kissed Bill and snuggled her head against his broad shoulder. "I love the way you carry me around," she said with a sigh, "and I love the way you feed me and I love the way you . . ."

He stopped the flow of her words with his lips as they reached the bed in the back room of the trailer. "And I love you, too, little one, but I'm afraid to others we might seem rather an odd couple."

"Odd?" She glared at him from where he'd laid her on the bed, her voice rife with frustration. She sat up and tugged at his hand to pull him down beside her.

"Bill, sweety, how can other people's stupidity affect us?" She had her soft hand on his cheek, pleading gently for his full attention. "Isn't our love strong enough to survive anything?"

She had a habit of brushing his hair behind his ear when they sat close together, talking. She was doing that now, and Bill was mesmerized by the sound of her voice and the feel of her fingers at the side of his head. He nodded in answer to her question.

"And wouldn't we be even happier if we didn't have to sneak around and hide our feelings?"

"Yes." His voice sounded alien to his own ears. She had that effect on him when she was so near and touching him. He kept his hands clasped between his knees, fighting the urge to touch back, not wanting to interrupt her.

"Was there anything wrong in the way we ran into each other last winter?"

He shook his head.

"Or in my coming here that first time for that lesson you gave me on how to stir-fry?"

"No."

"Or in all the other times we just naturally began to share our meals and try out new recipes together?"

He ran his hands through his hair, causing Mary's hand to fall away from his head. "I see what you're driving at, Mary, darlin'," he said, "it all started out innocent and we couldn't help falling in love." It was still hard for him to say the words, still hard to believe his good fortune, that she loved him back, when in fact it had been Mary who declared her feelings first.

"Clever man," she teased. "So, what have we got to be ashamed of?"

"It's not a case of shame. I've told you that over and over. I just want to be the one to tell Joe myself. And when the time is right."

He couldn't help but think of the promotion. He could give her so many things if he had the extra money. And she wouldn't have to work. And living in a trailer, on the marina property, wasn't right for a woman. Mary deserved a real home on a private piece of land with room for children and—and... He groaned. "And every time I think about kids I get cold feet."

"Then we won't have any!"

Mary's freckles stood out in gold relief against her pale skin when her dander was up as it was now. She jumped off the bed and paced the small room, hands on her hips, fire in her hazel eyes. "Who needs kids anyway? I never thought that was the be-all and end-all of life. I just wanted to get along in life."

She stopped in front of him and grabbed his face so he was forced to look at her. "Then I met you and suddenly I wanted more than just getting along. I wanted someone to get super close to, someone to share it all with. That's what I want now. That adds up to you. You and me, and now that's all I want, and if you want to keep it a secret I'll go along with that, too."

She bent and pressed her lips to his, sweetly though briefly. "I love you, Bill. And even if we're the oddest couple in the whole world, I don't ever want to be with anyone else as long as I live. So quit trying to find excuses to unload me and come give me something to smile about tomorrow in the midst of my lonely workday."

She plopped herself down on his lap and wound her arms around his neck. Seconds later Tabor had forgotten his reservations.

He was reminded again as they lay side by side, talking companionably. "I think Roxie and Jake are having an affair," Mary murmured, winding a shock of Bill's chest hair around her finger.

"What?" Bill almost pushed her off the bed as he sat up, rigid with alarm. "Jake and Roxie? Why do you think so? What do you know?"

Mary stared at Bill, eyes and mouth wide with disbelief. "Why, honey, what's the big deal? And why are you so surprised? They're absolutely adorable together. The perfect couple—after us."

Bill groaned and lay back against the pillows, shielding his expression with his arm folded across his face. The truth was, she'd just given him even more reason to keep their affair quiet. If Jake and Roxie were lovers, that meant one would be helping the other to get the promotion. He suspected Roxie would be the one to withdraw to let her man have the open field. She would work behind the scenes to help Jake achieve the promotion. What Bill didn't need was Joe's disapproval about Bill's love life, offset by the unbeatable combination of a Gilbert-Hilton campaign.

"Bill, are you all right?" Mary tugged on his arm.

"Yes, dear. I'm fine. Just fine." He sat up and began to pull on his clothes. He didn't know how, but suddenly he knew he had to do something drastic—dramatic—to impress Joe in a really big way.

He stood up and grabbed his jacket off the back of the closet door. A walk along the levee would clear his mind and help him come up with a winning idea.

"I need to get some air and stretch my legs." He patted her cheek. "Do you mind?"

"Now?" She pulled the covers up over her naked breasts, feeling inexplicably rejected. "It's so late."

"I won't be long. Why don't you get dressed and make a pot of espresso to go with the trifle. By the time it's done, I'll be back."

He walked the maze of slips twice. There was a ghostly atmosphere to the marina in the middle of the night, with the boats bobbing sporadically in their canopied lanes, the eerie sounds of metal clanking on masts and water splashing around the hulls. He loved the marina with its assortment of pleasure craft. He liked to think each boat had its own personality, and he considered them all his charges.

But the walk did little to stir his imagination. He was just turning back when suddenly he spotted a large, brightly lit vessel easing around the bend, moving downstream past the marina. He recognized it as the *Shark*. Both decks were filled with merrymakers leaning over the rails to view the river or dancing to music that he could barely hear.

He shook his head and traced his steps to the trailer.

Mary was getting her comb out of her purse as he walked through the door. She jumped, startled, and the bag fell to the floor, spilling its contents at her feet. "Damn. Clumsy me."

Bill knelt to help her pick up her things. "Sorry I startled you, love. Here." He picked up a small slip of paper with a circled phone number on it. "What's this?" he asked, handing it to her.

Mary frowned for a moment then grinned as she recognized the paper. "That was my poor attempt to keep Roxie from doing something foolish."

"What do you mean?"

"It's a number we found in the want-ad column in the paper. The advertisement offered boat charters at reduced rates. Roxie thinks it's Minto's ad, and I was afraid she planned to do something about it on her own, so I snatched the number when she wasn't looking." She laughed. "Futile effort. All she has to do is look the number up again in the newspaper."

Bill knew, suddenly, what he could do to insure that he was the one to earn the promotion.

THE PHONE WAS ANSWERED by a tape that asked for a
name and a number where the caller could be reached.
Bill hung up and sat at his desk, drumming his fingers
and trying to work out a plan. Would Minto check to
see that every caller who left a message was legitimate? And even if he didn't, he might return the call
while Mary was at the trailer. She was there almost as
much as Bill. That meant one of two things; either he
needed to keep Mary away from the trailer or he
needed to find an accomplice who had a safe phone
and who could keep a secret.

As if sent by celestial messenger, Mark Carter
knocked at Bill's door and opened it without waiting
for an invitation.

"You busy, Tabe?"

"Mark! Come in. Hell, no, I'm never too busy to see
you. What's up?"

Mark looked a little taken aback by Bill's enthusiasm. They were friends, but Bill didn't usually express
this much excitement over Mark's comings and goings.

"Did one of us just win the Publishers Clearing-
house Sweepstakes?"

Bill hid his embarrassment behind a sheepish laugh.
"Not that I know of, but I have something interesting
to propose to you."

Mark was as enthusiastic about Bill's plan as Bill
himself.

"And you're sure if Minto checks your number, he
won't be able to find out where you work?" Bill asked.

"Positive," Mark said, "the phone isn't even in my
name. It's in my roommate's name and he's overseas
in Malta, doing research for his thesis—won't be back
until September."

"Perfect." Bill rubbed his hands together. It was working out even better than he'd planned. "Okay. Now here's the deal: you set up your answering machine to give the message that you're him—your roommate—and what time you can be reached at your number. Maybe we'll get lucky and Minto will leave a number for you to call that isn't on tape."

"And then when he does, we nail him, right?"

"Not quite so quickly," Bill said. "First, you're going to set up a phony charter with him and we'll go from there."

They discussed the plan in great detail and when Mark left, Bill could feel his adrenaline flowing at the prospect of catching Minto in the act. He had to be careful, though. If Mary found out she'd hit the ceiling, and furthermore, she'd probably report the whole thing to Roxie, who in turn might tell Jake. It wouldn't do Bill any good if the whole company got in on the act.

CHAPTER THIRTEEN

MINTO REPLACED THE PHONE and sat staring, without really focusing, at the couple standing on deck near the railing.

What's wrong with this picture? He blinked and realized that the picture of the couple disturbed him as much as the phone call he'd just made. What the hell did Caryl and that wimp, Mayer, have to talk about all the time? Lately, they had their pointed little heads together every time he turned around.

"Mayer—get your butt in here," he yelled through the open cabin door. He saw their frightened response to his sharp tone and smiled inwardly. "Woman, don't you have work to do today?"

The woman followed Mayer to the cabin door but didn't venture over the threshold. "I was just taking a little break before I start making lunch, Harry."

"Take it somewhere else and make it a short one," he ordered. George Mayer had come into the cabin and was waiting a few feet away to receive Minto's orders. Minto couldn't fault the man, yet every now and then he got this uneasy feeling about the guy.

Minto rubbed his hand across his mouth and studied Mayer, not a bit concerned about keeping him waiting. He'd proven he was okay, hadn't he? When the deal went down on that last delivery, Minto had tested Mayer by having him make the exchange, and everything had gone according to plan. Still, Minto had had a feeling, lately, that the guy was up to some monkey business of his own.

"You wanted me, Harry?" Mayer asked. "Something you want me to do?"

"I want you to stand there and wait for me to tell you what I want until I'm ready to tell you," Minto snarled. "I don't like people pushing me."

"Sorry," the other man muttered.

Minto wondered if the word had been spoken in a sarcastic tone or if that was just his imagination. Naw...the guy was a wimp, he wouldn't dare use sarcasm on Harry.

"I just called some guy who left a message on the machine, and something doesn't smell right to me about it. I want you to check it out."

"How do I do that, Harry?" George asked.

"How do I do that, Harry?" Minto mimicked in his nastiest tone. "I tell you what, idiot, you figure a way to do it."

He laughed out loud, loving the sound of his implied threat and loving the look of fear on the wimp's face. It was fear, wasn't it? Minto squinted at Mayer. *It better be.*

He handed Mayer a slip of paper with a name and number on it. "I got a taped message when I called this guy. It said to call back after ten at night. Don't make sense to me. Why didn't he leave a number where he can be reached during regular hours?"

George shrugged. Minto was right, it did sound fishy.

"I gotta hand it to you, Harry," George said, filling his voice and his facial expression with as much reverence as he could muster without vomiting, "it'd take a genius to outsmart you." He looked at the paper and shook his head. "This guy must be a real jerk, or else..." George gave Minto an ingenuous look. "Maybe the guy is a cop?"

Minto grabbed the paper and stared at it. He hadn't thought of that. He'd just figured the caller for one of those Coast Guard snoops or some nerd from one of the charter boat companies along the river. Okay. This put a new slant on things.

"Call the guy," he told Mayer, handing the paper back. "Make it after ten like the tape says, and set up a meet. We'll check him out ourselves."

ROXIE SMILED at Bill Tabor and gestured toward the chair next to her desk. "Sit down, Bill, I'll get us some coffee."

"Is Jake coming in for this meeting?" Bill called after her as he took the designated seat.

"No. This is something you and I have to work out. It really doesn't involve anyone else." She came back carrying two mugs and set one in front of Bill.

"I even had Mary run an errand so we could discuss this in private."

"Sounds serious." Bill glanced at Mary's darkened office.

"Not really." Roxie went around the desk. "But I'll get right to the point." She took a careful sip from her cup and set it down. "Here's the deal," she began, as she seated herself, "at the present moment, I'm the only one doing payroll, the only one authorized to sign checks out of the accounts from this office, since Joe is away."

Bill nodded. He knew that.

"The point is, what if I get sick, or need to be away for some reason and a check has to be made out?"

"That could be a problem. Over at the marina, the guys know they can come and get a check from you if I'm not there to write one from that account."

Bill studied the bank forms for a moment before looking at Roxie. "Isn't Mary the logical one for this?"

Roxie shook her head. "I think it should be either you or Jake, but Jake is out on the river a good part of the time, and you are pretty much landlocked, as I am." She smiled at him and was gratified when he returned the gesture of friendship. Bill wasn't always easy to read, and recently she'd felt the rivalry established by the competition affected their relationship. She suspected that Bill was as ambitious as she.

Bill frowned thoughtfully, nodded, then picked up the pen and one of the forms.

There. It was done. Roxie used her coffee mug to screen any fleeting expression of unhappiness that might cross her face. Sharing this little patch of power was one of the hardest things she'd ever made herself do, but more and more she was learning that the good of the company had to come before the needs of her ego. No one was indispensable or immune from fate's little surprises, and that included her.

The amazing thing was that it was Jake who had taught her this; Jake, who seemed the least business-wise person she'd ever known. Maybe he'd inherited the bent for it from his father, even though he had no interest in running a business himself.

Bill signed his name in the designated places and returned the forms to Roxie.

"Thanks." She smiled again, this time a little more easily. "I'll return these to the bank this afternoon and then you'll be an official signer."

Bill gestured to the large black checkbook that sat on top of a file basket. "Anything I need to know about the account now?"

"On Wednesday, I'm going to teach Mary to do payroll. If you want you can sit in while I check her work sheets before signing the payroll, so if you ever have to sign it, you'll know what to look for. Aside from that, my procedure for making entries and writing checks is the same as yours since Martha set up both systems. And there's a list of account numbers taped into the front of the checkbook."

Bill nodded and stood up. "While we're on the subject of checks, I need you to transfer another chunk of dough into the Marina Expansion Fund."

Roxie almost said recklessly, "You may as well do that yourself now," then thought better of it. After all, there was no sense in giving the farm away before it became necessary. And she'd already taken a big step toward making herself less indispensable. Jake would be pleased when he learned of it.

So, instead, she said, "How much?"

He named a figure and Roxie raised an eyebrow at him. "Are you putting a private bath in each slip over there?"

Bill laughed and scratched his head. "I know what you mean. Seems like everything has doubled in cost since we did the last expansion. Is that possible, or am I remembering wrong?"

Roxie turned to the file cabinets behind her and pointed to the bottom drawer with her foot. "We've got all the paid invoices in there, going back seven years. Help yourself if you want to compare costs."

She stood up. "In fact, I'll get out of your way. I've got to run off the new flier ads for the dinner cruises." She made a notation on her calendar pad. "It's too late today, but I'll call in the transfer tomorrow." She left for the back room.

Bill was kneeling in front of the cabinet, going through a folder, when Mary returned from her errand.

Mary brought her usual scent of lily of the valley into the office, along with a waft of damp heat from outdoors.

Bill stood up, put his finger across his lips and gestured with his head toward the back. They could hear the mimeograph machine start up.

Mary laughed and slammed the door. "She can't hear us over that clunker," she said, striding toward her lover, her arms outstretched. "What are you doing here, anyway?"

"Looking up some invoices." He glanced toward the doorway then kissed her. "Mm, you're all warm and sweet and damp," Bill whispered, as his hands stroked up and down her back and came to rest at the delicious curve of her buttocks.

Mary snuggled closer and lifted her face for another kiss. "All over," she said, mischievously. Bill groaned.

Mary laughed and put her hand between their bodies to judge for herself the impact her words had had on him. "Ooh, William, you're such a stud," she teased.

He was pinning her down over Roxie's desk, punishing her with kisses that couldn't quite cover her squeals, when Roxie came into the room.

They leaped apart, Bill almost tripping over the open file drawer behind him.

Roxie stood, mesmerized, staring at her young friend and the middle-aged, graying marina manager, her mouth agape.

"Oh, Rox—I don't know what to say—I—Bill?" Mary put her hands to her mouth and fought back tears of fright. Would she be fired for behaving this way on the job? Would Bill somehow blame her and be furious that Roxie had found out about them?

"I forgot..." Roxie looked at the stencil in her hands, trying to recall why she'd come into the office. "I forgot the other stencil," she said, clearing her throat. She felt herself pale and then blush. Both Mary and Bill looked stricken. How awkward. How very, very embarrassing. "I...I'll just..." She gestured behind her. "I'll just go back."

She fled, not waiting to hear explanations or apologies, her mind roaring with the unbelievable words that played over and over in her head. *Mary and Bill Tabor? Bill and Mary? Mary and Bill?*

She sank onto the old wooden kitchen chair they kept in the back room and stared, unseeing, at the top of the mimeo machine racketing back and froth. *So this is Mary's secret lover. Bill Tabor.*

But he must be all of forty-five years old—maybe older—and Mary, Roxie knew for a fact, was only twenty-four. The man was old enough to be her father, and looked it. What did Mary see in him? Roxie had always found him a little taciturn, difficult to reach, not a particularly outgoing, friendly person—at least not with her.

Though come to think of it, he'd always seemed to take pleasure in teasing Mary Sanger, about her language, her freckles, her clothing. But of course, now Roxie could see that his ability to banter with Mary was born of intimacy. An intimacy they'd kept secret for months.

Why? Roxie stood up and began to pace the small room. Why would Bill make such a fuss about Mary letting people know about them? Did he have a wife, a family hidden away somewhere? Roxie had heard of such things happening. Oh, but Martha had told her once that they'd known Bill since they bought this property twenty years ago. Bill would have been in his twenties then and he'd already been with the Kenners for ten years. No, he couldn't have a wife without people around here knowing about it. And people on the river talked. It would be common knowledge.

Besides, Joe Harley was an old-fashioned man; if Bill had had that kind of skeleton in his closet, Joe wouldn't have kept him on when he bought out the Kenner estate. Joe would hire ex-cons in a minute if they showed signs of being rehabilitated, but he wouldn't have anything to do with what he would call a cad or a heel. And a man who left his wife would, in Joe's book, qualify as both.

It dawned on her then, what Bill had to hide. It was the affair with Mary itself. He was afraid, and with good reason, that Joe would disapprove of his involvement with a woman so much younger.

She stood up. That was their problem. Hers was to make sure that the office ran smoothly and that meant she couldn't let something like this undermine her authority. She couldn't hide in the back room for the rest of the day, avoiding Mary just because she was embarrassed by something she'd accidentally discovered. If they didn't want anyone to know, they shouldn't have brought it into the office in the first place.

Bill was just going out the door when Roxie marched to her office. Mary turned to Roxie.

"Bill wanted to stay and explain—apologize—but I thought it would be better if we spoke alone."

Roxie nodded and went behind her desk to sit down. "Go ahead."

"We shouldn't have been carrying on like that here in the office, and for that, we're both sorry."

She paused, but Roxie, sitting with her hands folded under her chin, kept quiet.

"Okay, but as for the rest, the fact that Bill and I are lovers is nobody's business but our own."

Mary's chin was thrust forward in that familiar, belligerent way. Roxie knew Mary well enough to know she'd go to the mat before she'd compromise, once she'd taken this stance.

Nevertheless, Roxie had some views on the subject, and she was going to voice them.

"Listen, Mary, it was a little awkward to discover you in an embrace with a man at my desk, but certainly not something criminal. Half the romances in this country would never occur if it weren't for people meeting on their jobs."

She smiled faintly at Mary. "It might be wiser to be more circumspect in the future—if this had happened in your office, with the door closed, I wouldn't have had to observe it."

She cleared her throat and leaned forward. "Mary, why Bill?"

Mary's complexion did that white-to-red-to-white trick and she frowned at Roxie. "What does *that* mean? Why not Bill? He's the most wonderful man I've ever known.''

"Well, among other things, the man's old enough to be your father."

"Since when is that so shocking? What's so uncommon about a man having a woman much younger than himself? And just what do you mean by 'among other things'? What other things?''

Mary was almost shouting at Roxie. Roxie took a deep breath and forced some restraint into her manner. Her voice followed suit and she asked in a more even tone, "What could you possibly see in Bill, Mary? He's one of the most middle-aged men I've ever known, he's absolutely stereotypic." She shuddered. The very idea of Bill, who was gray and dull as dishwater, and Mary, who was vivacious and feisty and pretty...

"No, Roxie, you're wrong," Mary said, almost reading Roxie's mind. Her eyes brightened and her face flushed with eagerness. "He's not at all the way you see him. He's...he's the most charming, funny, sexy man I've ever known."

Bill? Sexy?

Roxie slumped in her chair. "You've been brainwashed. Or hypnotized. It's not possible that you're this smitten over that man without undo influence."

Mary laughed. "You sound as old-fashioned as Martha sometimes."

"And we both know how Martha—not to mention Joe—would respond to this," Roxie said, pointedly.

The smile on Mary's face faded. "Oh, Roxie, please, you won't say anything to Joe, will you?"

"That's another thing I don't understand, Mary. If there's nothing wrong with your relationship, why is

Bill making such a case of not letting anyone know? That indicates to me that even Bill thinks it's wrong.''

"No. Bill just wanted to be the one to tell Joe himself. They're very old friends and Bill felt this was something he wanted to explain face-to-face, when Joe gets back.''

Yes, Joe wouldn't take kindly to hearing this secondhand, and Roxie doubted he was going to approve of it in any case.

She rubbed her eyes and looked over at Mary whose whole body seemed to strain with apprehension. "It's not my place to tell Joe," she said, and Mary's body visibly collapsed with relief.

"Thanks, Roxie, I'll be grateful to you till my dying day.''

"Or twelve thousand miles, whichever comes first," Roxie quipped wryly.

Mary giggled. It made her seem even younger and more vulnerable. And made Bill seem even older and more lecherous, but she decided to keep that thought to herself. Still, Mary had been like a kid sister to her over the years, and Roxie really cared about what happened to her.

"Just to satisfy my curiosity, would you mind telling me how this unlikely affair got started? I didn't think you saw Bill more than once a month, and then only if he dropped his journals off in person instead of sending them with one of his crew." It dawned on her then that all this season Bill had been bringing them over himself. Now she knew why.

Mary's face softened, her eyes almost glazing over as she remembered. "I ran into him at Dayton's this winter—in the kitchen department.''

Roxie couldn't help but imagine the scene as Mary described it, so vivid a picture did her friend draw. Despite her reservations, she was caught up in the romantic story.

"At first, it was just a couple of times a week, to prepare a new recipe together or for Bill to teach me how to make one of his specialties. Roxie, you should see his trailer—it's just one big kitchen with a bedroom and bath at the back. And he did the renovating all by himself," she enthused proudly.

Roxie nodded and smiled. "I've never been over there, but I've heard that he did a great job making the trailer work for him and I've tasted some of the treats he's brought to the office over the years so I know that he's a great cook."

"Oh, he's beyond cook, Roxie, he's truly a fine chef."

Mary looked so earnest, Roxie couldn't help but laugh.

"You'd think he'd be doing that for a living instead of running a marina," Roxie said, thoughtfully.

"Yeah. But see, in the winter, when the marina is closed, he has all his free time to study cookbooks and experiment with new recipes. It might not be as much fun for him if he did it for a living."

"True. I've heard people say that turning hobbies into careers takes the joy out of them. So, you started going over for cooking lessons. Then what?"

"Then, right in the middle of an Afghan meal we were preparing together, I looked over at him and knew I'd fallen in love." Mary sighed deeply. "His hair was falling over one eye and he kept using his arm to push it back because he was using his hands to peel lemons. All of a sudden, I wanted to get up and push that hair back myself.'' This she added almost shyly. ''After that, I found myself wanting to touch him every chance I got. So finally, one night while we were dancing...''

''Whoa,'' Roxie interrupted, ''how did we get from cooking lessons to dancing?''

Mary giggled again. ''Oh. I guess I left out a part.''

''I guess you did.''

''Well, see, Bill began to make sort of a big deal out of our dinners. He said that after going to all that trouble to prepare them, we ought to honor the finished product with the proper setting. So we began to set the table up the way it would be done in a nice supper club and then we added things like putting music on the stereo.''

Aha! The old romantic music-on-the-stereo trick— the dirty old man!

''That was my idea,'' Mary added, ''and then one night we were discussing the music that was on and I said I'd never really learned to slow dance, that my generation was more into new wave, punk and rock. And Bill said there was nothing romantic about the way kids dance today and I said show me what's so wonderful about slow dancing. And he did and it was.''

She had that dreamy look again. ''And then I told him I was in love with him and that I wasn't asking for anything in return but I needed to say what I felt. And Roxie, he began to cry.''

''Cry?'' It was difficult to draw up the image of rugged Bill Tabor doing anything as soft and sensitive as crying.

''Uh-huh.'' Mary nodded, her eyes misting up from the memory. ''He said he'd begun to love me from our first cooking lesson, but that he'd been terrified to let me know for fear it would scare me away.''

Mary took a deep, shuddering breath, and Roxie felt tears well up. She couldn't recall ever hearing a more charming love story, and if Mary hadn't exaggerated the details, it certainly changed Roxie's idea of what Bill was really like.

"I'm not going to tell you what happened after that, Rox, it's too personal, but I will tell you this, Bill is as strong and healthy and virile as any younger man I've known, and a whole lot more gentle and caring and damned sexy!"

Roxie sighed and wiped a hint of dampness from under her eyes with her fingers. "Okay," she said, clearing her throat, "you win. I'm convinced, it's the modern version of Romeo and Juliet."

She stood. "But let's not have any more hanky-panky in the office, where anyone can walk in and see you. And now, I've got to get back to work if we're going to have any customers for our first dinner cruise next Wednesday."

Today she was running off fliers, and a week from tomorrow their first cruise would be a sell-out, she hoped.

This was going to earn her plenty of points with Joe, she thought, as the old machine clunked out the pages. It was just this sort of promotion she was good at and it proved she was executive material even if thinking so made her less than modest. "Well, if you've got it flaunt it," she sang out, her words lost in the noise of the machine.

And that would put her one jump ahead of the others. She grinned. *All's fair in love and war, Jake, old buddy, and I want this promotion almost as much as I want you.* She lifted the stack of papers off the ledge and lined them up evenly.

She heard the phone ring, heard Mary's soft voice answer it.

Something in Mary's voice alerted Roxie. "I...I think you should talk to... I'm sorry, I think you want to speak with—"

And then Roxie heard a chair scrape the floor and fall, and Mary came running down the hall.

"Roxie, come quick! You'll never believe who's on the phone." Roxie's heart sank as she followed Mary and reached for the phone. Had something terrible happened to someone...to Captain Joe?

"Yes. This is Roxanne Hilton. May I help you?" Her response was automatic but her voice squeaked with trepidation.

"Ms. Hilton, I'm sorry, I seem to have flustered your co-worker. This is Susan Handel, Governor John Handel's wife." The caller paused, apparently used to a delayed reaction when she announced herself over the phone.

"Yes... Oh, my, yes, Mrs. Handel. Hello."

Mrs. Handel's gentle laugh made Roxie's color rise. She grinned at Mary and nodded her head. Mary's eyes widened with excitement.

"Ms. Hilton, someone in your office sent a brochure to the governor's office, and the governor's secretary brought it to my attention. It indicates you've held weddings aboard your boats?"

Roxie wrapped the cord around her hand twice and clung to it for dear life. Was this what she thought it was?

"Yes. Generally we do quite a few weddings, especially in June."

"Well, the reason I've called you is that our daughter is getting married and we've agreed that it might be fun to have the affair aboard the *Celebration*."

"I...we'd be honored. If you'll give me the date you had in mind, I'll check our schedule and..."

"Well, first, I thought we ought to make sure that such a thing is feasible," Mrs. Handel said, gently leading Roxie back to reality. "We realize this is awfully short notice for putting together a wedding, but my daughter's fiancé has just been posted to an embassy in Europe and they're determined to get married before he's due there so she can go with him."

Roxie drew a deep, quivering breath and held her hand up, fingers crossed, to Mary. "No problem, Mrs. Handel, we've been known to put together a wedding with only two weeks notice and done a top-notch job of it, if I may boast a little."

"Yes, well, I'm sure that's true—we've always heard good reports about your operation, though I must admit I have never personally been aboard either of your vessels."

Roxie murmured something politic and said, "I'm sure you'd find that we live up to our reputation, and I still have quite a few good dates open for the season."

"Wonderful. But before we decide anything for sure, we'd have to meet with you, see the facilities firsthand and assure ourselves that this is the best way to go."

Of course, first things first. One didn't just take an order over the phone from the governor's wife, the way one did for the average customer.

They arranged to meet the next day. When she said goodbye, Roxie's hand was shaking so badly she could hardly put the handset in the cradle.

"I don't believe it, I don't believe it," Mary intoned, over and over.

"It's true! We have a chance at the biggest social event of the year, right on the *Celebration*!" Roxie jumped up and began to pace the floor. "Do you realize what this means in terms of advertising alone?" She spun around, her arms flung out from her sides. "We could coast, for the rest of this year and maybe next, on the publicity."

"Just think, the governor's wife and daughter, sitting there, drinking coffee out of our cups," Mary said. "Oh, Rox, maybe we'd better have herbal tea available, too, you know a lot of people don't take caffeine anymore."

"And we must dress very professionally," Roxie said, looking pointedly at Mary's jeans and cotton sweater.

Mary nodded, her eyes gleaming. "Should I pick up some doughnuts or Danish or something on the way in to work?"

Roxie returned to her desk and picked up a pad and pencil. "I don't think so," she said, "I'm sure the staff at the mansion serves breakfast. But let's try to be ready with some ideas for the wedding to convince them we're the *only* way to go."

Selling the Handels became Roxie's obsession. There was no use going to lunch. She knew she wouldn't be able to force anything into a stomach that fluttered with nervous anticipation. She could barely concentrate on the paperwork for the charters she had already booked and had to make herself concentrate when she talked to anyone on the phone.

CHAPTER FOURTEEN

SLEEP THAT NIGHT was out of the question as she waited for Jake to show up after his run, though normally she'd have taken a nap in anticipation of a late night. She tossed and turned and kept reminding herself that she didn't want to look haggard at her meeting with the Handels.

But each time she almost succeeded in calming herself, another question would pop into her mind to stir her up again. Would the governor come to the meeting? And if so, would he have an entourage of important people with him? Secret agents? No. That was the president. The governor, she recalled, had only a state trooper for protection.

Hot milk hadn't worked, either, though at first it seemed to relax her a little. Then she considered the fact that the Handels would probably be checking out the other stern-wheeler companies, and what if they decided to go with the one in Stillwater on the St. Croix, which was a far more scenic river than this part of the Mississippi? *Too far from the governor's residence,* she told herself, but she worried about it all the same.

When she heard Jake at the door, using the extra key she'd given him, she rushed out to meet him.

"You'll never believe what happened today!" she shouted as she threw herself into his arms.

"Whoa, easy, Rox, you almost knocked me over," Jake said, laughing and easing her away. He caught his cap as it fell from his head and tossed it onto the hall table.

"Jake! The governor's wife called!"

Jake looked thoughtful. "You mean Susan Handel?"

Roxie stared at Jake. "You know her?"

"Yeah, of course. Man, I'm tired." Jake went into the living room and fell heavily onto the couch. "So, what did Susan want?"

Roxie stood in the doorway, deflated by Jake's easy manner. But of course he would know the Handels. His family was part of that special elite the top politicians courted for social and financial support.

"Well, it won't be any big deal to you," she grumbled, going over to the couch and pulling his feet off the cushion. She plumped down at the far end and gave him a look of scorn. "She just wanted to meet with me to discuss the possibility of having her daughter's wedding aboard the *Celebration*."

Jake sat forward and wrapped his arms around Roxie, pulling her against his chest. "So little Carla's getting married, huh? Well, I know you'll do a good job for them."

She turned and looked into his face. He did look tired. But that was no excuse for greeting her news in such a blasé manner. "Doesn't anything ever bowl you over?"

He nuzzled her neck and chuckled when she shivered. "You bowl me over, kid. In fact, you roll me over." He followed his words with a twist of his body that forced Roxie onto her back with him on top of her, his elbows propped on either side of her, his hands encompassing her face. He fit his lower body into the saddle of her legs and wriggled to show her his readiness.

"You want to talk, or what?"

She had to laugh, her miff forgotten. "What."

He slipped his hand under her gown. "What've you got under this?"

"Nothing," she gasped, lifting her body to facilitate his hand.

"I wouldn't call that nothing," he murmured, finding the spot he was searching for, "I'd call that something." He grinned when she moaned and called out his name, and then his expression grew serious and he covered her mouth with his own in a deep, sensual kiss.

Roxie's last rational thought was that this was just what she needed to take her mind off the meeting with the Handels the next morning.

CARLA HANDEL was a younger version of her mother, tall and slender with patrician features. Both women had Titian red hair and blue eyes, though Susan Handel's hair was streaked with gray and Carla's eyes were brighter and rounder.

Roxie showed them over the *Celebration* and the grounds of Harley's Landing including the marina, and Mary shyly served them coffee for which they both claimed an addiction.

They listened attentively whenever Roxie ventured to offer a suggestion.

One problem was that the lower cabin was too small to allow all the guests to watch the ceremony. It was Roxie who suggested they run a canopy from the top of the stairs to the boat landing and have the bridal procession start there. The guests could watch from the outer deck rails or from the cabin windows.

"Why not have the procession end at the gangplank and have the ceremony right there?" Roxie suggested. "When the bridal couple enter the boat, with the gangplank going up behind them, they will begin the reception cruise as Mr. and Mrs. Roger Johansson."

"What about keeping curiosity seekers and the press from crashing?" Carla Handel asked. "I don't want my wedding turned into a three-ring circus."

Roxie had never met anyone who had reason to be paranoid about crowds or about newspaper people hounding them. It had never occurred to her that sometimes fame could create anxiety and even unhappiness. She could tell from Carla Handel's tone that such had been the case in the past.

"I always thought that the press was invited to these things," Roxie admitted, not ashamed to show her ignorance in political matters.

"My wedding isn't an affair of state," Carla said, smiling at Roxie. "I'm okay with letting the society editor of the newspapers have the guest list and the details of the cruise, but other than that, this is to be a strictly personal event."

"I have another suggestion then. There is only one road into Harley's Landing. We can post a guard there to check guests as they come through and make sure they have invitations. You'll have to include something like tickets in your invitations or have the invitations state that guests must bring them to the wedding."

"That's a good idea," Susan Handel responded. "Now what about food? May we provide our own caterers?"

This was always the sticky part. "I'm sorry, Mrs. Handel," Roxie said gently, "but part of our revenue is based on our food sales. We use two very special catering companies, however," she added hastily. "We can provide you with testimonials from previous charter customers and I'm sure both companies would be willing to provide samples if you insist."

The Handel women exchanged a glance. "That won't be necessary," Carla said, turning to Roxie with a smile, "I've been on your boats a few times, I know you people do a good job."

Roxie was surprised she hadn't been aware that someone as well-known as the governor's daughter had been aboard. "I didn't realize that. When?"

"My high-school prom, for one thing," Carla said, laughing.

"Oh, that would have been before I came to work here five years ago." It was public knowledge that Carla Handel was in her late twenties and had just graduated from law school.

"Right. And before Daddy became governor. But I work for East Publishing," Carla said, "and they have had parties aboard the *Celebration*."

Roxie breathed a sigh of relief. Carla Handel had no complaints about her previous trips aboard the boat, so that was a good sign.

"Now, although we do work with an agent, and have access to most of the good musicians in town, you are allowed to hire your own band, if you prefer."

"Do you have a preference, dear?" Mrs. Handel asked her daughter.

Carla grinned at Roxie. "Could you get that Dixieland group that played last summer for my company's charter?"

Roxie nodded. "Of course—if they're still based here in the Twin Cities." She hoped her excitement didn't show. If the Handels decided to contract with Harley Marine, it would prove not only prestigious but, as it was turning out, very lucrative.

Apparently her memories of successful parties on the boat helped to persuade Carla Handel, and by the end of the week, Mrs. Handel called back to close the deal and asked Roxie to send the contracts out.

They chose July fourth as the date of the wedding cruise so that the wedding reception could end with a midriver view of the annual firework display at Harriet Island, just downriver from Harley's Landing. That also gave them four weeks to get the invitations out, which Mrs. Handel felt was cutting it close but Carla insisted was adequate.

Concern over the *Shark*'s operation was immediately pushed out of everyone's minds as the wedding of the governor's daughter became top priority.

Overnight the whole company was caught up in the preparations for the coming event. The media helped emphasize what a coup it was for Harley Marine and the phones were kept busy with reporters wanting to keep abreast of every new detail in the arrangements. Between the wedding and the other charters they'd booked, there was barely time to deal with the new business that evolved as a result of all the publicity.

It was almost a relief whenever they had a cancellation. Roxie and Mary were too busy to question the cause.

Bill Tabor put his crew to work, cleaning up the grounds around the marina and repainting the exterior of the buildings, and Jake had his crews touching up the paint on both boats.

Roxie had repeated meetings with the linen company, the two catering companies that Harley Marine used, and the agent who provided musicians when a charter customer wanted live music. She was always meticulous in her arrangements for any charter, but this one demanded extra care.

It was such a major event for Harley Marine that Roxie hoped it would lure Joe Harley back, at least for the wedding. She suggested it when he made one of his check-in calls the week after she'd booked the wedding charter.

His voice was filled with satisfaction when he told her, "You've outdone yourself, my girl. Martha, bless her heart, never would have thought to solicit the business of the governor's office." He laughed for the first time in all the weeks he'd been calling her from across the country; it held a note of proud triumph. "I was right about you—we both were. You're damned good at that job."

Too good, Joe, she wanted to say. *I'm more qualified for the job as general manager.*

"I'm glad you're so pleased, Joe," she said instead, "and won't you consider coming back to enjoy some of the prestige of owning the company that's putting on the affair?"

"Prestige doesn't cut it for me anymore, Roxie," Joe said. "I'm getting more and more pleasure out of the simple life. Why, right here in Montana, I feel closer to Martha than I have since she died, even though we were never here together. It feels like the kind of place she'd have loved. She always wanted to live near the mountains..."

His voice broke and Roxie had to take a deep breath before she could speak.

"Okay, Joe, I understand. We'll save all the newspaper stories of the event for you and I'll write and tell you all about it when I send you the monthly statement."

"Speaking of that, Roxie, I couldn't help but notice that the statement for June shows a reduction in reservations over the projected schedule from the May statement. Is there something wrong?"

Should she tell him about Minto? But then what? He'd only worry, maybe come back for the wrong reasons. She knew he needed this time away and that there wasn't anything he could do to change things. No, it was better to leave him in the dark about Minto's operation. "Nothing permanent, Joe. We...um...just had a change in dates for some of the June reservations. I guess a lot of people don't trust the weather here that early in the season. Anyway, I'm sure we'll fill those spots as we go along."

"I see. Funny, I've been listening to weather reports and it sounds like you're full into summer there."

"Well, yes, we are, in terms of temperature. But it's early to be this hot here and it could change any minute, as you well know."

He laughed, sounding relieved. "Yeah. I recall a time or two—before we put the furnace on the *Celeb*—that we canceled a charter in July because we had a drastic drop in temperature."

He seemed content to drop the subject of the lost reservations and they ended their chat on an optimistic note. "I have an idea for increased revenue, but I don't want to tell you about it yet."

"So, you're getting along all right with Jake?"

Curious that he'd think otherwise. "Why wouldn't we get along?"

"No reason. No reason at all. I couldn't be more pleased. Well, give him—and everyone—my best regards. And if you get a chance, tell the governor I'm delighted that he's partaking of my hospitality, even in my absence."

Roxie laughed and hung up, feeling incredibly pleased with herself. It was a feather in her cap to have booked the wedding of the year—maybe of the decade—and since Jake had approved her plan for weekly dinner cruises and they were soon to be underway, she'd have a firm lead over the others for the promotion.

If the Shark *doesn't eat up too much of our regular business.* She pushed that thought away. There wasn't time to deal with it now. And she felt too optimistic to let a cloud of anxiety darken her mood.

Joe had to see that she was the best person for the job, and if he didn't yet, he soon would. True, Bill Tabor had a construction crew working on the addition of fifty slips, and he'd added a small deli concession to the marina store so that people working on their boats could pick up a light lunch without leaving the area, but both those things only stretched Tabor's present operation. It would take more than a minor increase in revenue to impress Joe Harley. No, what was called for was a whole new face to the business, getting in step with the changing times, with the changing face of the waterfront.

It was going to speed things along in terms of the waterfront renovation project when the governor saw, firsthand, the beauty and versatility the river offered.

Roxie had a newspaper clipping of an artist's sketch of the projected plans for the riverfront proposal on the wall behind her desk. It was the proposal that had been presented to the commission studying riverfront development. She looked at it frequently, to remind herself of how the stern-wheelers were going to become a feature attraction of the river when that whole west bank promenade was in place. People strolling, window-shopping, picnicking in the riverfront park, going in and out of restaurants and shops, would gaze at the river and the first thing they'd see would be the boats steaming up and down, their bright red paddles churning white wakes at the sterns.

She was taking a moment out of her busy morning to study it, a dreamy smile on her face, when Jake came into her office through the back hall.

"Fancy meeting you here," he said, picking up a straight-back chair and turning it so that he straddled it with the back under his arms.

"Not as fancy as you think," Roxie said, as she turned from the picture. She tried not to notice how that peculiarly masculine way of sitting invited the female eye in the most personal way. After the incident with Mary and Bill, she was determined to keep her behavior perfectly professional while in the office. She picked up her notes for the Handel reception. "I'm usually here from the minute I arrive until the minute I leave," she quipped.

He chuckled. "Well, then, you definitely deserve a break. How about lunch—my treat."

She had to look at him then. She made a big deal out of looking at her desk calendar and riffling the pages. "I guess I could fit you in if we make it a short lunch."

Jake rocked back on his chair. "We could skip lunch altogether. Maybe get right to the dessert."

Roxie tried to hide her smile. "Desserts are fattening."

"Not the one I have in mind."

It was tempting, but she really couldn't afford the time right now. "Sorry, pal. You'll have to give me a rain check. I can't possibly get away for so long today."

The front legs of Jake's chair hit the floor with a bang. "Do you realize how long it's been since we last spent any time together?"

"Six days." She sighed and raked her hand through her hair. "Listen, Jake, I don't like this any better than you do, but we're fully into the season now, and with the Handel wedding coming up, and those dinner cruises, not to mention our regular schedule, we have to—"

"You know what the solution is, don't you," Jake interrupted.

"I don't think it would look right to move a bed into the back room, sweetie," Roxie said with an arch look.

"I'm serious, Roxanne."

He looked serious, and Roxie's heart sank as she realized where he was headed even before he said the words. She almost gasped with relief when the phone rang. She hoped, as she automatically answered the caller's questions, that Jake would drop the subject.

She saw him glance at his watch, checking it against the wall clock, and she thought he might leave before she finished her call. But he began pacing the floor, obviously determined to wait her out.

"If we lived together, this wouldn't be a problem."

He blurted the words the minute she hung up the phone, giving her no chance to find another diversion.

Roxie moaned and put her head in her hands. "Why do you have to bring this up now? You know, better than anyone, how hectic this job is right now."

"That's exactly why we need to simplify our personal lives as much as possible."

She lifted her head and glared at him. He was grinning, pleased with himself for making what he thought was a pertinent point.

"You can't be serious. There's nothing simple about two people moving in together, Gilbert. First of all, there's the question of where we'd live."

Jake didn't hesitate. It never occurred to him that they'd live anywhere else. "Aboard the *Tinker Toy*, of course."

Roxie stared at him, her mouth slightly open. "No 'of course' about it, Jake. Why would I move out of my beautiful apartment into the cramped quarters of a houseboat?"

"Because you love me, because I love you, because we need to be together, because living on the river is the most romantic life two people can share."

Roxie got up abruptly and went to stand in front of the windows. The heat of the day gave a hazy cast to the river's surface, as though it was simmering beneath the hot sun. "Jake, there's no way I can think about living with you right now, and certainly not aboard your boat."

She heard him get up and she steeled herself against his touch. When it came, his hand sliding under her hair to caress her neck, she fought back a telltale shiver.

"You look wonderful in this dress, honey," Jake whispered at her ear as his hand moved down to her waist, easing under the top of the two-piece cotton knit dress she was wearing. "Pink is a wonderful color on you."

She pressed her forehead against the cool windowpane and sighed heavily. He wasn't changing the subject, he was merely softening her up so he could charm her into doing what he wanted. She was beginning to recognize his manipulations. She made herself grow rigid and turned to face him, brushing his hand away as she did so.

"This isn't going to work, Jake," she said softly. "I'm not ready to make this kind of move. This isn't even a good time to be thinking about it."

The uncertainty in his eyes was fleeting, quickly replaced by a look of beguiling tenderness. His mouth was only a kiss away and Roxie felt the tremors of desire softening all her bones.

"People who love each other need to be together, Roxie. I thought that was a given."

"I want to be with you, Jake, you know that. But I'm not ready to commit to a full time, live-in relationship. Oh, Jake! Why do you have to complicate things?"

"I don't think there's anything complicated about wanting to spend more time with the woman I love." He shoved his hands in his pockets and grimaced. "I thought you felt the same way, but maybe with you this is purely physical."

Roxie stared at Jake then burst into peals of laughter.

Jake glowered at her and demanded, "What's so damned funny?"

"You are." She sniffled, wiped her eyes with a tissue and gave forth one more giggle. "You're such a baby at times, Jake." She blew her nose and grinned at him as she tossed the tissue into the wastebasket. "You can come down off wall now, Gilbert. If I were only interested in a physical relationship, moving in with you would be a cinch; in fact, in that case, it would suit my purpose perfectly."

He decided to forgive her for laughing at him. "So, if you don't want to move in with me, how about marrying me?"

Roxie's anger was instantaneous. "Not funny, Jake."

She picked up her notebook and tried to ignore him.

He leaned toward her, his hands on the edge of her desk. "I think I was serious, Roxie."

She eyed him balefully. "I don't consider a proposal of marriage a thing to be bandied about on a whim, Jake. And I don't appreciate your using it to try to manipulate me." She stood up. "The truth is, Jake, you don't really take anything seriously, not even love. Well, I know about marriage, and I take it plenty seriously."

Jake saw that he had gone too far and that he'd approached the subject of marriage the wrong way.

"I didn't mean to sound glib, Roxie, I just thought—"

"You don't think," she interrupted. "If you had, you'd know the last thing in the world I'd want from you is marriage."

JAKE PACED THE SECOND DECK of the *Princess*, watching the lights reflected on the dark water, playing and replaying in his head the blunder he'd made with Roxie.

Was she right? Was it that he didn't take love seriously? Or was it that something inside him refused to let him show his true feelings to anyone? And if that was the case, how had he got that way?

The lonely throb of a foghorn from downriver accentuated his mood. He went to the rail and gazed up at the lighted windows of the office. Roxie and maybe

Mary, too, were working late again tonight. Should he go up there and apologize?

But he still didn't understand her anger, didn't know why she'd taken his spontaneous proposal of marriage so badly. He breathed deeply. The air was damp and slightly fetid, but he was used to it, and for him it had the sensual attraction of perfume.

Had he jumped the gun, asked her to live with him too soon? Was she still harboring a yen for Montgomery? He thought of the hours they'd spent together. Not just the hours making love. No, she wasn't thinking about another man when she was with him. She loved him. Their friendship had made a perfect foundation for that love, and he didn't believe he could have been misled about her true feelings.

Below deck he heard the sound of the cabin door closing.

"I'm gone, Captain," Sara Winslow called up the stairs, "the bar's closed and I left the cash box on the table for you."

"Thanks, Sara. Good night," Jake called back.

He had traded runs with Mark tonight, not feeling up to the demands of the larger boat with its longer cruise after his argument with Roxie this afternoon. Even the two-hour run had taxed his nerves. On the one hand, he was eager to get back and mend fences with Roxie. And on the other, he felt as if he couldn't face her again until he understood where she was coming from.

He thought about how wonderful love and marriage could be. He'd seen it first in his own family, then in watching the Harleys over the years. It wasn't that he didn't take it seriously, it was that he took it for granted. He'd been truly alarmed in the past when he thought he was incapable of ever really loving someone. Now that he had finally found love, he was just doing what came naturally, accepting the joy, the pleasure, as his rightful due.

What examples did Roxie have? The thought popped into his mind as if from somewhere outside himself. Yeah. First her parents, who'd certainly made a bad bargain of it, then her failed relationship with Clay Montgomery. So how could she trust love, or for that matter, herself or her lover?

She was a serious little thing by nature. He recalled the way her eyes had clung to his, begging him silently not to find her wanting, that first time they'd made love. There'd been an uncertainty, a sort of shyness, about her every time since. Did she expect him to find fault with her, to reject her? The hesitation had only lasted for a few minutes, but it should have been enough for him to realize how insecure she felt.

"You've been an insensitive bastard, Gilbert," he muttered, looking up at the office again. Should he apologize? Or should he act as if nothing had happened and hope they could continue as they were until Roxie had worked through some of her doubts?

The lights went out as he was pondering his next move, and he decided that rather than run after her, he'd let it go for the night. She must be exhausted after such a long day. She didn't need the added stress of a confrontation with him.

He went to the lower deck, picked up the cash box, locked the door to the main cabin and left the boat. As he put his foot onto the dock, his shoe caught on a loose board, almost sending him headlong over the side. He righted himself, swearing under his breath, and continued to the parking lot.

CHAPTER FIFTEEN

ROXIE EDGED HER PLATE UP to make room for her elbows, clasped her hands under her chin and arched an eyebrow at Jake. "That's out of the question, Jake, there's no way I can approve such a major expenditure."

Jake crumpled his paper napkin, tossed it onto his plate and sprawled back in his seat, hands shoved into his pants pockets. "I don't see what choice we have, Roxie. The dock is rotting underneath, and it just won't take any more patch repair. We need a new dock before one of our customers has a serious accident."

"But Jake, ten thousand dollars! How can we spend that kind of money without Joe's approval?"

"When will he be calling again?"

"I have no idea. He calls when the mood strikes."

"What about an address—didn't you send some reports to him recently?"

"Yes, but I sent those to a general delivery postal station in the town he planned to be at next. I don't know where he is now and he hasn't called to give me the post office of the next town in which he'll be spending any time."

Jake ran his hand through his hair and frowned. "It will cost us a lot more than ten grand if anyone gets hurt on that dock and sues us. And didn't Joe say we should make decisions as though we weren't account-able to him?''

"I don't think he meant for us to blow all his prof-its.''

"Think what it will cost if we let it ride and some-one has an accident.''

"Why is Mississippi Barge letting the dock go so cheaply?''

"It was built for a company in Iowa that went bankrupt last week before the dock was ready for de-livery. Now, Mississippi Barge just wants to get rid of it without taking a total loss.''

Roxie pressed her hands into her lap. "So, this is what's meant by being between a rock and a hard place,'' she said, her face grim. "I really don't know what we should do. You're sure it can't wait until Joe calls again?''

"Do you know if that will be anytime soon?''

"No." She sighed and looked out the window be-side their table, not really focusing on the street be-yond. "There hasn't been any pattern to his calls. But since I talked to him only a couple of days ago, I don't expect he'll be getting in touch with me again for awhile.''

Jake leaned forward. "Listen, Roxie, Joe did say that if we had any problems in our individual areas we couldn't solve, we should contact one of the others for a majority decision. This is something that should have been taken care of long ago, but we kept putting it off. And if we wait for Joe, we'll end up paying full price, which amounts to another three thousand dollars. So I've come to you. I could have just ordered the dock from Mississippi Barge and taken the blame—or credit—myself. But I felt, in the absence of an official general manager, this was one of those decisions that should be made by two of us. If you'd rather, I can take it up with Tabor.''

Roxie felt the alarms going off in her head. She didn't want that! First of all, she liked the respect Jake showed by coming to her, and second, she didn't really want Bill involved with this end of the business.

''We have to decide something today, Rox,'' Jake prodded. ''Mississippi Barge told me they have another company that'll take that dock off their hands.''

''I guess I don't want to risk anybody in our gubernatorial wedding party crashing through the dock.'' And even Joe would jump at the chance to save that much money, wouldn't he?

''Thank you. I know I'll sleep better tonight knowing we're going to get rid of that rotting hunk of wood. The captain started talking about replacing it about five repair jobs ago but never got around to actually ordering the new one. You know how he was about things like that.''

Roxie laughed and relaxed in her chair. ''Yeah, I remember. Martha used to have a fit because the captain would procrastinate about certain purchases. She always said the cost of repairs would be the same as the cost of a new one by the time Joe took the plunge and bought a replacement.''

Jake's laughter joined hers. ''Remember how many times he fixed that air-conditioning unit on the *Celeb* before he broke down and bought a new one?''

Roxie grinned. ''Yes—about as many times as you'll fix that old ice machine on the *Princess*.''

''Hey, there's nothing wrong with that machine that a little special treatment can't take care of. It runs like a honey after I've tuned it up.''

His look of indignation turned to a smile as he saw the expression on her face. "Touché."

They were quiet for a moment, studying one another's faces.

Is it the wrong moment to bring up my clumsiness the other day and apologize?

Should I mention his proposition, tell him I'm sorry I'm not ready to live with him but that I do love him, do want us to go on as we are?

"How're the arrangements coming on the Handel wedding?"

"Fine. They've finally settled on a menu and after considerable maneuvering, I managed to get Marge's Menu and Cosmopolitan Catering to work together on this one."

Jake's eyes crinkled at the corners when he smiled. Why hadn't she noticed that before?

"Maybe you're missing your true calling, maybe your talents would best serve us if you'd negotiate peace in the Middle East."

"Don't laugh, two catering companies working on one party are just as much at odds and just as hard-headed."

The waiter came and removed their luncheon plates. "Dessert?" he asked, addressing Jake.

Jake threw the question to Roxie.

"I'll have a strawberry sundae." She smiled absently at the waiter and was surprised when he winked at her. She almost blushed when she saw that Jake had noticed.

"You know that guy?"

"Only since we sat down for lunch."

"Hmm."

She laughed at the look on his face. "You can't be upset by what might be only a little eye tic."

He chose to ignore that. Jealousy was a new emotion, one he wasn't prepared to acknowledge. He changed the subject.

"I need you to take a day off from work."

"When?"

"Tomorrow. I want you to go on a little trip with me tomorrow morning."

A trip. The words conjured up images of bed-and-breakfast inns beside large bodies of water, or facing each other across a white-clothed table in the dining car of a fast-moving train traveling over unfamiliar countryside.

Roxie blinked herself back to reality just as the waiter returned and set the sundae in front of her. "Enjoy," he said.

"Thank you," she said, barely glancing at him. She ate a spoonful of the dessert but hardly registered its taste. She spoke to Jake. "A trip? Where?"

"I want to drive down to Red Wing—to Minnesota Barge—and make arrangements to have the dock shipped up immediately."

"Can't you take care of it by phone?"

"Yes."

They stared at one another, questions darting silently between them, answers hovering in the wings.

She swallowed another mouthful of ice cream. "I really should work tomorrow—we're especially busy right now what with the wedding and all."

She looked at him and frowned, trying to hide her feelings. "Is this strictly business?"

Jake sat back, thinking about her question. He'd been so careful to put a distance between them these past couple of days, wanting to give them both time to be sure they weren't about to repeat past mistakes. How long was long enough? Looking at her now, just an arm's length away, he wanted to scoop her into his arms and run to his boat with her and make love to her from now until morning.

"Tomorrow's Saturday—don't you usually take Saturdays off?"

"Yes. But between now and that wedding, I ought to spend more time in the office."

Jake said nothing, but his expression spoke volumes.

"I guess... I suppose..." She wished he'd help—order her to take the day off and go with him. She cut into the mound of ice cream with the edge of her spoon, softening it into mush.

But that was silly, she didn't need a boss, didn't want anybody to control her. Did she? Was there some remnant of a weak, frail female within her who believed men should be in charge? She drew herself up, squaring her shoulders and lifting her chin. "I'd love to go with you," she said.

He grinned—a saucy, devilish grin. Had he read her mind, seen her moment of self-doubt? "It's a gorgeous drive along the river. If the weather holds we can take the top down on the Volkswagen."

She felt excited. There was something very intimate about driving a long distance with a man. What made it more so was that they were going to share a business experience, a major purchase. That was surprising. It would never have occurred to her before to think of a business venture as an intimate act.

"How long a trip is it?" she asked.

"About an hour and a half."

Jake began to feel excited. Roxie had never been to Red Wing. That meant she really didn't know how beautiful that whole area along the highway was. He would be able to show her his favorite places, take her to the best restaurant in the area. She'd like that. She loved good food and he would love to be the one to introduce her to the very finest. She thought his taste in food was at best uninspired. He would surprise her tomorrow. Suddenly, tomorrow morning seemed like eons away. It was going to be tough sleeping tonight.

"As long as we're down there, we might as well make a day of it so you can see what that end of the state is like."

"It sounds like fun."

"Yes. But let's not forget our primary reason for going." He grinned. "Bring the company checkbook."

She made a face. "I sure hope we aren't going to regret this."

"Look at it this way—we're in it together. At least we won't suffer alone."

Roxie bent to retrieve her purse from the floor beneath her chair. "Yeah, but some of us have a lower threshold of pain than others," she said wryly.

Jake chuckled and signaled for the check.

The waiter brought it and looked askance at Roxie's dish. "Something wrong with the sundae?"

Roxie shook her head and smiled at him. "No, really. It was delicious. I guess I was just too full."

But she knew that what had really killed her appetite was the way her stomach was rocking in response to the thought of her getaway with Jake the next day. It was going to be a miracle if she could concentrate on her work for the rest of the day, and most likely she wouldn't get a wink of sleep tonight.

THE DAY DAWNED crystal clear, and it was warm even as early as six o'clock, when Jake awoke after a restless night. He tried to take his time showering, shaving, dressing for the day, but still had two hours to kill before he could leave to pick up Roxie. He made an elaborate breakfast of eggs, toast, juice and coffee instead of the usual doughnuts or take-out food. He went on the deck to eat.

They'd agreed to leave at nine—if they got there early enough Minnesota Barge might be able to deliver the dock the same day. Now that they'd agreed to go ahead with the purchase, Jake was anxious to get it in place as soon as possible.

He looked out at the river, morning peaceful, and sighed, his breathing edged with nervousness. Okay, so part of the reason he wanted an early start was so that they would have the whole day together. No big deal.

But it was. Not a night had gone by that he hadn't fallen asleep thinking about Roxie, thinking about making love with her, laughing with her, watching the way she moved and the way her eyes lit up when she talked about something that excited her. Lying in his bunk aboard the *Tinker Toy*, the boat rocking gently in the water, his fingers could remember the silken feel of her skin, his mouth the taste of hers; he could smell the fragrance of her hair and her body warmed by passion.

His lungs filled with excitement. They'd be starting out in an hour and a half. Nervously he got up and began pacing the deck.

If he was going to act as jittery as a bridegroom over an ordinary outing, he might as well ease some of the tension by going for a drive.

THE SKY CREATED a clear blue cover over their heads in the convertible. Roxie breathed deeply and settled back comfortably.

"So, Jake. You were a little late picking me up—did you have a problem?"

"A problem? No. I just overslept then I guess I dawdled too long over getting ready."

Dawdled? She was struck by a feeling of disappointment, followed by one of irritation. Apparently he hadn't been as anxious for this outing as she.

She lay her head against the headrest and closed her eyes. The sun and wind felt good on her face. Fatigue was catching up with her.

Jake glanced over at her. Her eyelashes were dark gold spikes against the pink of her cheeks and formed soft shadows there. Oh, but she was beautiful.

"Bad night?" he asked.

"Bad night?" she repeated, her eyelids popping open. She sat upright. "No. No. I slept very well as a matter of fact."

She wasn't going to admit anything when he obviously hadn't been the least excited.

Silence ensued, disturbed only by the hum of the car's engine and the sound of the wheels whooshing against the asphalt road. Jake and Roxie were lost in private thoughts.

"I have to stop up ahead for gas—would you like something?"

He slowed down as they approached a roadside café and gas station and pulled in beside one of the pumps.

Roxie hesitated, debating. She hadn't eaten any of her breakfast, she ought to be hungry. But her stomach was still harboring waves of anxiety. She looked at Jake, who had got out of the car and was waiting for her decision. "Just some gum, maybe."

"There's some in the glove compartment," he said, "help yourself."

He was all the way inside the station office when he remembered and went dashing back to the car.

Too late. Roxie waved the citation at him and grinned. "This ticket for speeding fell out when I opened the glove compartment, and guess what?"

He tried to snatch it out of her hand but she was too quick for him. She held it behind her back and her grin widened. "It's got today's date on it."

But Jake's attention was suddenly captured by the picture Roxie made, her body straining against her shirt as she held the ticket behind her, her hair falling in a silver-blond sweep to her shoulder as she tilted her head to the side, her even white teeth glistening as her smile teased and enticed, and the tip of her tongue just peeking out between her parted lips.

The world around them seemed to come to a halt, sound became a muffled roar, as Roxie realized that Jake had halted midstep and was staring at her, mesmerized. She, too, succumbed to the power of the moment. Her mind and body registered the strength of Jake's physique in crisp khaki slacks and short-sleeve knit shirt. The shirt was blue and reflected in his gray eyes so that they became the color of heather.

"Tagged twice in one day." Jake cleared his throat. "And guilty as charged."

Roxie nodded, not trusting her own voice. She stared at Jake, letting him read the emotions that flitted across her face.

Jake took a step forward and stopped. He wanted to let all his feelings pour forth, venting the pressure that was building inside him. What he said, softly, was, "your hair is the color of sunlight."

"Yours is the color of wheat," she said just as softly.

Another silent pause hung between them, making the air shimmer.

"We have to start being open about what's going on with us," he said.

She nodded. Her hand was on the open window ledge. He placed his own over it and she shivered despite the heat of the sun.

He felt her shiver, tightened his grasp on her hand and felt his heart leap in response to the feel of her skin against his palm.

Oh, they definitely needed to talk, to get things out in the open. And after they did that . . .

He snatched his hand away, suddenly aware of how tempted he was to put the cart before the horse and drag her off to the nearest motel right now.

"After we finish our business," he said, his voice thick with pent-up emotion.

"Yes," she whispered and wondered if she was agreeing to the suggestion he'd made aloud—that they needed to talk—or to the one she'd culled from his mind telepathically—that they were about to embark on a whole new road in their relationship, one that would take them to far more intimate places than they'd been in the past.

Their business at Minnesota Barge was quickly completed. Roxie's hand shook slightly as she made out the check, but her nervousness stemmed as much from her awareness of Jake at her side as from the act of writing the large amount.

She was grateful for the few moments she had alone to compose herself while Jake arranged the delivery to Harley's Landing.

This isn't exactly a trip to Paris or Venice, she jeered at herself, *we're less than fifty miles from home.* But it may as well have been a foreign country; this place was just as new and unknown to her and she was just as tightly wound as she'd have been after an eight-hour flight across the Atlantic. And hadn't Jake's manner earlier suggested there was even more excitement in store for her?

It had been mostly farmland on the drive down, except for the town of Hastings, with its nineteenth-century downtown area that they glimpsed from the highway.

But Red Wing was the beginning of a string of river towns with a number of bed and breakfast inns and restored hotels like the St. James, built in 1875, which Jake pointed out as they drove up Main Street.

When he pulled into a parking space in front of the St. James, Roxie almost gasped aloud. What a hotel this was!

"We can't drive through Red Wing without showing you one of its most famous landmarks," Jake said. He peered into her face, his own face creasing in a broad grin. "Why, Roxie, romantic as the place is, it's only eleven-thirty in the morning. You didn't want to take a room did you?"

He had put his hand on her elbow to escort her to the door and she had to grit her teeth to keep from snatching her arm out of his grasp.

They had coffee and homemade cinnamon rolls in the coffee shop, which overlooked the river. They peeked into the two dining rooms on their way out to Jake's car. "What a lovely place to come for dinner," Roxie said as they got into the car. Jake only smiled and nodded.

She expected him to turn north to the Twin Cities, but he kept driving south, and now the highway wound along the river, giving them incredible vistas to capture the imagination.

Jake laughed aloud at each of Roxie's oohs and ahs, feeling intense pleasure at her response to the beauty around them. When they arrived at Lake City, where Lake Pepin was like a huge cup in the middle of the Mississippi, she reached over and hugged him in her exuberance.

"It's so gorgeous here," she said, clasping her hands together. "I can't believe it's been here all along and I've never seen it before."

"We can come again as often as you like," Jake said, laughing at the sight of her eyes wide with delight.

Neither of them realized the extent of the promise he'd made.

And he still had Café Pepin to present to her.

JAKE PUT HIS NAPKIN DOWN and smiled across the table at Roxie, who had just dipped the last of her bread in the remnants of sauce on her plate.

"Was it incredible?"

Roxie smiled back, but she could only nod; the way his eyes gleamed with the pleasure of pleasing her stole her voice.

Jake sat back, his hands clasped behind his head, and sighed happily. "I knew you'd love it. It's the best food to be found in the entire area, and I love the casual, comfortable feel of the place.''

Café Pepin was a converted saloon; the bar still remained as the focus of the room but the people sitting at tables were more concerned with eating than drinking. The decor was very simple, but it lent itself well as a background for the food.

"I love this street," Roxie said, pointing out the window. "It reminds me of the way small towns must have been at the turn of the century—just sleepy, lazy, sort of lost in the middle of nowhere."

"But this is actually a bustling community—neither lost nor lazy. On both the Minnesota and Wisconsin sides of the river, this area thrives on tourism, among other things."

"What else is there on this side?" Roxie asked.

He took a bill out of his pocket, threw it on the check and stood up. "We'll drive partway back on the Wisconsin side and I'll show you." He held his hand out to her and she took it, not letting go even after she'd risen from her chair. It seemed the most comfortable thing in the world to walk, holding hands, to the car.

"That was wonderful, Jake," Roxie said softly as they stood beside the car, hands still clasped.

"I'm glad you enjoyed it." He used his free hand to brush her hair behind her ear. "Your face is a little sunburned from the drive down—do you want me to put the top up?" He kept his hand on her cheek. When Roxie shook her head, her mouth inadvertently brushed the palm of his hand. He slid his hand around her head and into her hair and bent to brush her mouth tenderly with his lips. "You're beautiful," he whispered.

"Thank you." She didn't want him to talk about her looks—she didn't want him to talk at all. She wanted him to kiss her again, and this time she wanted him to kiss her ferociously.

He stepped back and opened her car door. Roxie climbed in and kept her face averted as she buckled her seat belt, unwilling to let Jake see her shock. What kind of game was this? She could have sworn he wanted her as much as she wanted him. Then why all these delaying tactics? *Maybe you expect him to throw you over his shoulder and drag you into the nearest motel, Hilton?* She put her hand to her mouth to muffle the frustrated sound that welled up in her throat. And why couldn't she just tell him what she was feeling?

Because I don't want him to think I'm ready to move in with him.

"So, all set?" Jake bent a bright, smiling look at her and put the car in gear.

Maybe I've been reading him all wrong. He certainly didn't appear to be caught up in emotion. Maybe he'd decided to end their affair if she wouldn't agree to live with him.

She tried to return his breezy smile with one of her own, though her face felt stiff and unyielding. She turned her head to concentrate on the view as they returned to the highway.

She jumped, startled, when she felt Jake lift her hand from her lap and encompass it in his own.

"Let's spend the weekend together," he said.

She looked over at him and felt something inside of her open up. "I'd like that," she agreed.

CHAPTER SIXTEEN

BACK AT ROXIE'S APARTMENT, they played Scrabble—Roxie won two out of three games—and they played Jake's game, gin—Jake lost $3.27 to Roxie—and they now were devouring the pizza Jake had ordered by telephone.

"What do you want to do after we eat?" Roxie asked, leering at Jake over the triangle of vegetable with extra cheese she held to her lips.

"Do you always win at everything?" he asked, looking more curious than put out.

She chewed, smiled and nodded. "I'm good at positive visualization. I will the right Scrabble tiles or the right cards into my possession."

He looked disgusted and bit off a large chunk of pizza, "Humbug!" The word, though muffled, was discernible.

Roxie frowned. "You really don't care if you win or not, do you?"

His good mood hardly ever seemed to falter. "No, I guess I'm not very competitive. The playing is more important to me than the winning." He leered at her. "Want to play a game we can both win?"

She matched him leer for leer and said, "I think I know the game of which you speak. I was beginning to wonder if we had anything at all in common, and now I see we do."

He was surprised. He thought they had lots in common. "What about our love of the river, and boats and river people?"

She looked surprised. "You're right." She helped herself to another slice of pizza and held it up. "And we like the same food."

Jake looked dubious. "What about that calamari you ordered at St. Anthony's Wharf? Come on. I'd never in a million years eat squid or octopus."

She didn't bat an eye. "So, we're even. I'd never in a million years eat one of those fast-food chain hamburgers you practically live on; which, by the way, might very well be made of something far more disgusting than squid."

"Touché." They laughed together and reached for their wineglasses at the same time. Jake raised his in a toast. "To our differences."

They drank and ate in silence for a few minutes. "Where did you learn to eat that kind of thing?" Jake asked, breaking the silence. "That seems a little exotic for a Wisconsin farm girl."

"That's why."

"What do you mean?"

"Well . . ." She turned on her stool so she was facing him more directly. "The truth is, when my folks walked away from the farm and we moved into a slum project in the city, I made up my mind I was going to live differently when I grew up. I was going to do everything differently from them, starting with getting a good education, never settling for doing less than my very best at a job, and enjoying the finer things in life."

"And calamari is one of the finer things in life?" he teased.

But she was still serious. "I didn't know if it was or it wasn't. I knew the only way to find out was to try it. I did, and I liked it, and so, yes, it became one of the finer things in *my* life. The big thing was that I wasn't passing up the chance to experience it—or anything else." She lowered her voice almost to a whisper, as if she was speaking to herself. "I was never going to be indifferent to what life had to offer."

He was reminded again of how much she wanted to change what she had come from, and that she was ambitious.

"It's more than just a job to you, isn't it?"

"Yes," she admitted, and he could see the sincerity in her eyes. "I would have had to make a success of any job I went into."

She got up and carried her plate to the sink. "Fortunately, the first job I got after graduation was this one, and I fell immediately in love with the whole she-bang—bosses, workers, the river, the boats, the operation—all of it."

She rinsed her plate and put it in the dishwasher. When she straightened, she was smiling. "It's like spending all your working hours planning parties. You can't beat that for fun."

Jake's expression reflected the hope that stirred within him. "Then you really understand how I feel about my job."

His words surprised her. "Of course. Why would you think otherwise?"

He shrugged, and when he raised his face again she saw that he looked sheepish. "Most people think I'm not ambitious enough, that this job is not fulfilling enough for a grown man."

She swallowed. Hadn't she been one of those people? She thought about his job as she knew it. "I'd like to see a wimp handle a three-story, two-hundred-foot stern-wheeler in any weather and all waters. And just how much more fulfilling can it be to add up columns of figures all day long or sit around in boardrooms complaining about what other people do or don't do?"

Jake's grin was becoming as vital to her as sunlight. She returned it and removed his plate. "Don't be a sap, Gilbert, you don't have to account to anyone for what you choose to do with your life."

"Yeah." He stacked their glasses on the empty pizza box and carried the works to the sink. "Does that include you, Roxanne?"

When she looked at him, he was close enough to kiss. She nodded. "Yes, that includes me—you don't have to take any of my crud anymore than anyone else's." She looked at her hands. "I don't know why I attack you so much—sometimes I feel like we've been quarreling all our lives rather than just five years of them."

He closed the little distance between them and tilted her head with gentle fingers at her temples. "I love you, Roxie, more every day."

"Even though I beat you at Scrabble and—" His lips closed over hers, cutting off her taunt, and Roxie forgot what she'd been saying as his sweet tongue met hers and his arms pulled her body into his.

But later, as she lay beside his sleeping form, his arms still holding her, she wondered how long he would be willing to settle for this part-time arrangement. He hadn't brought up the subject again, but she knew it was still on his mind.

She had no intention of falling into another bad relationship, so what was she going to do with her love for Jake?

Could she really trust him when he offered her a commitment? He'd had at least three involvements with different women in the five years she'd known him, and that didn't include the casual dates between his semipermanent relationships. And even if he was sincere, what about the future?

Sure, she thought he had the right to choose his own career, and she'd meant what she said when she told him he didn't owe explanations to anyone for what he did with his life. But that was fine as long as he was the only person he had to worry about. Being half of a couple meant considering the other person's needs, feelings and wishes. She wasn't sure Jake was really up to it. But he loved her, she was sure of that. Was that enough to change the habits of a lifetime?

"Want to talk about it?" Jake asked quietly, startling her out of her reverie.

"I thought you were sleeping."

Jake stretched, yawned and put his arm around her again. "I was. But I don't like sleeping alone."

She stiffened, afraid he was going to bring up the very subject she'd been worrying about.

Instead, he asked, "Do you think you've really got Montgomery out of your system?"

Roxie sat up, shocked at his question. "How can you think otherwise? I've told you I love you, doesn't that mean you're the only man in my heart, my thoughts? Do you think you'd be in this bed if I still cared for him?"

Jake pulled himself up and plumped a pillow between his back and the headboard. "It's just that I never really saw you go through a grieving period after the breakup. I've always heard that's necessary."

"Are you over Taffy?"

"What's she got to do with this?"

"Same issue—you didn't lose much time hitting on me after your breakup with her, did you?"

They stared at one another for a long moment.

Jake observed that Roxie's chin was thrust forward in that fighting attitude that he found strangely enticing.

Roxie made note of his arched eyebrow, the masculine set of his jaw, and realized that she was continually intrigued by his mood changes and the way they defined his face.

"I guess you've got a point there, hon. But I'm the one who's willing to commit to something permanent," Jake said.

"I'm just not willing to commit until I'm sure that it *is* a commitment."

"Are you saying that my attitude is frivolous?"

"Did I say that?"

Jake thought, *I could end this squabbling just by taking her in my arms.*

Roxie's eyes filled with the sight of Jake's bare, broad chest, soft hair the color of a golden dawn, and her heart filled with joy at his presence. If he reached out and touched her now, she'd experience that same delicious meltdown he always created with his touch.

Jake sighed. "I could never understand why some part of me held back from Taffy. At first, I thought she was exactly the kind of woman I was looking for. She was exquisite in a flashy kind of way—sort of voluptuous."

I know. Roxie nodded.

"She was fun, that's the best way to describe Taffy back then, I think." He chuckled, remembering. "Her friends called her Daffy Taffy, but I didn't heed the warning in that. I called her delightful."

Roxie swallowed and noticed the lump that had formed in the back of her throat. "I'm not sure this is such a good idea..."

He put his hand up to stop her. "Bear with me. I think this is really important." He looked at her. "The two mistakes people make when an affair ends are either they talk endlessly and boringly about it, or they hide their true feelings and don't ever deal with them. I want you to know why I'm so sure of us now."

He peered at her profile, trying to see if she agreed. When she said nothing, he went on.

"Almost from the start, Taffy and I changed, maybe brushing off on one another in a way. Anyway, she began to want the life I'd left behind up on the hill, and I began to want to do nothing but play."

He cleared his throat and was silent for a few seconds, gathering his thoughts.

"I see now how unfair I was to Taffy, never really admitting my feelings, but constantly avoiding anything that smacked of seriousness." He brushed his hand over his forehead and through his hair.

Roxie noticed that his mouth was drawn in a straight line and his jaw was clenched. She didn't want to hear about Taffy, didn't want to compare her own thin, moderate prettiness to Taffy's rich, full beauty. But something about what Jake was saying and the way he sounded fascinated her, compelled her to keep silent and listen. Though she could admit she didn't like to be reminded of the intimacy he'd shared with another woman, she also had to admit she was greedy to learn everything about him that she could. And wouldn't it help her to deal with him if she knew why his relationship with Taffy had failed? That was, assuming he could honestly see what he'd done wrong and was man enough to admit it.

"I really couldn't give her up, but I also couldn't take the relationship one step farther. It was a most painful impasse. At one point, I even considered asking her to marry me because I thought it would end her threats to leave me and would keep the status quo. But even that would have been taking a step, and I was too paralyzed to do that."

Roxie asked, "Where did the pain come into it? You obviously didn't love her..."

Jake faced her squarely. "Oh, but I did. As much as I could. And what made it all so painful was the fear that I couldn't love *anyone* any more than I loved Taffy, and that, obviously, wasn't enough to build a stress-free weekend on, leave alone a lifetime relationship. I saw the whole thing as some failure of mine, some weakness or flaw in me. I've only recently begun to believe that we were just two average people—each perfectly nice—who were wrong for each other."

He paused and looked at his clenched fists. "I see now that my attempts to fill every waking hour with play, with fun, were my way of trying to divert her from what she really wanted and needed."

The lamp beside the bed shadowed his face. Were those tears in his eyes? Roxie rubbed his shoulder soothingly. "Go on," she urged gently.

"Sometimes I used to think, why don't I just give Taffy what she wants? Why don't I try harder to be what she needs?"

Was that a break in his voice? Was he weeping?

"And then I'd ask myself, will I ever be able to give enough to make a woman happy? Or am I doomed to a life of selfishness, or loneliness?"

His shoulders were hunched, and she was sure now that he was weeping. It stunned her into immobility even though she wanted to throw herself into his arms, to comfort him.

She couldn't imagine, in a million years, Clay Montgomery weeping. And the kind of weeping her father had done had been the self-pitying sort all drunks indulge in—not to be confused with real emotion.

"I think you're overlooking the obvious, Jake," Roxie said, hoping her words would accomplish what she couldn't make her body do. "The fact that you care about making a woman happy proves how unselfish you really are."

He took a tissue from the box on the nightstand and blew his nose. "I always envied my parents, they seemed so right together, so in tune with one another. They're so totally a couple, you can actually *feel* their togetherness when you're around them."

She could remember from the night of the dinner dance that she had had something of that feeling about the older Gilberts. "Some men would go their whole lives without noticing that sort of thing about a married couple—particularly their own parents," Roxie pointed out. "I think it's a tribute to them that you do notice and probably a guarantee that you're going to be a very caring husband yourself someday." She hoped the warmth she felt didn't manifest itself in a telltale blush; it seemed pushy to bring up the subject of marriage, especially when she had no intention of marrying him herself.

"What about you, Roxie?" Jake said, slipping the focus from himself to her. "You went with Clay for a couple of years—I find it hard to believe you didn't feel an ounce of hurt or anguish over the breakup."

She could feel the belligerence building in the area of her chest. She crossed her arms and shook her head. "I don't know what can be gained by my discussing Clay and I—first of all, we weren't like you and Taffy, we didn't live together."

"But he led you to believe he loved you, that marriage was a very real probability?"

She shrugged. "Maybe. Or maybe I just read him wrong all the way. In which case, I've no one to blame but myself."

"We're not talking blame here, Roxanne. We're talking grief. After going with him for two years, you must miss him sometimes or resent him for letting you down. You must feel some kind of loss."

"Must I?" She shook her head and began to explain in an offhand manner.

"Clay was someone it was easy to have illusions about; he was an attentive escort, he remembered occasions like birthdays, and was always on time." She paused. She had summed Clay up in one sentence—but she hadn't intended to make him sound so shallow.

"It was easy to fall into the trap with him because he was so expert at pretending." Roxie frowned and touched her forehead with her fingertips. Strange, she'd never before tried to describe her relationship with Clay—nor, for that matter, any other man she'd gone with. It was kind of spooky.

"Go on," Jake prodded. He lay back, propping his head on his hands. *Typical jackass,* he thought. *Mr. Perfect!*

Roxie's eyes dimmed as she grew more thoughtful. "I guess in a way he was like Taffy—very handsome, always well groomed, and everybody liked him."

Is that what he told you? Jake bit his lower lip and forced himself to remain silent.

"Funny, I seem to be making him sound sort of—I don't know, sort of... plastic."

Mmmph! Jake was determined to keep his big mouth shut, to show her the same courtesy she'd shown him.

"I don't mean to. I guess it's just that he was almost too perfect, too together, if you know what I mean."

When she looked at Jake, he nodded, rather forcefully, she thought.

"Is something wrong?"

"No. No. Go on, I'm listening."

"Well, we got into a routine because Clay liked to know he could depend on me for special events and regular dates on Saturday nights and Sunday afternoons. He liked me to be there for him when he had a cold or the flu, and sometimes he'd ask me to come up to his place and cook dinner if he had a lot of work to do."

She pulled the sheet up to her neck, feeling suddenly chilled. Was it bizarre to be sitting in bed, nude, discussing their previous love affairs? She glanced at Jake and saw that his gray eyes had darkened and that they were riveted on her. Maybe the way he seemed to be hanging on every word was what was making her so uncomfortable.

"We went along like that for two years and..." Her words trailed away and her expression grew dazed.

Jake sat up, alerted to the change in her manner.

She rushed in to cover her hesitancy. "He was very secure, very safe to be with. You knew what to expect from him...he never broke a date or was late or drank too much or..." She stopped again, confused. *What? What did I say? Oh, yes, about drinking.*

She covered her mouth with her fingers. They seemed to be trembling and she thrust her hands together in a prayerful gesture.

"Clay was the kind of man you could depend on... He wouldn't let you down." Had she said that already? Was she repeating herself? Jake had a funny look on his face, was almost leaning toward her as though to reach out and touch her. As though to comfort her. But that was silly, she didn't need comforting, she wasn't in the least upset.

She took a deep, quivering breath and thrust her chin out.

"Clayton Montgomery was the most reliable man I ever met!" she blurted, and burst into tears.

Jake muttered an obscenity and wrapped his arms around her, making a haven for her against his warm chest. He should have seen this coming, should have realized it would only cause her pain to rehash the past. Why did he always have to put his foot in it with her, wreak havoc where he meant only to offer love?

He'd bet she hadn't cried like this since she was a child. She reminded him of Sissy and Beth when they had been hurt as children. Beth, especially, would cling to him as Roxie was doing now, as if she'd fall if she let go. He tightened his arm at her waist and stroked her hair. Her tears warmed his skin. He held her closer.

"Yes, good, cry, darlin', it's good to get it out. Let it go, Roxie, let it go."

After long moments of crying she began to stammer an explanation through her sobs. "I was using—using him to m-make up for m-my dad."

"Yes." Jake nodded. *Right on, Roxie honey. You're getting a clear picture now—great!*

She pushed him away and he saw that her eyes were large and made dark by rage. "And he—he let me down. Just the way my f-father..." She hiccuped, laughed uncertainly and burst into a fresh spate of tears. When he tried to take her into his embrace again she drew back and reached for a handful of tissues.

"No," she said, sniffling and blowing, "let's don't make a big thing of this. I'm not really hurting." She blew her nose again and wiped her eyes with the back of her hand. "This isn't hurt, Jake, it's anger."

"You're right, I shouldn't have started this business."

"No, not at you, Jake, darling, never at you." She threw her arms around his neck and hugged him. "I'm mad at myself because I wasted two years in a fantasy that had nowhere to go."

She almost purred as Jake smoothed her hair and held her tight. "I guess I'm angry, too, because I don't like making a fool of myself," she added.

"With me?" He pushed her away and looked into her eyes.

"No," she said, laughing, "with Clay—and with myself."

Jake sighed with relief. "You're quite a woman, Roxanne. And I'd be honored if you'd reconsider my proposal."

Roxie lurched away, pulling the sheet up to cover herself as she jumped off the bed. "Damn it, Jake, you just can't help spoiling things, can you? Just when I think you really understand me, you use the moment to manipulate me."

THE NEXT TWO WEEKS became one long memory of working and sleeping for everyone who worked at Harley Marine. Both boats were scheduled for day and night charters almost continuously and when there wasn't a cruise scheduled, there was work to be done to prepare for the double celebration coming up on the fourth of July—the Handel wedding and the annual fireworks party cruise.

Both Bill and Jake saw to it that their crews spent every free minute of the day cleaning the grounds. Jake even planted flowers so the drive from the road would be lined with color.

One day Roxie drove in and saw the Larsen brothers cutting back underbrush in the wooded area that lined the property to the south. As she pulled into the parking lot she saw Jake doing the same thing along the bank leading down to the levee.

They hadn't really seen each other since the night of their trip to Red Wing. Roxie responded to his cheerful greeting with a wave of her hand and hurried into the office building.

She recalled the way she'd hidden in her bathroom until she heard him leave her apartment, determined to avoid argument about his proposal. The truth was, she was scared to death he'd either coerce her into something she wasn't ready for or force her to break off their affair. She couldn't bear either.

No, what she needed was to put the relationship on hold until she could gain some control.

But she found herself looking up frequently to catch glimpses of him from the window overlooking the side of the building.

Like the Larsen boys, Jake wore only cutoff jeans and sneakers. But she didn't notice if the Larsen brothers' muscles rippled as they worked, or if the sheen of perspiration directed the eye downward from the vulnerable place at the base of their throats to the mysterious place below the gaping waistband of their denim shorts.

Her mouth grew dry as she craned her neck to watch Jake sit on his heels to get at some particularly stubborn roots. His bunched-up thigh muscles looked steely hard and masculine.

When she could no longer see him without going right up to the window and running the risk of him seeing her, she forced her attention to her work.

She put a contract form into the typewriter and began to type. But the image of Jake, bare-chested in the sun, kept coming between her and the page.

She sighed and pulled the form from the machine. "Minneapolis Manufacturing," she muttered, glaring at the word "muscles," which she'd typed in place of "manufacturing."

He acts as if we never had a single shared, intimate moment. She rolled another sheet of paper under the platen.

Mary came out of her office as Roxie was swearing and throwing her third balled-up contract into the wastebasket.

"Aha! Even the big chiefs make mistakes," she gloated. "That makes me feel lots better. I don't think I've ever seen you make a mistake before. Have you got the flu or something?"

"Don't be absurd, Mary," Roxie snapped, "of course you've seen me make mistakes—nobody's perfect."

Jake's body is perfect. She swallowed hard, amazed at her delinquent train of thought, and averted her face from Mary's frank study.

Mary frowned and shook her head. "Wanna go to lunch? We haven't had any time to get together in weeks."

"I'm not the one who's been tied up with my lover," Roxie said pointedly. *I'm not busy with anyone but myself and my miserable thoughts.*

"Oh, I haven't been tied up," Mary said, attempting to keep a straight face, "we don't go in for that kinky stuff."

"Very funny, Mary," Roxie said and wished she didn't sound so huffy. She made an effort to soften her tone. "I guess I can make it to lunch, I haven't anything better to do."

Mary pretended shock, throwing her hands up in the air. "Gosh, Rox, that's got to be the most gracious acceptance of an invitation I've ever heard. Care to share what's needling you?"

Roxie was about to make a snappy retort when the door opened and Jake and Doug Larsen came thumping in, letting a wave of heat into the air-conditioned room. Doug was carrying a thermos and Jake was wiping sweat from his forehead with his arm.

"We need some ice water," Doug explained, heading for the back room.

Jake threw himself into the swivel chair behind the other desk and gasped. "Lord, it feels so good in here I might stay for a week."

Suddenly the large room seemed smaller, filled with bare skin and male heat and sweat. Roxie could feel her lungs filling with something other than air, and her need to gasp made her jump from her chair angrily.

"Have you forgotten this is a business office, Captain Gilbert?" she demanded. She used his title sarcastically. He didn't look anything like a ship's captain now, he looked like... She licked her lips, trying to relieve their dryness, and sat down, ashamed of her outburst.

Jake stood up and stared at her, his eyes suddenly darkening with understanding. "You're right. I apologize." He looked serious. "Doug," he called out, "when you finish filling the thermos, go out the back door and walk around, will you?"

They could hear the puzzled tone in Doug's affirmative reply. Jake went to the door and nodded at the two women. "Sorry. It won't happen again."

Roxie couldn't help but see the golden hair that furred Jake's strong, well-shaped legs. The cutoffs were damp from sweat and clung to his buttocks in a most inviting way. She almost choked as she tried to say goodbye.

Mary discovered she was holding her breath. She let it out in a long, noisy sigh. "Is there something happening around here that I don't know about?" She looked at Roxie with an eyebrow raised in question.

"I don't know what you mean," Roxie said, fumbling for the pen she'd dropped when Jake stood up. "But we certainly can't have the crew coming in here half naked anytime they feel like it. What if we'd had customers in here just now?"

Mary's quizzical look turned to a grin. "I kinda liked it. What's the use of working for a charter boat company if you don't get to see a few half-naked sailors once in a while?"

Roxie had to laugh at Mary's brash remark, and even as she did she realized that it had been some time since she'd had her sense of humor out for airing. Since when? Her trip with Jake. Well, she'd had two weeks in which to ponder what she'd learned about herself, and to admit to herself that she didn't want to lose Jake.

"I guess I owe Jake an apology," she admitted to Mary.

"That should prove interesting—will you promise to make it while I'm within earshot?"

This time Roxie's laugh was a full-bellied sound of humor. "Sure enough, pal, and while you're enjoying that little scenario, you can be thinking of how you're going to have the June disbursements journal done by the end of today."

Mary saw she'd met her match and scurried to her office, shaking her head. She called over her shoulder, "See you at noon, Chief."

Roxie settled to work, still smiling, and wondered when would be the best time to let Jake know she was ready to eat crow.

CHAPTER SEVENTEEN

JULY FOURTH brought the most perfect weather any bride or, for that matter, anyone setting out for a day on the river, could ask for. Both boats were draped with red, white and blue streamers of dyed flowers and sailed under full flags.

The *River Princess* spent the day doing two-hour public excursions, which were in such demand that the office was filled with people seeking shelter from the sun while waiting for the next ride. Others brought picnic lunches and dined alfresco along the levee as they waited their turn.

The big event for the *Princess* would come at nine, when it carried a capacity crowd to the middle of the river to watch the fireworks. Reservations for that cruise had been sold out for weeks. Every year there were rumors that scalpers were selling tickets and making a fortune, but so far it was only rumor. All the riverboat companies in the two states would be sold out for fireworks displays along the two rivers.

The *Celebration* teemed with activity of a different kind as caterers and florists and the staff from the governor's residence joined the Harley crew, making sure everything was ready for the wedding, which would take place at eight o'clock that night.

Roxie stole away from the office every few hours to see the progress being made and was enchanted by the decorating of the florists, who'd been hired by Mrs. Handel. Even the gangplank was festooned with red, white and blue carnations. Each table had a center-piece of red and white tea roses in a small blue basket. There was a tall white taper in the center of each bou-quet. Roxie could just imagine what it was going to look like when night fell on the river and all those can-dles were lit on both decks.

She sighed as she visualized the romantic setting, then started back to the office. She almost knocked Mrs. Handel down.

"My goodness. Ms. Hilton—Roxie. I'm afraid I didn't see you."

"My fault entirely," Roxie confessed. They shared a giggle. "Are you nervous about tonight?"

Mrs. Handel grinned. "What, nervous about the wedding of my only daughter? I should say not." She clutched her hands to her chest in a melodramatic ges-ture. "After this, I shall never again complain about having only had one child."

Roxie patted the older woman's arm. "You're doing just fine. Most of the mothers of the brides threaten to abandon ship the minute the boat hits deep water."

They laughed again and Roxie took a step away. "I have to get back to work, but just in case I don't see you again, I want to thank you for giving us this job and tell you I know all will go well and that this will be a happy and memorable occasion."

"What do you mean, in case you don't see me again? Aren't you sailing with us?"

Roxie stared at Mrs. Handel. "Well, I hadn't planned on it. You see we do employ regular hostesses for these affairs and the caterers bring their own staff. I usually don't go along."

"Oh, but I'd hoped you would so that my husband could meet you. We've just raved about you to him, about all the help you've given and your good ideas. I know he'd want to thank you himself."

"You're very kind, Mrs. Handle, but I was just doing my job."

"Why, Roxie, if we'd known this, we'd have sent you an invitation. Don't you want to see the wedding with the other guests, to see the fruit of your labor come to life?"

She couldn't admit she'd been envying the rest of the crew and wishing she could justify going on this particular cruise.

"I would love to, Mrs. Handel, but I didn't want to use my job to intrude on a private affair. After all, I don't normally go out on these things anymore."

Susan Handel leaned toward Roxie and took her hand. "Would you come along to keep a nervous mother from making a fool of herself in front of three hundred people?"

"When you put it that way..." They laughed again and Roxie squeezed the woman's hand. "All the more reason to get back to work if I'm going to have time to get home and dressed and back here in time."

On the way to the office, she couldn't help but picture herself with Jake beside her in the romantic setting of the reception. When Mary asked about her high color, she blamed it on the heat and the climb up the stairs.

Mary was elated that Roxie was going on the wedding cruise. She had elected to work behind the bar on the *Princess* for the public fireworks cruise. "Now you can tell me all about it firsthand. And take notes if you have to, I don't want you to miss a single detail."

She didn't need notes, even if she'd entertained the idea of taking them; every facet of the event was to be indelibly and forever imprinted on her mind.

She was stunned but not surprised, when she thought it over, to see that Jake's brother Martin was one of the ushers and to find the rest of the Gilbert clan among the guests. What surprised her was that Jake had never mentioned that his family would be attending, and that neither Susan nor Carla had mentioned it, since they knew Jake would be piloting. Roxie decided there must be an unspoken rule of privacy among the upper classes that prevented anything that even hinted at gossip, at least among outsiders.

Was she an outsider? She couldn't see the governor's family making a personal friend of the woman who helped make such a success of Carla's wedding. But Governor Handel couldn't have been more gracious, and Roxie was gratified to discover she didn't feel the least bit patronized.

Yet it wasn't until Jake came down from the pilothouse, dazzlingly handsome in his formal white uniform, that Roxie began to feel comfortable among the important wedding guests. Jake's gaze found her immediately and sent a message of warm approval for the way she looked in the mauve silk two-piece dress. Her palms instantly grew damp and her breath heightened as he pushed through the crowd to join her.

"Having a good time?"

This was no time for a philosophical discussion about the mixing of the classes. She smiled at him and nodded. "The best. Wasn't the ceremony gorgeous?"

"Thanks to you. What a great idea to have it on the dock—it was a perfect touch."

"Thank you." For the first time in memory she was having trouble accepting kudos for her work. "Thank God you insisted on the new dock. And wasn't it a stroke of genius for the florist to create a movable canopy of flowers across the dock, leading up the gangplank for the ceremony and the procession?"

"Great," Jake agreed, almost absentmindedly. "Listen, Captain Fellows and Terry are both at the wheel, so I can take a little break. Would you dance with me?"

He made it seem as if he was her date for the evening. They danced for awhile on the second deck where a small band played nothing but romantic love ballads that invited slow, dreamy dancing. The Dixieland band would take over after dinner.

And before he went up to the pilothouse to spell Captain Fellows, who'd agreed to come out of retirement for this one special cruise, they had a glass of champagne together and shared a plate of hors d'oeuvres. He took her to the table reserved for his family and asked them to keep her entertained until he could get away for another break. She couldn't deny that they treated her like an old friend and made her feel wonderfully welcome.

The best part of all was when, after the second break, he invited her up to the pilothouse to watch the fireworks with him. Captain Fellows and Terry Johnson were tickled to join the revelers below, so Jake and Roxie were alone in the darkening night, far above the rest of the world, when Jake anchored downriver from Harriet Island.

It was the most extraordinary vantage place for viewing fireworks. The cabin filled with light and color, and it was as if they were being bathed with both.

Jake's face glowed eerily in the green light of a starburst when he took her face between his hands and bent to kiss her. All around, the world seemed to explode with the pop and whistle of rockets. Blue fire cascaded from the sky and merged with red wisps of fallout before fading into billowing clouds of shimmering, silver-streaked smoke. Jake's lips, so gentle, so searching at first, seemed to take warmth from the dancing flames, and the smell of spent gunpowder seemed to heighten his passion. His kiss deepened, plundering, demanding, wrenching such excitement from Roxie's very innards that she almost collapsed against him. Pinwheels and Roman candles screamed in the sky above them then hissed past them as sparks and colored flames fell to the water below.

She tried to draw back, to loosen the ropes of emotion that bound them together almost against her will. Nothing had prepared her for this kind of excitement. No man's touch had elicited such pain, such longing, such intense pleasure. Or was it the fireworks, the drama of the night creating an illusion of passion that couldn't possibly subsist on its own in any normal situation?

"Don't pull away from me, Roxanne," Jake murmured, attempting to draw her back into his embrace.

She felt as spent as a burned-out firecracker. "No, Jake, don't, please." She turned from side to side, frustrated that there was no place to go in the tiny cabin except to leave it altogether, and that she could not do. She looked at Jake, helpless, pleading silently for understanding.

"I won't pressure you," he promised, reading her mind. His features seemed even more intense in the red, white and blue glow of a spinning pinwheel.

"You think that now, but how long will it be before you forget your promise and start pushing me again?"

"Will you give me a chance?" The tail end of his question was muffled by an explosive burst of gunpowder nearby but she was able to read the word formed by his lips. She could hardly look away from those lips, from that sensuous mouth that had sent excitement thrumming through every pulse point in her body. The cabin filled with a burst of rainbow colors signaling the finale of the display just as a huge arrangement of lances lit up to produce a fiery American flag on the shore of the river at Harriet Island.

Jake caught Roxie's gasp of pleasure in his own mouth as he silenced her with a kiss that caught her off guard. He felt her body give way and he caught her against himself and moved his lips to the soft, silken spot at the side of her neck. She moaned softly in his ear, and he lifted her arms to wrap around his neck and pulled her into the hardened saddle of his torso with his hands clasped to her buttocks.

Roxie could feel wet heat surging from within her body, and her desire for Jake strengthened even as her limbs weakened.

"Ahoy, Captain, last call for champagne," Derek Fellows' voice called from just below the open cabin door.

They sprang apart as they felt the old pilot's weight moving up the ladder. Roxie covered her mouth with her hand, hoping she'd already worn off her lipstick before Jake began kissing her. Jake turned his back to her and made some adjustment to his clothing.

It was immediately clear that Captain Fellows had celebrated the fourth of July and the wedding party below with great enthusiasm. They could smell the bourbon on his breath.

"I'll take her in myself, Cap, why don't you go have a nightcap?" Jake said, sending Roxie a silent apology with his eyes. "I'll just take Roxie down and be right back."

He slid down the ladder quickly and held his arms up to her. Roxie sat on the top rung and went easily into his embrace. "Will you wait for me?" Jake whispered. "We can go out somewhere and then go to the *Tinker Toy* or to your place."

She was relieved to have her feet touch the deck and to hear and see the crowd around her. She shook her head. "No. I'm really exhausted, Jake. Let's wait until tomorrow."

Everything about the wedding cruise had been wonderful. But it was like overdosing on rich food and fine wines, too much and too soon. Her feelings for Jake were all mixed up with the romantic excitement and beauty of the wedding and the fireworks. Tonight she'd have been putty in his hands, agreeing to anything he asked. She needed to know that if and when she ever decided to make a lifetime commitment to him, it was out of trust and faith, not a romantic fantasy.

He seemed to understand and let her go with only a shrug to show his disappointment.

Roxie went home alone but her mind and heart were filled with memories and she knew that sooner or later Jake would have what he wanted.

SHE WAS JUST SHARING the last detail of the event with Mary, leaving out only those parts that pertained to her and Jake, when he came into her office talking and laughing with Bill Tabor.

"Well, we certainly can congratulate ourselves on a double success," Jake said, throwing a check on Roxie's desk and plunking a metal cash drawer beside it. She picked up the check and saw the governor's signature immediately.

She stared up at Jake wide-eyed. "He paid the balance last night? How did you manage that?"

Jake shrugged. "It was his idea. The only figure we didn't have on the bill was the cost of the bar, and he asked Floyd if he minded counting the bottles right then. Floyd didn't mind, we did it together, and the governor whipped out his checkbook and wrote us a check on the spot. Said this was out of his private checking account and he knew how small businesses needed to be paid right away."

"We're not that small," Tabor said.

"No," Roxie agreed, "but it's nice to keep the cash flow coming in on a daily basis, it looks great on the books." She was delighted with the size of the check; the bar, their major source of profit, had done very well.

"Yeah, and by the way, the governor wrote a separate check for the crew and bar people so you don't have to tip them out of that."

Another unexpected surprise. "How much?" she asked, curious.

Jake and Bill exchanged a grin. "A thousand dollars."

"What?" Roxie and Mary screeched in unison.

"Yup. Said he appreciated good service more than anything and that this had been the best and that when a man's only daughter got married, it was worth it to have everything go so well."

Roxie was busy putting figures into her ten-key, Mary looking over her shoulder.

"Wow," Mary gasped, when Roxie hit the total key. "That's $167.00 each! Well over what I would have paid them."

Jake laughed. "Right. And he wrote a similar one for the caterer's crew. They all earned it."

"That's true," Roxie said, "I've never been more proud of our people." She sat back in her chair and looked at Jake, who was hovering in front of her desk, playing with the pens in the cup. "So now it's time to get busy with the weekly dinner cruises."

"I haven't had a chance to discuss the mechanics with Mark yet."

"Do it soon," Roxie said, reaching for the ringing phone. She covered the mouthpiece with her hand. "I want to get the first one lined up for the end of this month, if possible."

Jake nodded and sat down to watch her as she talked to her caller. She whipped a pen out of the cup and began jotting notes on a yellow ledger pad, answering and asking questions as she wrote.

She'd been a sensation last night at the wedding, smashing in that mauve party dress and even more smashing in the colored light of the fireworks in the cabin. He ran his hand through his hair then rubbed his mouth. God, he'd have made love to her right there if he'd had his way, forgetting where they were and what they were supposed to be doing. She made him lose all control of himself, and if he didn't make love to her again soon, he thought he would go crazy.

But there was a fragility about her that kept him from pushing her when she backed away. Maybe it was the way she reminded him of Beth. Or maybe it was because he loved her so damned much that she was on his mind constantly these days. He wanted to spin cartwheels for her, rob a bank, walk a high wire...

Go to work in the family business. His stomach lurched violently at that thought. Where had that come from? He was really losing it.

Mary and Bill had been talking quietly across the room. Mary went to her office and Bill came over and said, "I'd better check on my guys, they're apt to fall asleep on the job the day after a holiday."

Jake thought Roxie looked like she was going to be on the phone awhile. He stood up. "Yeah, I need to make sure my guys aren't spending their tip before they finish cleaning up the *Celeb*."

Roxie finished her call and looked up from her notes. She saw that Bill was leaving and Jake was right behind him. "Jake, would you mind staying a moment?"

He patted Bill on the back. "See ya later, pal," he said, and turned to Roxie with a smile. "You think you can con me into being your escort for the first dinner cruise if you get me alone?"

"Would it work?" She smiled back and found she was pulling nervously at the tab of her belt.

His face had softened with the smile, restoring the humor and sexiness he seemed to reserve for when they were alone. "It might." He glanced at the doorway to Mary's office. They could hear the murmur of her voice as she spoke on the phone.

He strode across the room, leaned over her desk, put his hand on her elbow and pulled her around the edge until she was up against him. "Talk me into it," he whispered. His mouth was only a breath from hers.

Her legs began to tremble, and when she inhaled, her breath snagged on the edge of her throat. She put a hand against his chest to steady herself. "How?" Her lips vibrated as the word escaped from her mouth into his.

His tongue shot out and caught the word and eased it back onto her lips. "Like this."

The sound of a chair banging against a metal desk made them jump apart guiltily, and Roxie scurried around to her seat and grabbed a paper out of a basket on her desk.

"...and I really think we ought to consider charging an increased rate if they want to go upriver this time of year," she improvised as Mary came out of her office.

Jake brushed his hair back and tried to look serious. "I agree. Do whatever you think best," he said, heading out the door.

Mary stared at Roxie. "What's going on with you and Jake?" she asked.

Roxie tore her eyes from the door. "Me and Jake? What do you mean?"

"What were you talking about?" Mary grinned and cast a pointed glance at the paper in Roxie's hand.

"Oh. This. I was pointing out some of the Danvers party's special cruise requests."

Mary eased the paper gently out of Roxie's hand and held it in front of her. "That's funny. This doesn't look like a contract. It looks like a cash bar liquor inventory sheet."

Roxie could hear Mary's laughter long after Mary had left the building to go to the post office.

Roxie was still swearing under her breath when the phone rang. She snatched it up, almost snarling into the mouthpiece. "Hey." Jake's voice was a husky whisper in her ear. "Is this the same soft, feminine, sexy lady I left about twenty minutes ago?"

She laughed. She had to admit to herself that she was thrilled to hear from him, that she was sorry their intimate moment had been so abruptly shattered.

"What do you want, Gilbert?" She didn't have to admit any of that to him, after all. Responding to his humor was all right. It was safe. Responding to his sexiness was another matter altogether.

"I forgot to tell you that I'd be honored to escort you on the night of the dinner cruise."

"I forgot to ask you to."

"I'm willing to discuss it further."

"Over dinner?"

"Your place or mine?"

Roxie laughed. "How about someplace neutral. Say the St. Paul Hotel?"

"How about a compromise, like a coffee shop?"

"Ugh. How romantic is that?"

"What else did you have in mind?" he asked with a leer in his voice.

"Very funny."

He laughed. "Indeed. So, let's say about seven-ish?"

"Okay." She hung up, ordering her heart to resume beating at a normal rate, and tried to concentrate on the contract she was typing.

When the phone rang again almost immediately, she was sure it was Jake with an afterthought.

She answered, laughing.

"You won't be laughing for long if you keep messing with me."

Despite the shock, this time she was able to answer Minto's threat.

"I've taken steps to assure that the police will know it's you if anything happens to me," she said quoting a line from a long-running television series. Certainly no more bizarre than picking up a telephone and listening to a thug threaten her.

"I told you to lay off me in the papers."

In the chaos of the wedding and the holiday, she'd forgotten that the *Waterfront Journal* had printed her interview with Meg Curley. But she wasn't going to let this oaf scare her again.

"And I'm telling you, I'm not going to rest until you're off this river."

"Lady, you're asking to be hurt."

"No, I'm not," she persisted, "but if you want to play rough, I'm prepared to go to any measures to have you stopped."

She hung up the phone and bit down on her fist to keep from screaming. Eight deep breaths with her eyes closed helped her achieve a level of calm. Shock caused her to giggle. She felt like Goldilocks confronting Papa Bear. Any one who heard her would have thought she'd lost her mind. But maybe the kind of man who tried to intimidate women over the phone was really a coward at heart, and maybe, just maybe, she'd been able to bluff him into backing down.

CHAPTER EIGHTEEN

ROXIE HAD BEEN NERVOUS and jumpy, especially when the phone rang, ever since Minto's call. But after a while she began to relax. By the end of July, she was sure she'd been right to call his bluff, that he was all bark and no bite.

Now she was caught up in the excitement of the maiden voyage of the weekly dinner cruises. Jake would be at her apartment in half an hour to pick her up. Terry, licensed now, was taking the *Celebration* out on his very first totally solo charter, and Jake, with his first night off in a long time, had accepted Roxie's invitation to join her for the cruise, mostly, she suspected, so he would be on the river and able to keep an eye on Terry and the *Celeb*. He was as nervous about Terry's solo run as a mother letting her child walk to school alone for the first time.

She was pretty nervous herself, dropping first her hairbrush and then the mascara wand as she thought about tonight. If everything went as planned and the dinner went well, word-of-mouth advertising would assure the success of the cruises.

She was just slipping into a strapless ivory moiré cocktail dress, purchased especially for tonight, when the buzzer announced Jake's arrival. She carried her shoes to the door and peeked through the telescopic eye he'd insisted she have installed. She opened the door.

"It's you," she said, grinning happily.

"Naw, just someone who looks like me." He took time to brush her hair from her face and to study that face before bending to kiss her. "You're beautiful," he said, wrapping his arms around her waist.

"Thank you. Where is the real you, then?"

"Looking over Johnson's shoulder every minute for the next—" he lifted his arm from her waist to peer at his watch "—three hours."

She laughed and pushed him away. "You're going to make a very attentive date tonight, I can see."

She held onto his arm as she slipped into her heels. "I'm just grateful the dinner cruises are on the *Princess* and not the *Celeb* or you'd probably want to spend every minute in the pilothouse."

He shook his head and grinned. "Uh-uh, then it wouldn't qualify as a solo run, would it?"

"No," she teased, "but that wouldn't stop you, would it?"

"No." He laughed and pointed at the ivory shawl that was on the little hall console. "You wearing this?"

He draped it across her shoulders after first bending to plant a few kisses along the scented skin from the back of her neck to the little mole in the middle of her upper back.

"Mmm." Roxie shivered and turned to kiss him on the mouth. "We haven't been out together in quite awhile," she said breathlessly as the kiss ended.

"And we may not be out again tonight if you keep kissing me like that," Jake warned, his equilibrium visibly threatened.

"Ha," Roxie said as she moved toward the door. "No way are you going to stay away from that river tonight of all nights. Terry Johnson may be alone in that pilothouse but he sure as hell is not alone in spirit.''

He protested halfheartedly all the way down in the elevator and in the car as they crossed the bridge. But once aboard the *River Princess*, both were totally absorbed in the romantic ambience of the first deck cabin and in one another.

Mark Carter, debonair in his whites, saluted Jake and Roxie smartly as they came aboard. All the staff wore the uniforms she'd ordered especially for the Handel wedding, the crew in khaki pants with short-sleeved cotton shirts and the bar people in navy and white. They looked attractively professional and eager for this new venture to begin.

Roxie had opted for Japanese lanterns, knowing what a lovely sight they would make from the shore. They would also cast a mysterious golden glow over the outer deck of the boat for the passengers to bask in.

A single red rose lay on each of the tables, an exotic contrast to the pristine white linen cloths. Tall red candles were set into wisps of fern and baby's breath tucked into milk glass candlesticks. They would be lighted, along with the lanterns, just before the passengers came aboard.

In the far corner the members of the combo she'd hired were setting up their instruments. Their leader, Marty Conroy, waved at Roxie. The leer he sent her way told Roxie that he'd spotted her arrival with Jake and put two and two together. The three of them were old friends, since his group frequently played for charter parties. Tonight, he had been told to play only the most romantic music he had in his repertoire.

She waved back and took Jake's arm in an obvious gesture. No reason to keep their affair secret, the whole world could know she loved him. Which made her think of Bill and Mary and their clandestine affair for the umpteenth time that day. She thought briefly of telling Jake about it—later, maybe.

"Hi, guys," Jake called out to the band, "I see you're on time for a change."

They laughed and Marty sent an obscene gesture Jake's way. "You look spiffy in your dress-up clothes, Jakie," Marty yelled. The trumpeter blew a raspberry on his horn.

Roxie laughed and let go of Jake's arm. "I see you're still batting a thousand at winning friends and influencing people," she said. "I think I'll check on the caterer while you and the band do your little boys' thing."

Jake caught her arm as she started to move away. "First, this little boy wants to play a little game."

"Let me guess—you want to play doctor?" She kissed him lightly on the mouth.

"You've been reading my letters to Santa." His lips were only another kiss away from hers and his breath was warm and sweet on her face.

She wet her lips and played her fingers up and down the lapel of his charcoal gray blazer. The coat made his eyes even more gray. "How else would I know what it would take to really please you?" she asked, her voice husky with an upsurge of desire.

"And you do that so well," Jake said, brushing her mouth lightly with his. "Just thinking about it makes me want to take you straight home to bed."

She turned her face into his coat as she whimpered in agreement. "Why do you do that?"

"What?"

"Talk about our lovemaking when we're out in public and can't do a thing about it? It makes me—"

"Ready?"

"—crazy."

"Same difference. Okay, I'll quit teasing you and let you get to your inspection if you give me one real kiss."

She did and was rewarded for her boldness by an outcry of catcalls from the members of the band.

She pushed Jake away and took her blushing face to the galley where Floyd was helping the caterer set up the electric warmers.

"You're becoming more beautiful every time I see you, Roxanne," Floyd said.

Marge, the caterer, looked up and nodded. "Oh, yes. My goodness, Roxie, have you gone and done something extreme like falling in love?"

It hit the nail so exactly on the head that Roxie felt her blush deepen. "I suppose this is the price one pays for going public," she said with a mock groan. She looked over her shoulder and saw some of the musicians slapping Jake on the back and shaking his hand.

Floyd shook his head and affected a hangdog look. "I take it this means I'm no longer in the running?"

"You'll always be special to me, Floyd—what we have transcends romance and sex."

Easy for her to say," Floyd said, addressing Marge.

"Friendship is what you give to the girl who has everything—and is getting it from somebody else," Marge quipped.

"I came back here to see how you're doing, not to talk about my love life." Roxie dipped her finger in a bowl of white sauce and laughed when Marge glared and slapped her hand away.

"Okay, sorry. Mmm, but that's delicious, Marge, what is it?"

"Horseradish sauce for the prime rib."

"It's better than any horseradish sauce I've ever tasted."

"That's because I'm the best chef you've ever known."

Sara Winslow came into the galley from the bar, which was located just around the corner. "Am I really supposed to put a bottle of champagne on ice at your table and replace it every time the bottle empties?" Her wide blue eyes seemed even wider when she was surprised or puzzled. "I thought tonight everyone gets champagne and we pour?"

Jake. Roxie laughed. "You tell Captain Gilbert you take your orders from Floyd Dubrov and no one else—no, never mind, I'll tell him myself."

Jake was nowhere in sight when she went to the main cabin. Marty Conroy called out, "Roxie, I thought you ordered easy listening for tonight."

Roxie stopped in her tracks. "And so I did. What's the problem?"

"Jake said we're to play nothing but heavy metal."

"And try that on an accordion," Mike Saunders, the pianist, said. The others joined in the laughter.

Roxie shook her head, gave the band a baleful look and continued her search for Jake.

On the upper deck, the caterer's crew were setting tables to match the ones in the cabin below. Roxie recognized one of the waitresses and called out a greeting.

"Hey, Rox, how ya doin', babe?" Darlene responded.

"I'm fine but I'm looking for a tall, blond man, did he come through here?"

"You mean Captain Jake?"

Of course, the catering crew would all know Jake from their jobs aboard the *Celeb*. "Yes."

"Yeah, he was here. He tried to tell me that you wanted all the coffee cups turned upside down on the saucers and placed on the tables. I told him we're not a schlock operation, that we don't do butcher work and that we put the cups on when we serve coffee, after the meal."

"Good for you," Roxie said. "Which way did my little helper go?"

Darlene gestured upward with the handful of forks she was holding.

"I might have known." Roxie went out of the cabin and around the deck to the bow where a flight of metal stairs led to the pilothouse.

"Are you trying to sabotage this dinner, Jake Gilbert?" she demanded as she entered the cabin, which was much roomier than the one on the *Celebration*.

Jake was lounging back on one of the two captain's chairs. His feet, minus his cordovan loafers and encased in gray socks that matched his blazer, were propped up on the control panel. He was peering downriver through a pair of binoculars. He lowered the glasses, grinned boyishly over his shoulder at Roxie and turned back to his study of the river.

Mark Carter turned from the log in which he was making notations and gave Roxie a look of exaggerated relief. "Boy, am I glad to see you. Can you get Papa Bear out of here? Somebody else is sitting in his chair, and he's going nuts."

Roxie laughed. "I should have expected something like this, but I hoped the romantic ambience of this affair would help take his mind off his latest little problem."

"Little problem?" Jake shouted, as he spun around in the chair and lowered his feet to the deck with a thud. "We're talking a couple of tons of vessel here, folks. And in the hands of a novice."

"A novice trained by the Great Gilbert, remember," Roxie said, taking Jake's arm. "Come with me, pal, tonight you don't get to play anything but passenger."

He leered at her. "Is that anything like playing doctor?"

"That depends on how well you behave from now on," she teased.

Jake slipped his feet into his loafers and hurried after her. But at the cabin door he turned back and said, his tone serious, "Keep an eye on Johnson for me, will you, Mark?"

Mark saluted. "Aye, aye, Cap." He smiled and waved at Roxie and turned to his logs.

"I've never been a passenger on either of the boats," Jake said, as they entered the first deck cabin. He sounded surprised.

"Well, then, you're in for a treat, aren't you?" She looked at him and a warm glow filled her chest and caused a lump in her throat. He looked so handsome. He was a man who wore dress clothes and casual wear equally well. She supposed that sense of style came from his background. For a moment she could see herself in that little dress shop in Madison, where she had worked after classes and Saturdays, and hear her boss, Mrs. Danvers, saying, "Nobody's born with clothes on, so nobody's born with clothes sense—it's learned knowledge."

Martine Henderson, the hostess, came toward them carrying a clipboard under her arm and smiling.

"Are you going to want to greet guests yourself, Roxie?" She gave Jake a look that made Roxie put her arm possessively through his.

"No, tonight Jake and I will be observers. You can treat us just as you do the other guests."

"In that case, let me show you to the table we reserved for you." She led them to a table near a window where they could look out and see the string of lanterns swinging over the rail. Because it was still quite light, the lanterns were not yet as effective as they would be when the sky and the river turned black.

A waiter filled their tall flutes with champagne. Jake lifted and touched his glass to Roxie's. "To the most beautiful woman in the world, and to another success to enhance her career."

Their eyes met and held over the rims of their glasses as they drank. Feeling suddenly shy, Roxie lowered her glass and glanced around the room. She was surprised to discover the band already playing a medley of ballads from the musical *Showboat* and to see the room almost filled with guests. A sigh of satisfaction mingled with the excitement that rose in her chest.

"It is beautiful, isn't it?" she said, turning to Jake.

"Beautiful," he murmured. There was no doubt he was referring to her. She smiled and placed her hand in his.

He laughed suddenly.

"What?"

"I just had a flash of recall. Remember the night the crew all went out for pizza after an electric company cruise—and you bet Andy you could match him beer for beer?''

"Ugh," she moaned, "don't remind me. I had a headache for a week afterward."

"I'm not surprised. Before the evening was over, you two were drinking straight from the pitcher. Floyd had to carry Andy out fireman style and drive him home."

A question that had always disturbed her came to mind. "How did I get home?"

"I drove you."

"You did?"

"Yeah." His laugh was deep bellied and caught the attention of the people at the next table, an elderly couple who smiled at the sound. "I slung you over my shoulder, too, and you and Andy yelled across at one another all the way out to the parking lot about how sober you each were and what drunks the rest of us were and how we were all party poopers."

Roxie groaned and hid her face in her hands. "I'm so glad I have no memory of that, I would never have been able to face you again. Even now, I'm embarrassed."

He pulled her hands down and shook his head, his expression tender. "You were adorable. I thought you were the most fun girl I ever met." He sipped more of his wine. "I thought the reason you never mentioned it—or thanked me—is because you didn't want me to get the wrong idea and think you were interested."

"I always thought you were so cool because I wasn't your type."

"Cool? I was never cool to you. We were pretty good buddies over the years."

"Well, you know what I mean. Not cool, but not really interested in me in—you know, in a personal way."

"I thought you thought I wasn't your type."

"Why? I didn't have a type."

"Come on, Roxie. How about Montgomery? And before him, Don Mueller, from whom I always suspected Montgomery was cloned. And before Mueller there was Pete Olson who followed David Ankers, not to mention..."

"Jake Gilbert! What did you do, memorize the list of my male acquaintances?"

"Acquaintances? Come on, Roxanne, this is your old pal and previous confidant you're talking to here."

Roxie felt her anger growing. "Oh, yeah, I wouldn't cast any stones if I were you, Jake, old pal, old buddy. Not with the way you kept a steady stream of Daffy Taffy types flowing through your private little pontoon penthouse."

Jake's body was shaking with mirth and Roxie was having a hard time keeping her temper from creating a scene.

"You're lucky we're in public, Gilbert," she said.

"So are you, my sweet," Jake said, patting her cheek and leering at her even as another chuckle escaped his throat.

"What is so damned funny?"

"Realizing how jealous we were of one another all that time without realizing it."

"Jealous? Don't be silly. I was never..." She grinned. "Yeah, you're right."

"We really used to get a lot of laughs out of your little shenanigans," he said. "Particularly when you were trying to outsmart Martha or Joe."

"God, they never let me get away with anything," she moaned, "they always either caught me in the act or found out later." She smiled wistfully. "I don't know how Martha managed to have any hope for me and to see my potential."

"Oh, girl, even when you were up to your eyeballs in mischief or making mistakes left and right, your ambition shone like a beacon in the night."

Somehow that nettled. She responded out of irritation. "I suppose that was no worse than the way you had your antenna out for any hint of an easy make, no matter the time or place."

"What's that supposed to mean?" Good. That'd certainly wiped the grin off his face.

"Come on, Jake, how about the way you always managed to come down, sniffing around whenever you got a hint there was one of those blond bombshells aboard?"

He looked all hurt and defensive. "I had to take a break once in a while."

"Funny, you didn't seem to need so many breaks when we carried a load of men, or senior citizens, or any school groups younger than prom kids."

"What's this about prom kids?" Floyd demanded, helping himself to one of the vacant chairs at the table without waiting for an invitation. "I thought we were through with the little darlings for the season."

"Here's an objective observer," Roxie said, delighted to have a witness to Jake's past.

"What, have I landed myself in the middle of a domestic quarrel?" The bartender made a move to get up. Roxie and Jake each grabbed an arm and forced him to stay seated.

"Tell this woman I have always behaved with absolute decorum toward the female passengers on our cruises."

"Admit the truth, both of you—he's been a regular libertine!"

"Libertine?" The two men shouted the word in unison, their guffaws of laughter drawing the attention of quite a few of the people at neighboring tables.

Roxie felt her face stiffen. "It was Martha's word." She said it softly, but the men heard and instantly grew serious.

"Yeah," Floyd said, "old Martha could turn a phrase."

"She'd have been proud of you for creating this, Roxanne," Jake said, his face reflecting that emotion as he gestured toward the room with couples dancing, people eating their salads and drinking wine, and the hum of conversation and laughter, all signs of a successful party. What made it more special was that these people were all strangers to each other, except to the people at their own tables, and yet everybody seemed to be relaxed and having a good time.

Roxie's heart filled with satisfaction. It was what moved her to an act of generosity. "Why don't you have dinner with us, Floyd?"

Jake's hand on her knee, under the tablecloth, punished her reckless invitation with a squeeze. Roxie put her own hand on his and patted it though she refused to meet his gaze. "We'd love to have you join us," she gushed.

Floyd looked from one to the other of them and shook his head. "I make it a point never to allow myself to become a third wheel." He stood up. "I'm going back to work. Thanks anyway." They watched as he ambled away, stopping at various tables the length of the room to greet people.

"Nice guy," Roxie said, looking after him.

"Yeah. Floyd's the greatest." This time his hand caressed, and Roxie felt her breath draw up in her throat. She turned to give him her full attention.

"Let's dance," he suggested.

"Better not," she said, pushing his hand away and dragging it onto the table. "I'm not sure I could handle too much touching and holding right now."

"Arguing gets you excited," he commented, picking up his salad fork.

"You get me excited." She picked up her own fork and hoped her comment sounded as matter-of-fact and passionless as his did, but her hand trembled, belying her tone.

"Eat your salad," Jake said gently.

Marge had outdone herself with the dinner; even people who might have groused about the set menu were soon digging into the delicious food with enthusiasm. A perfect vinaigrette laved the crisp greens, interspersed with chunks of walnuts and spears of baby asparagus. The main course, prime rib, barely pink, was served with fluffy baked potatoes and fresh, steamed green beans tossed in a bacon and onion sauce.

Roxie looked around frequently and observed that everyone was enjoying the meal. And when the waiters served Marge's outstanding dessert—a light, cool, unusual grapefruit mousse—the oohs and ahs could be heard around the room, ending in applause for the chef. One lady asked if Marge gave out any of her recipes.

"You did good, going with Marge," Jake compli-
mented Roxie.

Roxie put her napkin down with a sigh of contentment. "I get the shivers thinking about how I almost
went with Continental just because Pete offered me a
slightly lower bid."

"Pete's good—it wouldn't have been a disaster if he
did it, but then it wouldn't have been the perfection this
meal was, either."

"Let's go for a walk," Roxie said, needing to exercise after the rich meal.

They found themselves in the middle of a promenade of couples on the deck. They followed along,
holding hands and enjoying the balmy night air and the
golden glow caused by the swinging lanterns, until they
arrived at the foot of the stairway.

"Let's offer Mark a break," Jake said, his voice
suddenly husky.

Roxie answered in a whisper. "Won't he mind?"

"Why should he? He'll understand."

He pressed her hand and she followed him up to the
pilothouse.

Mark picked up his dinner dishes and carried them
out with him. "Thanks," he said, over his shoulder,
"I'll be back in ten minutes."

The cruise was almost over; they could make out the
landmarks along the shoreline indicating they were
only about twenty minutes from Harley's Landing.

Jake made an adjustment to the wheel, pushed
something on the instrument panel, then pulled Roxie
into a rough, hungry embrace.

"You taste like grapefruit," she said, licking his
bottom lip with her tongue.

"You taste like heaven," he said with a groan, and thrust his tongue past her lips into the warm, sweet interior of her mouth. She suckled him gently then pushed her tongue into his mouth. The rhythm of his suckling made her body go limp and her breasts ache with a longing to be touched. She pulled his hands around to her breasts and thrust her hands under his sport coat and into the waistband at the back of his slacks, urging his pelvis against hers.

"Yes, do that," she whispered throatily as he ground against her. "Oh, Jake, yes, yes, that . . ."

Jake pulled the strapless bodice of her dress down and exposed one pebbled peak of her swollen breast to his eyes and then to his hungry mouth.

He drew away, his face flushed, his eyes glazed and his breath rasping, and looked over his shoulder at the helm. He made another adjustment, and Roxie shivered as the cool night air struck her wet breast.

His mouth was still hot, still wet, when he turned back to kiss her.

He laughed shakily and drew her top up. "Maybe we'd better cool it until we get home."

Dazed, Roxie looked around, surprised she'd forgotten, so quickly, where they were. She straightened her clothes and ran her hand over her hair. "See, I told you. You've got to stop getting me all excited when we're out in public."

"Yeah," Jake agreed, "but you don't know how hard it is to keep my hands off you, Roxie. I'm not going to be able to drive us home fast enough to suit me."

They went to the helm, arms around each other's waists, and looked out toward the landing. "Oh, look," Roxie said, pointing toward shore, "the *Celeb* is back in."

Jake slumped onto the captain's chair with a heavy sigh. "Thank God, that's over."

"You haven't been worrying all evening, have you?" Roxie asked, laughing.

"You bet."

"Not three minutes ago, you weren't," she said, pretending to glower.

"Well, no, not three minutes ago." He reached up and pulled her down for a quick kiss as they heard Mark coming up the stairs. "And not ten minutes from now, when I get you home."

But no sooner had the gangplank lowered to the dock than Terry Johnson came running aboard, shouting, "Jake, come on, bring Floyd and Mark—and hurry!"

"What's happened?" Roxie demanded, pulling on Terry's sleeve as Jake, responding instinctively to the urgent tone in Terry's voice, sped up the gangplank to get the others.

"Bill Tabor's in trouble—I think he's gone after Harry Minto."

Behind her, Roxie heard Mark Carter yell, "Oh, no, don't tell me the dumb son of a bitch went without me."

CHAPTER NINETEEN

ROXIE PACED THE FLOOR, stopping every few minutes to peer out a window into the dark night, trying to catch sight of the launch, with the men aboard, heading upstream to where the *Shark* was anchored.

Mary sat at the desk, her head in her hands, her face tear-drenched, as they waited to hear news of her lover and of his friends who'd gone to his rescue.

What if Jake is hurt going to Bill's rescue? What if they're all hurt? Roxie squinted, trying to see past her own image reflected on the night-backed glass. She looked the way she felt, frenzied, disoriented, frightened. She pushed her hair behind her ears and leaned closer to the glass.

Hard to believe that only a short time ago, she and Jake had stood near the rail on the *Celebration*, holding hands, waiting for the gangplank to come down so they could be first off and rush to the apartment to make love. She bit her lip. She mustn't let herself dwell on the frightening possibilities. She would think positive thoughts, think only of Jake's safety—the safety of all the men.

Thinking of the men and their mission made her furious with Bill Tabor. What could he have been thinking of, to set up a meet with Minto by himself?

There'd been so many rumors about Minto's proclivity for violence, his possible connection with the syndicate. Could such a thing really exist in St. Paul, Minnesota? It had always seemed only fiction—something that existed in literature and movies. Suddenly, tonight, it had become real.

She shivered, turned to Mary and said, "Take it easy, Mare, I'm sure they're going to be all right."

She didn't know how sure she sounded, but Mary seemed to take heart; she blew her nose, rubbed her eyes and took a deep, quivering breath to steady herself. "I pray you're right, Rox. I'll never forgive myself if anything happens to any of them. If I hadn't told Bill about that ad in the paper..."

"Don't think that!" Roxie took a breath and softened her tone. "Just concentrate on it all coming out all right." She made herself leave the window, return to her desk and pick up her coffee mug.

"Want more coffee?"

Mary's hair was coming loose from the usually neat braid. Her eyes were red-rimmed, her freckles standing out like blotches on her pale skin. She shook her head. "No. Thanks." She blew her nose again and got up to take Roxie's place at the picture window.

"Mary, I know Bill left a note telling you where he'd gone, but did he tell you why?"

Mary turned away from the window and smiled wanly at Roxie. "I know why. He thought if he was the one who proved Minto was pirating business away from us, he'd earn more of Joe's esteem and move ahead in the race for the promotion."

Roxie frowned. "He put his life at risk to get the general manager job?"

Mary nodded and faced the window again. She leaned forward, her breath fogging the glass. "Why doesn't the Coast Guard call back?" she cried out.

Roxie put her mug down and swiveled restlessly in her chair. "They said they'd call when they knew something."

"Why don't we drive along the river and see if we can spot them?"

"That doesn't make sense, Mary, there are too many places where the river can't be seen from the road. You know the road doesn't stay parallel with the river for more than a few blocks on either side of Warner Road."

Silence prevailed again as Mary stood sentry and Roxie sipped the hot, now-bitter brew and willed the phone to ring.

Roxie tried to convince herself that Bill had either changed his mind and turned back without ever approaching Minto—or that he had got away with his amateur detective work and had some proof to bring to the authorities that would convince them to put Minto out of business—and, even better, behind bars.

Everyone safe and Tabor a hero. She put her mug down and stared at her hands. *Would* that impress Joe so much that he'd give Bill the job?

She twined her fingers and squeezed her palms together prayerfully. *Too much risk even for the juicy plum Joe is offering.* She shuddered. How far would *she* go to get the promotion?

Across the room, Mary leaned her hot face against the cool pane and said angrily, "What could be taking so long? And what's the big deal about a few stolen charters, anyway?"

"THERE IT IS," Terry said, pointing upriver to where the mock paddle wheel of the *Shark* could be seen.

"Pull in there," Floyd told Jake, who was at the wheel of the motor launch. He gestured toward a cove that would hide their boat. A narrow peninsula of land separated the cove from the *Shark*. They would be able to reach the pirate boat by foot.

Jake did as Floyd suggested, and Terry jumped into the shallows to carry the line to shore to tie up.

"Let's keep our voices down now," Floyd told the others, "we don't know what we're going to find over there. We all know how voices carry on water, and we don't want to give away our approach."

Floyd reached past Jake and took a pair of binoculars off the dashboard. He slung them around his neck by the leather strap and pulled a small handgun and a flashlight from the deep pocket of the yellow slicker he'd brought with him from the *Princess*.

"Where the hell did you get that?" Mark asked, jumping back and almost knocking Jake over when he saw the revolver.

"I don't go out on any charter without it. I keep it in the petty cash box, out of sight. Don't worry, I know how to use it."

"That's what I'm afraid of," Mark said.

"You guys bring anything you can find that will serve as a weapon," Floyd said, ignoring Mark's comment. "We don't know how many people Minto has working for him."

"Come on, you guys," Terry called out in a harsh whisper, "let's get going."

The others slipped over the side to follow Terry through the shallow water to land.

When they reached the bank, Floyd moved to the front, and handed Terry a spanner he'd found in the hold of the launch. "Mark," he said in a whisper, "let

Jake bring up the rear." Mark and Jake traded places; both waited, quietly poised, alert for Floyd's next order. Jake briefly wondered if it was the possession of the gun that gave Floyd the authority, or if it was just that they all recognized that he had had experience at this sort of thing. The thought left as quickly as it came—whatever the reason, Floyd was welcome to the position of leader since he seemed best qualified to handle it.

"Okay, I suggest we cut across the head of that outcropping and when we see the boat, we can move down and hide in the brush until we get the lay of the land."

They moved as quietly as possible in single file, keeping close to one another in the dark night. The light from Floyd's flashlight bobbed ahead of them, outlining the semblance of a path.

"If only there was a moon tonight," Mark grumbled as he tripped over a surface root, "that flashlight isn't much help back here."

"Yeah," Jake whispered, "and then we'd be totally visible to whoever might be watching for us."

"We're going to have to forgo the flashlight in a few minutes," Floyd called softly. "It'll mark our approach if they've got guards posted." Just as they reached the top of the path, Floyd stopped short, quickly dousing the light, and turned to put his hand up to warn the others to silence.

Jake stood without moving, scarcely breathing, listening to his own heart beating. He could hear Mark's breathing, too, and around him the sporadic night sounds of the river—the plaintive cry of a loon answered by the bleating of an owl, the choking sounds of bullfrogs, the slap of water against the hull of a boat and the splash as a fish searched the dark river surface for food. As his ears became accustomed to the quiet, Jake could hear more of the rustlings of tiny nocturnal life in the grass around them.

His blood seemed to freeze in his veins as an alien sound penetrated the quiet. A footstep in the brush, just to the right of them.

"Floyd?" Mark whispered, "what was th—"

Jake heard the sound of a scuffle just ahead of him and moved stealthily toward where he thought Mark had been crouching. A hand clamped over his mouth and iron bands seemed to squeeze the air from his lungs as his nose detected the odor of tobacco. He struggled vainly against the assault and found himself pinned to the ground. A flashlight shone briefly in his face and a voice above him whispered, "Keep quiet or we're going to have to put you out." Jake let himself go limp, no longer resisting his attacker.

Another voice called out in a low tone, "Charley, I got the leader, he had a gun."

Jake shivered. The voice must be referring to Floyd. So much for the advantage of weapons; his own choice, a short crowbar, had fallen from his hand when his attacker brought him down.

"Hear that?" a voice said, close to his ear. Must be the guy called Charley. Jake nodded. "I've got a gun," Charley said, and just as that moment Jake felt something hard push into his ribs, "and I'll use it if you force me to." Jake nodded again.

"Okay, when I tell you to, you're gonna stand up nice and easy." Jake felt the other man's weight lift away from him, and the hand came away from his mouth. He wondered if he could find the crowbar before the guy hauled him to his feet.

He blinked as a flashlight punctuated the darkness just a few feet from where he lay. "Okay, you guys," the first voice said, "I've got a gun on this man. Get to your feet and move ahead of me, single file."

"Where are you taking us?" Jake heard Terry ask. Terry sounded plenty scared. Jake took stock of his own emotions and was surprised to discover he was more angry than frightened. What the hell had Tabe got himself into, and why? With the *Shark* taking bites out of all the businesses on the two rivers, there wasn't much chance of it doing too much harm to any one of those companies. And now they were all in danger just because Tabor fancied himself some kind of hero.

Well, he wasn't going down without a fight—he had too much to lose, too much to live for. An image of Roxie's face floated across his mind and with it the memory of their first lovemaking aboard the *Tinker Toy*. In the night, along a deserted, wild shore of the river, surrounded by men with guns in their hands and retribution on their minds, Jake realized he wanted to make a commitment to Roxie. He would even give up his houseboat for her. He wanted to marry her.

That means staying alive, you jackass!

"Okay, get to your feet, nice and slow," Charley whispered from somewhere above him.

He had maybe a minute before the others would reach them and he would once more become Charley's prisoner.

Stealthily, he felt around for the crowbar, his fingers scrabbling quietly in the direction he thought he remembered hearing it fall in the fracas. He held his breath and almost exploded it out of his lungs when his palm closed around the cold, rust-roughened instrument. He let his breath out with caution then inhaled with relief.

He slipped the crowbar behind his back and began to rise carefully to his feet. In the darkness he couldn't identify the man called Charley, but he thought he could make out the bulky outline of his captor. Counting on the fact that Charley's vision would be as limited by the dark as his was, he crept toward the shape, raising the crowbar over his head as he moved.

Just as he neared the mass, the weapon was snatched out of his hand and an arm caught him around the neck.

"You aren't going to be needing a weapon," a man said, emitting a low, rusty laugh. "We're with the Coast Guard."

JAKE TURNED from the radio phone and went to join his friends at the rail of the Coast Guard launch. Floyd looked at Jake. "Roxie and Mary all right?"

Jake nodded. "Worried, but holding up." He didn't tell the others that Roxie had burst into tears when she heard his voice and knew he was safe.

He gestured toward the brightly lit riverboat across the river. "Anything yet?"

"Naw. Charley says the narcs weren't planning to make their move until they got a signal from one of their men they had planted aboard the *Shark*. Seems Minto has a woman living with him and the undercover agent says she's not part of his dealings so they want to get her out of there if they can."

"What about Tabor?"

Floyd shrugged and Mark answered, his voice thickened by guilt, "They don't know if he's actually aboard the *Shark* or if Minto was meeting with him on the bank.''

"Why would Minto have set up a meet with Tabe on the very night he'd arranged to pass on the drugs?'' Floyd asked of no one in particular.

Charley came out of the cabin just then and joined them. "Could your friend have been in on the drug thing with Minto?''

They all stared at the Coast Guard officer.

"Maybe Minto wanted to unload Tabor and was planning to use him for a scapegoat if the drug transfer was discovered by the narcs.''

Terry scoffed. "Get real! The cops'd take one look at Tabe and know he was no drug dealer—the guy's as square as a sandbox and just about as interesting. I can't believe he actually had the balls to try this little stunt on his own.''

"I wouldn't sell Tabe short, if I were you,'' Jake told his young protégé, "he's landlocked now, but he's done his time on everything from ocean craft to coal barges and he did Navy time before that.''

"Yeah, well, this sure was a dumb move!''

Jake punched Terry on the arm then draped his arm across the younger man's shoulders. "So see that you always remember the buddy system before you set out in pursuit of the bad guys when you grow up,'' Jake said. The other men laughed and Jake laughed with them as he ducked away from Terry's futile attempt to take a swing at him.

The momentary levity brought relief from the tension.

Their little skirmish ended in a quick snap to attention as a gunshot rang out across the water. In the quiet night and with the river acoustics, it sounded like a cannon going off.

"What was that?" Terry rushed to the rail where he was joined by the others.

"Sounded like a shot."

"Hold on," Charley said, "we're going to move in."

Please, Jake prayed, *let Tabe be okay. It'll break Joe's heart if he loses his best friend so soon after losing Martha.* But it wasn't only Joe who'd be affected if Bill Tabor was hurt. They were all fond of the marina manager. Jake had spent many a pleasant evening over the years drinking beer and talking boats with Tabor.

He didn't understand why Bill had felt the need to do this, and to do it alone. Roxie said he'd left a note for Mary. Why Mary? What did she have to do with Bill?

They were nearing the north shore, and Jake could see men outlined against the lighted windows of the lower deck of the *Shark*. As they drew closer, he could see that a large group of men surrounded a smaller group of men who had their hands up. So it was over, and all there was now was to count the wounded. One shot only had rung out. Was that shot aimed at Bill Tabor? And had it struck its intended target?

THE RED ROOF LIGHT lit up and began to turn as the siren shrieked in the night air and the wheels of the government car kicked up gravel as it climbed the bank to the paved road.

Floodlights, lined up under the eaves of the building that housed the offices, bathed the dock area in artificial daylight.

From where she stood at the window, Roxie could see Bill helping Mary into the marina launch. Mary paused and looked at Bill, putting her hand to his cheek. Roxie could see her young friend's expression clearly. The look of love was so blinding in its purity that Roxie had to close her eyes to shut out the intimacy that no outsider should witness.

She turned from the window as Jake came into the office.

"Are all the government people gone now?"

"Yeah, the last one just left."

"Did Bill ever explain his part in all of this?"

"Yeah." Jake ran his hands through his hair and went to retrieve his coffee mug from Roxie's desk. He stared into it, took a swallow and said, "Apparently Bill had set up a meet with Minto at Vitner's Cove for tomorrow night. Then he figured if he went there tonight, unexpected, he'd be more apt to uncover the operation."

"But he didn't know about the drug traffic."

"No." Jake shook his head and laughed, the sound hoarse in the quiet office. "No, he fell into the exchange by accident and the minute he showed up, the leader, a guy named Yong, shot Minto. Tabe said all hell broke loose then and agents started coming out into the open from everywhere. Said the dealers never had a chance."

Roxie watched as Jake drained his cup and fell onto a chair. He looked exhausted. She wanted to go to him, but there was still so much she needed to say before she could feel at ease with him again.

"Man, I'm beat," Jake said, rubbing his eyes. "This wasn't your run of the mill kind of cruise."

Maybe this wasn't the time for it, she thought, turning to the window.

"Thank God Bill is all right," was all she said in a hushed voice that vibrated with feeling.

Jake surprised her from behind, pulling her into the cradle of his embrace, his arms snaking around her waist, his lips nuzzling at the softest part of her neck.

"You really mean that," he said.

"Of course. Oh, Jake!" She turned to face him without leaving his arms. "Surely you didn't think I wished him any harm?"

"No, not really. But just sometimes, sweetheart, your ambition seems larger than life."

Roxie frowned, looking thoughtful as she caressed her lover's face with her fingers. Beloved face, that she'd feared she might never see, never touch again. "It's true, I've wanted that job above all else—or so I thought until tonight."

"And tonight?" He nipped her earlobe with his strong teeth, and Roxie shivered and pressed her body against his.

"Tonight I...Jake, I can't think, let alone talk when you do that." She moaned and opened her mouth as his tongue slid along her lower lip and begged entry. The kiss dizzied her, reminding her of their unfinished business. Had that really been tonight? It seemed eons since she'd crossed the gangplank on Jake's arm, proud to be with him, proud to be going out on the maiden dinner cruise she'd created.

Jake drew back, holding her away with his hands at her shoulder. "Talk first, love later."

As if to insure that they would talk, he moved across the room and took a seat behind the desk.

"Tell me about Mary and Bill."

"They're lovers," Roxie said, clearing her throat and putting a shaky hand to her disheveled hair. How did Jake turn on and off like that? Would she ever know?

She went to her desk and sat on the edge. "At first I was really horrified at the thought, because of their age difference. I was really judgmental about them. But when Mary described her feelings for Bill, and his for her, I began to see things differently." She smiled weakly at Jake.

"Tonight I had a lot of time to think about things while I tried not to think of you—of any of you, hurt or worse..." She shuddered again but kept her eyes firmly fixed on Jake's.

"I realized tonight that I'd picked Clay because he was the opposite of my parents and I disapproved of my parents because they were so different from the mainstream. And then I thought, so what? They didn't abuse me or withhold love. They didn't desert me or give me up for adoption." Her smile was stronger now.

"They just played at life like children. And I realized that I had been seeing some of their playful attitude toward life in you and that it had scared me to death."

Jake had all he could do to keep from leaping to his feet and going over and grabbing her. She'd learned a lot about herself in a very short time. He remembered Martha used to say what a quick study Roxie was. He clenched his hands in his pockets and nodded at her, settling for words instead. "I can dig it, Roxie. I must look like the world's biggest dropout to someone like you."

She shook her head. "Don't get me wrong, Jake, I always admired you and respected you, it was just that

I couldn't understand anyone not wanting the penthouse, the executive suite, the top of the mountain.''

"I know." He nodded again. He was so damned proud of her, he could have shouted and made himself heard around the world. "You know, I realized something tonight, too, hon. I realized that I started to fall in love with you way back when you first came to work here and used to get into so much mischief.''

"Before my ambition turned into a monster, you mean?'' she asked, laughing sheepishly.

"Uh-uh. There was never anything monstrous about you, Roxanne. You just focused on the one thing and shut out everything else. In a way, that's how your parents lived their lives.'' He cleared his throat and stood up, but he stayed behind the desk. "I've been doing a little of that myself, Roxanne. I'd like to remedy that, if you'll have me.''

"Have you?'' They stared at one another, but neither moved.

"Yeah. I don't want to push you into anything, but I'd like to move into your apartment with you, if you'll let me. Maybe a kind of trial run. I promise, if you hate living with me, I'll move out without a fuss.''

Roxie shook her head and blinked back tears that welled up. "You...you want to live in a regular apartment? You'll turn into a regular yuppie. While I...''

"While you...?''

"While I was thinking life's too short to waste it on a job. And maybe we could go south together this winter.'' Her eyes were large, begging him to come to her, to assure her that a relationship between them was worth any sacrifice.

"Yeah. I'd like that." A familiar stirring in his loins reminded him how much he loved her.

"Listen, I think you should know what Bill told me just before he and Mary left. Apparently, you're not the only one who did some real soul-searching tonight."

"What?"

"Bill said the sight of all those guns being drawn made him realize how content he'd be to spend the rest of his life with Mary and his job as marina manager. He said he doesn't think he wants to put in the time required to run the whole show."

Gray eyes sought brown, and two chests heaved ragged sighs.

Roxie wished he'd make the first move. Her legs were too weak to allow her to cross the room.

"What are we going to tell Joe now that Bill has decided to withdraw from the race? Because, you see, I don't think it's right for me, either."

He fairly leaped across the distance that separated them.

Roxie breathed a sigh of relief as his arms enfolded her and his beard-roughened cheek pressed hers. Jake's face glowed with love as he drew back and smiled at her.

"Damn, sweetheart, don't go all wimpy on me now. I've finally got a handle on what makes you tick and I'm ready to make the big leap to join you in the grown-up world."

"I'm not sure I'm getting your message," Roxie said, grinning at Jake. "You want me to be your boss?" She didn't know why, but the idea almost disappointed her.

"No, no way. I've got a much better idea."

"What's that?" She had one, too. She wished they were through talking and could get back to basics, things like kissing and caressing and... She slid her hands under his shirt, eager to touch his warm, bare skin.

"We'll remind Joe that this has been a ma-and-pa business for thirty-five years and suggest it's still the only way it can be run properly."

"What do you mean?" She could hardly concentrate when he was touching her that way. She almost purred as she moved closer to him, happy to discover that he was as turned on as she.

"I mean, you and I will run this business together, as a team."

"Oh, Jake, darling, that's a wonderful idea! But do you think Joe will..."

"I know he will. He'll be getting two great minds instead of one, and you know Joe can never pass up a good bargain. And now," he fairly growled, "shut up and kiss me." He nipped at her lips.

Roxie lifted her face obediently. She wouldn't always be so compliant, but this was one of those times when it was sheer pleasure. Working with Jake was going to be far more fun than working alone, she decided, as his mouth moved hungrily over hers. She couldn't have planned it better if she'd planned it herself.

CHAPTER TWENTY

THE PATH WAS A BLAZING ARROW of red and gold leaves that crunched beneath Joe's feet as he made his way around the building to the door of the office. Everywhere he looked he could see evidence of work on the place, from the flower beds lining the driveway onto Harley's Landing to the fresh paint that sparkled on every building, and on the boats, as well.

He stopped a moment to catch his breath, leaning against the building as he fumbled in his pockets for his pills. Those stairs from the levee had taxed his heart, another sign that the decision to resign might no longer be voluntary.

The tablet melted under his tongue. After a few moments, to let the medication do its stuff, he squared his shoulders, took a deep breath and went in to meet with his staff.

They rushed him at the door, the men pounding his back while Roxie threw her arms around him. Joe laughed and pushed them away, determined not to let them see the effort it took to catch his breath.

"Get back! I want to look at you."

They drew away, all three grinning happily and talking at once. Joe eased onto the nearest chair. He laughed and put his hands to his ears.

"One at a time!"

"You look wonderful," Roxie said, her eyes glowing.

He looked at Jake, whose grin was beginning to look foolish. Jake was glowing, too, and nodding agreement with Roxie. Joe turned to Bill. "How ya doin', Tabe?"

Bill's glow was a little tarnished around the edges. "Great, Joe, just great. And you're a sight for sore eyes."

Joe studied Bill, his old friend. "Something you want to get off your chest, Tabe?" he asked quietly.

The three exchanged glances. "Maybe we should leave," Roxie offered.

"Stay," Joe commanded waving toward chairs, "it's plain you already know what's going on." He grinned and pulled out his pipe, putting the stem between his teeth without filling it.

They'd all seen that particular grin before. They stayed. And they sat. And they felt the tension circle the room as Joe waited, quietly sucking on the pipe stem.

"Mary and I are...we're getting married," Bill blurted, unable to tolerate the tension.

Mary. Joe had to think a minute. The only woman he knew named Mary was the waitress over at the River Diner—but the woman was at least fifteen years older than Tabe. *"Not for us to judge what brings two souls together, Joe,"* he heard Martha say.

Joe took the empty pipe from his mouth and nodded. "I always thought you needed a good woman in your life, Tabe. And one thing about Mary, she's used to taking care of people. I'm sure she'll make you a fine wife."

Roxie and Jake exchanged surprised glances, and Bill looked startled.

"I guess so, Joe. She has been doing a lot of work with the customers since Roxie promoted her."

A dense hush hung in the room as Joe absorbed what Bill had said. He opened his mouth, shut it, opened it again and squawked, "You mean *our* Mary? Little Mary Sanger?"

The others flinched. And then Bill squared his shoulders and thrust his chin out and said, "Yes, and much as we'd like your blessing, Joe, nothing is going to change our minds—not even losing our jobs."

Joe could feel Martha's ghost getting ready to rise up with one of her homespun lectures on tolerance and understanding. *Time for me to test my own mettle, old girl,* he thought, pushing her to the back of his mind. He stood up and held his hand out to Bill.

"We've been friends too long for me to risk that by attempting to choose your bride for you, Tabe."

Bill's scowl of assertion turned to a surprised smile and then widened into a glorious grin as the two men shook hands heartily.

"Okay, so if that's all that's been bothering you, let's get down to business." Joe eased into his seat and began to turn the pipe over and over in his hands.

It was Jake who noticed. "Joe! You're not smoking your pipe."

He had no intention of burdening them with his medical problems.

"Too many places they don't let you smoke anymore. I figured I'd quit before it was outlawed in the privacy of our own homes."

Their laughter assured him they believed him. He relaxed and looked at the clock. "The lawyer is going to be here in about fifteen minutes, so let's get anything said that needs saying just between the four of us right now."

"You never told us your criteria for choosing the general manager," Jake pointed out.

"You thought it was a matter of heroics," Joe said, looking at Bill. Bill flushed and shrugged.

"I figured it couldn't hurt."

"You surprise me, Tabe. I never gave brownie points for anything but quick learning and dedication to the assignment."

Bill nodded.

Joe smiled. "Have to admit, I'd like to have been here to go with you, Tabe. The two of us would have made an unbeatable team." They exchanged a shared wistful smile. Those days were gone, and they both knew it.

"I've been talking to Roxie pretty regularly, so I know that revenue is up in all areas. But the truth is, it was never a matter of who created the most new revenue, either."

Now they all looked blank. Joe laughed. God, he missed his pipe at moments like this. The smoke screen he used to create between himself and others always used to make a special moment stretch out a little longer.

"Do you really want it, Tabe?" He looked Bill Tabor full in the face and he saw the play of emotion that ranged from surprise to excitement to honest appraisal.

Bill shook his head. "I guess not, Joe. A young wife likes lots of attention. So between Mary and managing the marina, I guess I'll be too busy to take on anything more."

"All wives like lots of attention, not just the young ones," Joe said, chuckling, remembering. Why, even now that she'd passed on, Martha still managed to flit in and out of his life anytime she felt like it.

He turned to the two younger people. Funny, he'd had a fleeting impression the two of them were holding hands, though Roxie was sitting behind her desk and Jake was leaning against the window four feet away.

"Roxie, I sure have reason to know you can *handle* the job. But do you really want to tie yourself down to a business this demanding, and give up things like marriage and kids and all that means?"

Roxie stared at Joe, stood up, then stole a glance at Jake. Was it her place to speak for both of them? Jake's nod was almost imperceptible. She nodded back.

"Joe, Jake and I have a proposition to offer you."

Joe looked over at Jake, his expression impassive, and nodded to Roxie. "Let's hear it."

"Well, when Bill told us he'd decided he didn't really want the promotion, we talked it over and Jake and I . . . well—" she rushed the words "—we'd like to run the business together, the way you and Martha did."

"The way Martha and I . . . ?"

He leaped out of the chair with no concern for his frail heart as Roxie's meaning sunk in. "The two of you? Jake? It's true?"

They were all laughing. Joe didn't even realize that tears were sliding down his face through his laughter, and now he saw Jake had gone over and put his arm around Roxie.

"They look just the way we used to when we were young and in love for the first time, don't they, Joe?" he could hear Martha saying.

Shut up, woman, he ordered silently, *I can see some things with my own eyes.*

He took out a handkerchief and mopped his eyes. Jake was grinning at him, and Roxie was flushing prettily. They did indeed make a handsome couple; Martha had been right about that.

A telltale flutter made him fall heavily back on the chair. "People around here've been pretty busy this season," he said gruffly. "It's a wonder you got so much work done with all the shenanigans you've obviously been up to."

Lord, those two didn't know what a gift they'd given him; if he died on the spot, he'd die happy, knowing they'd found each other and were going to carry on the Harley tradition.

But that wasn't his plan. The thing to do was to get this legal business over; he'd already made his will, leaving the marina to Tabe and the rest of his holdings to Jake; all that was left was to sign over the general managership for the remainder of his lifetime.

He'd worried a little, sitting in the lawyer's office, that he was forcing Jake into taking over the business by leaving it to him. But Roxie's weekly reports had assured him that Jake was more interested in the business than maybe Jake realized himself. And now his fondest dream was coming true. He hoped his heart could withstand the good news just a while longer.

"I take it you approve, Cap?" Jake asked around his grin. "Especially when you know we won't be asking for double raises."

Joe didn't get a chance to respond to Jake's teasing because the door opened just then and the lawyer, Dave Bellows, came in, brushing a leaf from his overcoat and letting a draft of chilled, autumn-scented air into the building.

"Getting nippy out there," the lawyer exclaimed, putting his briefcase down and extending his hand to Joe and then to each of the others.

"My favorite time of year," Roxie said as she took Dave's coat and hung it on the rack. Dave accepted a mug of hot coffee and Roxie offered him her desk to sit at. She went to stand beside Jake, and his arm around her dispelled the chill the newcomer had brought in.

The business of assigning two names rather than one to the agreement took a few minutes, and the signatures of agreement, with the transfer of power of attorney, only a few minutes more.

They were talking about a celebration dinner over at Bill's trailer when Joe pulled Dave aside where the others couldn't hear them.

"I'll be leaving in the morning, Dave, but there's one more thing that needs changing in my will, and I'll come in and initial it on my way out of town, if that's all right?"

"Sure, Joe, tell me what it is and I'll have it revised and ready for your signature by ten."

"The place where I've assigned Jake Gilbert as my heir?"

Dave nodded and grinned. "I think I can guess what you want to change." He glanced over at Roxie and Jake.

"Yeah," Joe said, his smile broadening, "make it read Mr. and Mrs. Jacob Gilbert, or whatever is legal for the two of them as a couple. You can copy the way Martha and I were listed as co-owners.''

Roxie caught the look the lawyer had sent her way and moved a little closer to Jake. The season was over; they'd had their last color cruise yesterday, and now they'd have a couple of weeks to marry and honeymoon before they started the trek down the Mississippi with the stern-wheelers. The carpenter had been here this morning, starting the work on the sleeping cabin she and Jake would share during the trip. Sleeping bags in the main salon were all right for the crew, but they wouldn't do for the captain and his bride.

She looked at Joe, wanting to share an unspoken moment of happiness, and for a moment she could have sworn she saw Martha standing beside her husband. Roxie blinked and the vision was gone. But better than anyone, Roxie knew that wherever she was, Martha would be giving her blessing to Roxie and Jake.

* * * * *

*Praise is well, compliment is well,
but affection—that is the last and final and
most precious reward that man can win.
(Mark Twain)*

COMING IN 1991 FROM
HARLEQUIN SUPERROMANCE:

Three abandoned orphans,
one missing heiress!

Dying millionaire Owen Byrnside receives an
anonymous letter informing him that twenty-six years
ago, his son, Christopher, fathered a daughter. The
infant was abandoned at a foundling home that
subsequently burned to the ground, destroying all
records. Three young women could be Owen's long-
lost granddaughter, and Owen is determined to track
down each of them! Read their stories in

#434 HIGH STAKES (available January 1991)
#438 DARK WATERS (available February 1991)
#442 BRIGHT SECRETS (available March 1991)

Three exciting stories of intrigue and romance by
veteran Superromance author Jane Silverwood.

This April, don't miss #449, CHANCE OF A
LIFETIME, Barbara Kaye's third and last book in the
Harlequin Superromance miniseries

A powerful restaurant conglomerate draws the best and brightest
to its executive ranks. Now almost eighty years old, Vanessa
Hamilton, the founder of Hamilton House, must choose a succes-
sor. Who will it be?

Matt Logan: He's always been the company man, the quintessen-
tial team player. But tragedy in his daughter's life and a
passionate love affair made him make some hard choices....

Paula Steele: Thoroughly accomplished, with a sharp mind, perfect breeding and looks to die for, Paula thrives on challenges
and wants to have it all...but is this right for her?

Grady O'Connor: Working for Hamilton House was his salvation
after Vietnam. The war had messed him up but good and had
killed his storybook marriage. He's been given a second
chance—only he doesn't know what the hell he's supposed to
do with it....

Harlequin Superromance invites you to enjoy Barbara Kaye's
dramatic and emotionally resonant miniseries about mature men
and women making life-changing decisions.